BY OWEN NICHOLLS

Perfect Timing

Love, Unscripted

Perfect Timing

Perfect Timing

A Novel

OWEN NICHOLLS

DELL
NEW YORK

A Dell Trade Paperback Original

Copyright © 2021 by Owen Nicholls
Book club guide copyright © 2021 by Penguin Random House LLC

Published in the United States by Dell, an imprint of Random House, a division of Penguin Random House LLC, New York.

DELL and the HOUSE colophon are registered trademarks of Penguin Random House LLC.
RANDOM HOUSE BOOK CLUB and colophon are trademarks of Penguin Random House LLC.

Published in the United Kingdom by Headline Review, a member of the Headline Publishing Group, London.

LIBRARY OF CONGRESS CATALOGING-IN-PUBLICATION DATA
Names: Nicholls, Owen, author.
Title: Perfect timing / Owen Nicholls.
Description: New York : Dell, 2021
Identifiers: LCCN 2021016172 (print) | LCCN 2021016173 (ebook) |
ISBN 9781984826893 | ISBN 9781984826909 (ebook)
Classification: LCC PR6114.I274 P47 2021 (print) |
LCC PR6114.I274 (ebook) | DDC 823/.92—dc23
LC record available at https://lccn.loc.gov/2021016172

Printed in the United States of America on acid-free paper

randomhousebooks.com
randomhousebookclub.com

2 4 6 8 9 7 5 3 1

Book design by Dana Leigh Blanchette

To Mum and Dad
For everything

Perfect Timing

Prologue

Be still, he tells it. Be still, my beating heart. As this poetic refrain rattles around his mind, Tom berates himself for meaning it so literally. There is no romance in the situation. The panic in his blood. The pit in his stomach. The fight-or-flight response of a long-gone relative who chose not to face his fate. The worst part of it all? That this chain reaction of physical agony, this panic attack, is all because someone smiled at him from across a coffee shop.

Or maybe she didn't. After all, the "someone" in question is waiting for the man she's with to bring their drinks over. Tom saw them walk in together and asked himself, "What if I could be someone like him?" His answers offered nothing positive. When eye contact was made between Tom and the stranger for the second time, Tom left for the freedom of fresh air and solitude.

The truth was, Jess *was* smiling at him. In the short walk from their meeting place to the coffee shop, Jess had made up her mind about her quasi-blind date. She knew he was looking for a submissive type, and Jess was anything but.

That he'd already decided and dictated their plans for the entire evening was enough for Jess to start looking elsewhere. Her eyes found Tom.

As Tom stood and left, Jess felt a compulsion to go after him. It was an impulse she couldn't dismiss. Outside the café she looked left and right and left again, like a child crossing a road alone for the first time. The figure she'd been inexplicably drawn to was no longer in sight. Baffled by her own response, she returned to her date.

Tomorrow, there would be two hundred and fifty miles between Tom and Jess.

That distance, however, would not be there for long.

Part One

BEGINNINGS

1

"A Nice Dream"

Tom

Cemetery Road, Sheffield
July 15, 2015

I don't talk out loud to my grandad. It feels unnatural when I see other people do it. Like they've seen it in a movie and thought it worth copying. I do still talk to him, though. Just in my head. I tell him about what's happened over the last month. I tell him about my band and the music and how things are going pretty well. And today, I tell him about the girl in the coffee shop, because, why not?

"It would be handy," I confess through the power of thought, "if I didn't instantly fall in love with anyone who threw a smidgen of attention my way. I mean, all she did was, maybe, smile at me and I was fantasizing about us owning a cat, a cot, and a cottage by the sea."

I conjure up a response from him. "That sounds like a nice dream."

The cemetery is deserted. The sun high enough in the sky

to cast only tiny shadows on the rows and rows of head-
stones taking the form of crooked teeth in the ground.

Grandad reminds me, "Back to this girl in the café?" His
invented interruption takes me back to drinking coffee an
hour before. I couldn't describe what she looked like now.
For any would-be criminal, me doing an e-fit of them would
be the equivalent of a get-out-of-jail-free card. I do remember her brown hair and brown eyes. I have a type, after all.
But as time and distance grow between us, her face fades.

"What would Sarah think of all this?" Grandad replies
with his bark of a laugh.

Sarah is my girlfriend. Sort of. She, rather coincidentally,
also lives in Sheffield, so when I take the trip from Edinburgh
I can kill two birds with one stone. Visit my grandfather's
final resting place and see my fictitious other half. I made
Sarah up after the boys in the band started questioning why
I wouldn't talk to any girls after our gigs. Instead of confess-
ing that I have crippling anxiety—that seems to be worse
around the opposite sex—I thought it slightly more manly to
just pretend I had a girlfriend who lives far enough away that
they'll never have to see her. "Sarah" is a junior doctor and
so she works *a lot*. She's also incredibly intolerant of all
forms of social media. Handy, that.

Sarah's been "alive" for over a year now and, to date, her
invention has had no negative consequences. When people
ask when they'll meet her, I offer loose plans about soon or
maybe at such and such, then when the day comes "Her work
is a bit busy" or "She has some family stuff going on." It's a
lie that will eventually be caught out, but for now it works
wonders.

It's a long way to come to Sheffield from Edinburgh, but

it's a journey I'm always glad I've taken. Grandad is the one family member I get on with. And while, true, he's been dead for five years, in many ways I still prefer his company. He was the reason I got into music.

Patrick Delaney, while never a household name, had a following of some pretty devout fans. He left behind three studio albums and one live record, as well as lending his skills to a number of other albums by better-known bands. His death, and the circumstances surrounding it, only added to his mystique. But to me, his only grandchild, he was a hero before I knew he'd toured the world. Before I knew he'd been praised by everyone from Dylan to Bowie. Thus began my journey to what is undeniably an all-encompassing obsession with music. It's why I'm so resolute that we will make it. I am driven by an absolute certitude that our music will one day take us to places we could only dream of.

Who cares if, right now, I'm rendered unable to speak to anyone I deem remotely attractive? Because in a few years' time, when me and the rest of our band are gracing the covers of every music magazine still in publication, then, well *then* I'll have confidence. I want that so-called normal life, and ironically, my best hope for getting there is through unbridled success. And with that success, in my own way, I'll keep my grandad's legacy alive. When they ask me what my biggest inspiration is, I'll say, Patrick Delaney.

I'm suddenly motivated, for the first time ever, to say this last bit out loud.

"Love you, Grandad. See you next month."

2

Little Wiener Men

Jess

Matilda Street, Sheffield
July 15, 2015

The messages from Matt start off nice. Lots of checking if I'm OK. Concerned but respectful. About five minutes after my weird manic moment of running after a complete stranger, I decided our first-date setup really wasn't going anywhere and so I let him down gently. Actually, I didn't do that. I said I wasn't feeling well and asked if we could rain-check, knowing full well that no matter how sunny the next day, there was no way I'd be seeing Matt again.

Within the first few minutes he'd wittered on about TV and films I just *had* to be watching and explained to me the virtues of the *beans* we were drinking and why they were *so special*. He was undeniably handsome. But I prefer a face with a little character. I'm not saying I'd love a partner with a gigantic nose or a mug with tattoos, just something unique so I won't get bored gazing at it if we end up together for the next several decades.

Like that guy in the corner of the coffee shop. He had something interesting going on. Heavyset, sure, but he wore it well. His Scandi-look of scarf and hat, even though it was inside and July, set him apart from anyone else I'd seen since the leaves turned green. I don't know. Maybe I was just looking for a distraction from Matt's disappointing introduction.

The nail in the coffin for Matt was his reaction to me finally getting a word in edgeways and telling him about my comedy. His response? "I dunno. I just don't find women that funny. Is that so wrong to say?" Yes, Matt. Yes, it bloody well is.

My phone buzzes. Speak of the devil.

I hope I didn't say anything to upset you.

I'll reply when I get home. Let him know that we're just incompatible. It's fair that I'm honest rather than playing the game of "Let's do this again sometime!" in the hope that he knows exactly what that means.

Another buzz. I'm Captain Popular today. Oh, it's Matt again.

I just don't understand what I did wrong. Please reply.
Please.

All right, Matt, bit needy. It's only been ten minutes. If you're acting like this between the time it takes for me to get to the next bus, I'd hate to think what you're like if you couldn't get ahold of me for . . . *Buzz* . . . Seriously? . . . *Buzz.*

Why are you being like this?
What's wrong with you?

Well, this is escalating quickly. To reply or not to reply? That is the question. Sort of intrigued as to where this is going if I don't. Another two buzzes.

> I meet women like you all the time. You think your so special.

It's "you're" not "your" and what does "women like me" mean? You spent approximately five minutes in my company. "Women like me." Oh. Right. Yep. I can see where this is heading. He's going to call me a bitch in the next one.
Just wait.
5, 4, 3, 2 . . .

> Screw you. I wasn't into you anyway. And you've got fat legs.

Fat legs? I love my legs! I'm not always keen on the rest of me but, buddy, if you're looking to draw blood you can do better than insult my legs. Well. At least he didn't call me a . . . *Buzz*.

> Bitch.

There it is.
So bloody predictable. Self-entitled tool. Should I reply? Chastise him for his unacceptable behavior? I could, but my silence is clearly infuriating and I'm getting a cheap thrill out of him sitting in his chinos, sweating over what he may have done wrong. And really, what do you even say when someone is that thin-skinned? Why did I even hope for more?

I'm done. Done. Done. Done done done. Comedy career first. Little Wiener Men a very distant second.

"It's good material for our next show," Julia says, buzzing around our kitchen making herself a gargantuan sandwich.

In the few years we've been housemates she's really made an art form of turning negatives into positives. It's why, whenever we bomb at an improv class, or one of our stand-up shows tanks, I always feel like it went better than it did. She's the Queen of Optimism by Osmosis and has prevented me throwing in the towel on many occasions.

"That's one way to look at it, I suppose," I offer, as she hacks into a loaf to make a doorstop that would hold open the gates to Fort Knox. I'd like to see the funny side of this but this Dark Side of the Man is becoming a little too commonplace of late.

"Where was this one from?" she asks.

"Birmingham. '*This one*'—you make it sound like I go on a million dates. I'm twenty-seven. People aged twenty-seven are allowed to go on a few dates. And this is only, like, my third in a year."

She affects a dodgy Brummie accent. "Birmingham, eh?" It's not Julia's strong suit. "We could do a series of sketches, call it 'Date Britain.' I'll play the horror dates from across the UK, you play the poor unfortunate subject of their affections."

"Why do I have to play the sap?"

"Because you have beautiful big brown eyes and thighs that make me very fucking jealous. Men love you within seconds."

I throw a tea towel at her head because it's hard to take a compliment, even from your best friend. Even if I do like my thighs very much, thank you, Matt. If I'm honest, I give the tea towel a little more force than needed, because if anyone in this duo gets men to fall in love with them in seconds it's her. She has cool blond hair (that always falls the way she wants) and flawless porcelain skin (that would make a china doll weep).

"If all men loved me within seconds," I reason, "I think I'd be able to find someone that doesn't make me want to scratch my eyes out with my own severed toes."

"Oooooh, dark." Julia adds half a bag of lettuce to her sandwich, rendering the monstrosity half the size of her head. I gaze at it in wonderment. When she sees me, she radiates pride. She continues, "Maybe that's where you need to go next. Dark and edgy. And sexy, with great thighs."

"Because that's how we make it in the world of comedy?" I trowel on the sarcasm. "By having nice legs?"

"They helped get us booked for the show tonight."

I've been working on my death stare and deliver it with aplomb. Jules retreats and changes the subject back to my latest car-crash date.

"Don't worry, you'll find someone who isn't a complete knob. One day. And you'll make them very happy."

She assesses how best to tackle her lunch, measuring it from every conceivable angle, trial and error. Then in a breathtaking act of physicality I didn't think possible, her jaw widens and the sandwich goes in.

"I'm not the only one," I add.

Through a mouthful of half-masticated food, Julia tells me that who knows, I might meet someone at our next gig.

"An 'industry boyfriend'?" I reply with dripping disdain.

"They won't all be like Olly."

The mere mention of his name sends a shudder down my spine. Olly, the boyfriend who genuinely had me believing in the existence of "good men." Until the texts and the lies and the ex, who he just couldn't live without, but didn't have the balls to tell me about until he was sure she'd take him back.

I shake his existence away.

"Nope. None of that, thank you," I tell her, while pinching a crisp off her plate. "I've decided, after today's disaster date, that *all* of my attention needs to be on the comedy if I've any chance of making it."

She senses the despondency and I know what she's gearing up to do.

"Jess," she begins, leaning into it, "who's going to be a huge success?"

"I am."

"Sorry, I missed that. Who's going to be a huge success?"

"I am."

She puts down the sandwich and grabs me by the shoulder, her mouth thankfully now free of food.

"Who. Is. Going. To. Be. A. Huge. Success?"

"I am!"

"One more time for the people in the cheap seats!"

"I AM!" I scream it with all my heart.

Our neighbors must love us.

3

Clean Teeth

Tom

"How's Sarah?" asks Scott as I arrive at our rehearsal space.

I've never got used to lying to my best friend. Keeping my fibs short and boring seems to do the trick to prevent any follow-up, but the act of deception itself stays with me long after the interaction has ended. I often think if I just fess up to the fact that I go to visit my grandad's grave once a month, the secondary lie about a whole made-up person might not be so hard to reveal. On many levels I've convinced myself I'm failing a test of my masculinity with both of these acts. I think it's going to be a long, long time before either is revealed.

"Sarah," I parrot. "Yeah, she's good."

I've learned that keeping it vague is the best way to avoid tripping yourself up later. It also seems to be, or so I've gathered from my twenty-five years of observation, how other men effectively communicate about their significant others.

Scott reveals, "Y'know we've been talking with a couple of people in Sheffield about a gig."

I swallow hard and grin to mask my fear.

"That would be great!" I exclaim, possibly too ecstatically. I yawn, a real yawn, and Brandon yells out from behind his drum kit, "Tired from a weekend of rutting, are ya, Ken?"

Calling me Ken, despite my name being Tom, stems from me being a big, soft southerner. I was in fact born in Scotland, in the house my parents live in now. But we moved south from the age of five to thirteen. Two awful ages to uproot your only child and change countries. When I first moved to Edinburgh, I thought everyone was calling me Ken because they'd finish every other sentence with "d'yae ken," a phrase I would later learn could be best translated as "Do you understand?" I didn't, of course.

Secondary school was tough for this, until I met Scott. He was the first to take pity on me and help me get reacquainted with the Scottish tongue. We became friends when I walked into school wearing a BLUR: ARE SHITE T-shirt I'd recently acquired from a Mogwai concert. Being a Mogwai superfan was the initial spark for our friendship, but when he also found out I could play anything from drums to keyboard he quickly recruited me into his band. And now as we all enter our mid-twenties, we're pretty confident the time is right for our fortune and glory to be presented to us by the music industry.

I genuinely feel like I could tell Scott anything, including the fact that I've been lying to him for the past twelve months. It's the others in the band I worry about, Colin (bass), Brandon (drums), and Christian (vocals). As the band sets up, with Colin retuning, I look around to see Christian hasn't arrived yet.

Like a telepath Brandon says, "Prince Charmless ain't here yet."

My fellow bandmates are all good people, but for some reason, known only to men who have been friends since their teens, we communicate almost exclusively in insults and put-downs. Prince Charmless was a name given to our lead singer behind his back about five years ago, and it just stuck.

As the de facto leader of the band, I should have put a stop to it. But I'm sure they call me worse when I'm not around. It's one of those "things men do," which I'm pretty sure we all secretly wish we didn't. Just as I'm about to get antsy with his tardiness—to exhibit a little leadership and professionalism—Christian saunters in fifteen minutes late for practice.

God, he's gorgeous, I think as he walks through the door. I say this in a completely heterosexual way. He has the flowing locks of Jennifer Aniston circa 2000 and the jawline of her former husband Mr. Pitt. Whereas I, at best, look like the guy that would play Brad's best friend in a shit romantic comedy.

I'm a biggish guy and that biggishness has nothing to do with protein shakes or lifting weights. My excess baggage is down to a love of battered sausage and real ale, and an evolutionary aversion to treadmills. I try to wear it well. Expensive haircut and beard neatly shorn. But I know I'm no one's idea of a perfect specimen. It's reason number one—on a list of a few hundred—why, until we're successful, I'll never be the guy to go up to a woman like the one in that café and say the three little words: "Fancy a drink?"

"Sorry I'm a bit late," Christian announces with perfect diction. Whatever the equivalent of the Queen's English is in Scottish, Christian speaks it.

"I thought practice starts at four," Colin says, as if Christian hadn't just apologized.

Scott and I, always the Switzerland, step in and play mediators.

"It's OK," I say.

"Let's just get cracking, shall we?" Scott adds.

Christian takes his long black coat off and tosses it onto the beat-up orange sofa that sits at a right angle to our stage setup. At the front is his mic, to his left my keyboard; Scott is level with me and Colin, with Brandon at the back. It's a big old room and the acoustics in it are gorgeous. It's a little way out of the city and we're all often late for one reason or another. Today, though, Christian's lack of punctuality is enough to kick-start hostilities. Hostilities that have way more to do with hidden jealousy concerning his looks (and popularity) than poor timekeeping.

"We've got a couple of gigs coming up," Colin nags again. "Make sure you're not late for them."

Scott and I share a look, as if to ask each other, *What do we do?* Sometimes band dynamics need to hit a crescendo, but these little jibes could bubble for days. Something bigger is brewing.

"I don't think I'm the first to be late to rehearsal," Christian counters. "And I have apologized."

There's tension in the air as Christian steps up to the mic. Colin petulantly flips him a V-sign. Scott and I ignore it, as though he's a child acting out.

"Right. Number four," Scott announces before counting us in.

After less than a minute of play, you can tell we're all off today. Brandon's too quick. Christian's mumbling the lyrics and the rest of us are finding little synergy. I let it play out for a couple of songs but it starts to get painful to listen to. After a few more stops and starts from the beginning, I hammer my fist down on the low notes and everyone looks at me like I've let off a stink bomb.

"Time out," I announce.

There're a few shakes of the head and grumbles (and I'm pretty sure I hear Brandon mutter something about that being my catchphrase), but they all set down their tools and file over to the corner of the room where a small table and four chairs are set up for this very eventuality.

They all sit, and I stand.

"What's going on?" I ask.

I'm met with a collective shrug and a few kicked heels. It's like they're all ten years younger and the headmaster has caught them smoking behind the bike shed.

"Come on, guys."

"You were off too," Brandon argues. "What's your excuse?"

The way that everyone is looking at me makes me think this is a *Them vs. Me* thing. I look to Scott for support, but he's still pretty baffled.

"I'm not having a go," I say to try to temper the situation. "It's just something clearly isn't working. I want to know what it is so we can fix it and move on."

Christian looks at Brandon conspiratorially. Brandon nods and Christian stands.

"I'm still not entirely happy about the decision not to audition for the Fringe Showcase."

My blood boils at the fact that this argument has risen again. Only a week after I was sure we'd decapitated it with a clear vote against this being our way into the Edinburgh Festival.

"We've done this. The decision was made. This band isn't going on a sodding talent show."

"As two fifths of the band, don't we get a say?" argues Brandon.

Colin is the next to speak, with a pretty lazy put-down that Christian and Brandon should "get a room." It's a comment that riles Scott, and before long the five of us are making more noise with our mouths than we had minutes earlier with amps and an undampened drum kit.

"LOOK!" I yell above the din. Silence descends. "We had this vote. I get it. Two of you want the exposure. Three of us don't. That's it. All right?" If I thought the look Brandon gave Christian was conspiratorial, the one they share with Scott is like something from the Illuminati playbook.

"Scott?" I ask with the quiver of a man who knows he's about to be stabbed in the back by his best friend.

Scott asks the others to give us a minute and they step outside for a smoke. Once they're gone, we trade the arguments and counter-arguments we had before. This time the counter-arguments are all mine, whereas before he'd played a pretty neutral position until it came to the crunch and he decided to side with me and Colin.

"I just can't believe you want to sell out."

"It's not bloody *X Factor,* mate. It could be good for us."

"It's a popularity contest, Scott!"

"And?! It's a local contest. In our city. We are *actually* quite popular around here."

"Christian is popular. I don't know what we are." My words cause Scott to drop his head and I try to come up with something that might pick him up, yet also get him back on-side. "Just believe in the band. It's a waiting game some-times. The timing is off at the moment . . ."

He sighs heavily and looks me square in the eye.

"Mate, you just came up with three different ways of say-ing let's do nothing. I'm saying let's do *something*." After a decade of friendship, I know when Scott has made up his mind about something. And on this, he's sure.

"I don't want to side against you, Tom." He puts his hand on my shoulder and searches for a sign that this isn't going to be something we won't recover from. "It'll be OK." His tone of voice is comforting enough, but my stomach still lurches at the prospect. I offer a petulant see-if-I-care shrug.

As a little olive branch, I joke, "I just can't believe we gave everyone equal voting rights."

Scott smiles at me as we make our way back over to the rug to find the others fiddling with their equipment.

"OK," Scott proclaims. "I propose a new vote on whether we play the Fringe Showcase." I feel nauseous as soon as the vote is made final and very much not in my favor. As if to add another coat of shite to proceedings, the door to the ware-house opens and in walks Christian's newest girlfriend, Gre-tel.

"I thought this was a no-partners zone," Brandon says grouchily. Gretel waves hello to us all, and the nausea I felt at the band's decision moments earlier gets turned up to eleven by her presence. I know it has nothing to do with her person-ally. She's actually really quite lovely. Smart and funny. She brushes past me and the smell of her perfume causes my breathing to suddenly become shallow.

"Sorry for crashing rehearsal," Gretel says, before pulling

a set of keys out of her leather jacket pocket. "You might need these if you're to get home tonight."

We all back off as she hands the keys to Christian. They embrace and he kisses her on the lips. I realize I'm staring directly at them both as they make out, while everyone else is being normal and looking away. As they separate, Gretel looks right at me. She smiles uncomfortably and says her goodbyes.

But it's too late. Something has been tripped inside me. I shuffle nervously and tell myself to count my breathing in and out. Dry my hands. Get rid of the signs and the symptoms might follow suit. I scrunch my feet up in my shoes as my heart beats like a bass drum in my chest. I know this action doesn't help, but muscle memory causes me to try regardless. Scott sees me shuffling from foot to foot and asks if I'm OK. If he hadn't asked, I might have got through this.

"Just need a little fresh air, that's all."

I mercifully make it outside and round the corner of the building. I find a quiet spot to get the weight off my feet. I wait for the dizziness to subside. Is this all because of the presence of Christian's girlfriend? Or is it the talent show decision going against me? The frightened part of me easily convinces myself it's the former. The part that says I'm not good enough for anyone else.

My first-ever panic attack was in the dental hygiene aisle of the Broughton Road Tesco. And that had nothing to do with the opposite sex. I was nineteen. I'd just come back from a heavy week of truth, beauty, and freedom at the Glastonbury music festival when the toothpaste attacked.

I was actually seeing someone at the time. My second

girlfriend, who, just to be clear, was an actual real person. Beth, the only substantial relationship I've ever had, had texted asking if we were meeting later. We were due to see each other that evening for the first time in a fortnight. I wanted to make myself as presentable as possible and thought it best to start with getting rid of the bum-mouth I'd developed over a week of dirty campsite living.

It was the choice that undid me. There were—and I swear to everything holy I'm not exaggerating here—forty-seven different types of toothpaste in front of me that day.

These were the options:

Colgate—Total Original
Colgate—Total Active Fresh
Colgate—Total Advanced Deep Clean
Colgate—Total Clean Breath
Colgate—Total Whitening
Colgate—Advanced White
Colgate—Sensitive Sensifoam
Colgate—Sensitive Pro-Relief
Colgate—Cavity Protection
Colgate—Maximum Cavity Protection
Colgate—Max White
Colgate—MaxFresh
Colgate—Deep Clean Whitening
Colgate—Triple Action
Colgate—Max White Expert Complete
Colgate—Charcoal + White

And that's just one brand. Then there's . . .

Oral-B—Complete
Oral-B—Pro-Expert
Oral-B—Pro-Expert Healthy White
Oral-B—Pro-Expert Strong Teeth
Oral-B—Pro-Expert Sensitive and Gentle Whitening
Oral-B 3D White—Perfection
Oral-B 3D White—Enamel Care
Oral-B 3D White—Whitening Sensitive
Oral-B 3D White—Arctic Fresh
Oral-B Gum & Enamel Repair
Arm & Hammer Advance White Extreme
Arm & Hammer Charcoal White
Arm & Hammer Sensitive Pro Repair
Sensodyne—Rapid Relief
Sensodyne—Rapid Relief Extra Fresh
Sensodyne—Rapid Relief Whitening
Sensodyne—Deep Clean Gel
Sensodyne—Repair and Protect
Sensodyne—Repair and Protect Extra Fresh
Sensodyne—Repair and Protect Whitening
Sensodyne—Daily Care Original
Sensodyne—Daily Care Extra Fresh
Sensodyne—Daily Care Whitening
Sensodyne Pronamel—Daily Protection
Sensodyne Pronamel—Extra Fresh
Sensodyne Pronamel—Gentle Whitening
Macleans—Fresh Mint
Macleans—Whitening
Aquafresh—Triple Protection
Aquafresh—Active White

And finally, there's number forty-seven: Tesco Essentials Toothpaste.

I'd been living in a field with limited access to running water for the past five days. I just wanted clean teeth. If I were normal, if my brain functioned the right way, I'd have focused on one aspect, like the prices, realized I had £13:12 left in my bank account, and picked the store brand because it was only fifty pence. But I didn't. I just stared at them, reading each one in turn, my eyes flicking between two at a time, my brain firing questions I didn't understand, questions I didn't have the answer to, even if I had understood them.

The strip neon lights buzzed miles above me in this cathedral of things. My hands started to get clammy, my legs weak. And then I noticed my heart. The heart that's always there, doing its job just fine in the background. But, my God, once you notice it . . . When you think about the damage your heart could do if it wanted to. And right then, as Aisle 4 and Aisle 5 seemed to close in against each other, my heart very much felt like it wanted to hurt me. It was crying to be let out. I fell and hit the highly polished linoleum of the supermarket floor, taking some store-brand mouthwash with me. I came around, a few minutes later, to a crowd of unfamiliar faces and one name badge that said DEBBIE—HERE TO HELP. My shoulder and ego were both bruised but I was on my feet and out before too much damage was done. All because I couldn't decide between MaxFresh and Gentle Whitening.

The next day I went to the doctor to see what the diagnosis was. Once I let slip I'd been at a week-long music festival I was sent on my way with a friendly pat on the back and an oral subscription to "take better care of myself." She said to come back if it happened again. I never mentioned it to Beth, and we split up a few months later.

My next attack wouldn't be for another year.

A lady carrying shopping bags stops on the other side of the street and looks at me sitting on my arse, ashen-faced. She's about fifty or sixty. I don't know, I'm rubbish with ages and right now it's the least of my worries. I blink a few times and get my bearings. I glance at my watch and see that not much time has passed.

"You all right, love?" she asks. "Just, you look like a sack of shite."

"I'm fine." The old dear looks at me with skepticism and sniffs to try and work out my level of intoxication. "Honestly. I'm fine. Just a bit tired. Been burning every end of the candle, that's all."

My excuse seems to be enough for her as she nods, picks her shopping back up, and trudges off. I brush off any dirt I may have collected from the ground and make my way back inside the building. Gretel has gone. The band are in a circle chatting, a beer in each hand. It looks like a mini celebration. Even Colin seems to have been converted to the cause.

"All right, Ken," Brandon says, chucking me a beer. "Thought we'd lost you then."

I open it and chug. It's finished in under ten seconds. It's my most self-destructive party trick, one that I honed during college. As someone who felt like an outsider, I learned pretty quickly that if you can be seen as the one who parties well, people will forgive your less attractive qualities. Self-annihilation by alcohol gets you cool points. I lob the empty can into a bin ten meters away to the sound of ironic cheers.

"Right, if we're entering this piss-poor pissing contest, we better win. Let's get on it." As if my words are magic, they put down their drinks and assume their positions. I look to Scott.

"Number four?" he suggests.

"Number four," I repeat.

Now the music works. It fits. The tension's gone and we play as one. Any roughness, any rawness, is exactly as intended. When we're in the middle of it, I don't feel pleasure or pain. Everything fades away. It's just the music.

Everything is in its right place.

4

Exposure

Jess

"You're not funny!" yells out Arsehat #1.

Arsehat #2 offers, "You're not fit either!"

It's always a tough choice between giving them the attention they want with a witty put-down and a comeback to a heckle, or persevering and sticking to the script. We choose the latter, because Julia and I both know we have a secret weapon up our sleeves for the closer. The room is almost three quarters full, about eighty punters, and we're doing well enough that "The Arsehats" are pissing off those who paid their money to see some "new" and "exciting" comedy.

Julia and I have collectively generated a nice little following in Sheffield and some very favorable reviews for these shows of ours. It's a real mismatch of sketches and stand-up, and it would be fair to say a large portion of my stuff on stage is impressions. But when the Academy votes for actors who are basically mimicking real-life people year in year out, I'll be damned if I'm gonna see it as a lesser form of comedy. And my Angelina Jolie is on point. It's all in the lips and the hips.

We're coming to the end of our set. Our penultimate skit is one of Julia's favorites—a "what if" where the "what if" is "What if Harry Potter never got his invite to Hogwarts and had to go to a state school." I'm not as big a fan of it as Julia clearly is, but it's going down well tonight.

Arsehat #1, completely oblivious to the applause and laughter which shows that what we're doing is working, yells out, "Don't give up your day jobs, loves!" Their reentry into proceedings is perfect timing for what's to come. And when comedy is all about timing, really, we should be thanking them both.

Julia moves to the back of the keyboard. I turn and smile as sweetly as I can at our two hecklers, before purring with a Jessica Rabbitesque piece of seduction, "This song is for the two handsome fellas in the front row." And then we launch into our "Tiny Wanger" song, with "wanger" being my absolute favorite synonym for a man's joystick. "Joystick" being second.

Our song is a reasonably well-crafted reworking of Elton John's sing-along hit, which substitutes observations about seventies California with reasons why we know men have got a small penis. It's crass for sure, but it always gets a laugh. Thanks to our hecklers it should prove even more of a hit tonight.

And so it does.

As we reach the final verse, Julia changes our usual line "Because you heckle us on the street" to "Because you heckle us at our shows" and brings the house down. The objects of our ire slope off before we take our bow.

It's a good show and one that was badly needed.

One of my absolute favorite parts of stand-up comedy is after-work drinks. It's always the relief that you made it through an entire set that feels so good. Even if no one turns up and nobody laughs, you know you did a thing that few people have the guts to do. That sense of accomplishment and the release that comes with it is palpable in everyone sharing the lineup, so then you get to spend the early hours of the morning with completely relaxed—usually a bit squiffy—people who also happen to be pant-wettingly funny. You do, however, need a very thick skin to be out on the lash with fellow comics.

There are five of us tonight (including me and Julia), with Tariq, Jim, and Hannah. Hannah is Sheffield born and bred and specializes in character comedy. Everyone is convinced her "Patty C"—a white girl hip-hop star—is going to be huge one day. We all get a turn to be roasted and, because I was foolish enough to state an unhealthy attraction to Labour politician Chuka Umunna, it's now my turn to be mercilessly ribbed. Tariq kicks things off: "Er, Jess, I'd like to show you the, er, inside of the Labour HQ."

I eye-roll. "That's more Obama than Umunna, you big fat racist."

In character, Patty C offers up, "Obama, Umunna, you

know Jess wanna do ya. If you got a cheese-face, she'll dip ya like fondu-a."

Julia applauds this like a seal because she's been in love with Patty ever since she met her. That she's still yet to admit this to me makes me sure it'll be a helluva long time before Patty finds out. I sometimes wonder if Julia knows herself.

I turn to Jim who's stayed surprisingly quiet thus far. "OK, Jim, what have you got?"

He sips on his neat whiskey, a pompous drink that is so unbelievably Jim.

"First, I don't think a white girl from Sheffield," he points an accusing finger at Hannah, "should use the term 'cheese-face,' and secondly I can't believe you'd fawn over some neo-liberalist Blue disguised as Red, metropolitan elite . . ."

The four of us boo in unison, drowning Jim out, until he holds up his hands in surrender. Hannah slides over to me and whispers, "Don't look now. But there's a guy at the bar who's been checking you out for the last half-hour."

I look and I make eye contact. He's wearing an expensive suit, has slick black hair, and is carrying a black A4 legal pad. The whole look is a little bit eighties yuppie/serial killer. As soon as we lock eyes he starts striding over.

"I told you not to look," Hannah chides.

As he approaches, he sticks out his hand to me and says with an American twang, "Julia?"

We shake. "No, I'm Jess. This is Julia." Julia stands and shakes his hand too.

"It's a pleasure to meet you, Jess and Jules." He says our names as if we're one word, like we're the iconic brand we'd like to be. "Can I join you?"

In unison, we realize he's an industry type and it might be best to act professional. Hannah does not get this memo and lets out a really teeth-rattlingly disgusting belch.

He ignores it and says, "I work for Topanga Talent. My name is David Matthews."

Hannah snorts and is about to say "Like the band!" but Julia kicks her under the table as we all take our seats again. David has his back to Tariq, Jim, and Hannah, and faces me and Julia.

"I really liked your set. I thought you did a great job in holding off on those two fools in the front row until the last possible moment. It showed great—"

"Timing," Tariq chips in. David turns and gives him a withering look—not of contempt so much as somewhere between pity and annoyance—then he turns back to us.

". . . it showed great commitment to your act. I've seen older, more established comics lose their way under that sort of pressure. You've also got a fantastic—"

"Timing," Tariq tries again and gets a death stare from all three of us.

David continues ". . . surety of who you are. A real voice."

Behind his head, Hannah—or to give her the benefit of the doubt, let's say it's Patty C—mimes a double blow job.

"And let's not forget your—"

"Timing?" Julia and I ask in unison.

"Exactly. Do either of you have plans for Edinburgh next month?"

It's a conversation we've had countless times. While playing Edinburgh is the Holy Grail for upcoming comics, we're not naive to the fact that attendance for first-timers in Edinburgh is about one to one. As in, one member of the audience for every one comic. We've got a semi-good thing going on in Sheffield. A reasonable crowd, some good material. Are we ready to jettison a fair bit of money on what could turn out to be a big fat plate of rejection? But he wouldn't be asking if he didn't have an offer of some kind.

"We're thinking about it," Julia says with the sort of come-hitherness I'd usually reserve for gangsters' molls in the forties. I squeeze her knee under the table to stop myself laughing.

"Giving it serious thought, certainly," I add. "Why do you ask?"

"It's a couple of weeks away, but there's a little showcase I'm putting together. I suppose it's a little like a talent show, but y'know, not as lame as I'm sure that sounds. Would you be interested in that?"

Julia nods and I reply, "As long as it's not named something godawful like *Edinburgh's Got Talent,* I think we could be game. What's it called?"

The professionalism of Mr. Matthews flies out of the window as he goes a shade of red that would make a beetroot blush. "Well, it's not called *Edinburgh's Got Talent* anymore, that's for sure."

"Is there money in it?" I ask directly, causing Julia's butt muscles to flinch so much I can feel them quiver through our shared seating.

David points a finger at me. "I like you. You'll go far in this business." He tilts his head like he's doing maths on the spot. "We had contemplated a purse for the winner . . ."

"What, like a Mulberry one or something nice like that?" pipes up Tariq to stifled laughter.

". . . but exposure would be the real prize." A groan comes up from the other comics. Jim leans over as if he's absolutely entitled to join our conversation.

"Ah, the great 'exposure'! The thing that's been keeping artists warm since time immemorial."

"Quick, everyone," Hannah joins in. "Take a bite of this lovely 'exposure.' It tastes so good and fills you up for weeks."

David Matthews holds his hands up in surrender. "OK, OK. We could probably stretch to a grand or two for the winner."

"How many are on the bill?" Julia asks.

"Ten acts. There are four bands so far. Three comics and two poets. You'd be taking the last spot."

"OK, how about a guaranteed two hundred quid for each act?"

The businessman among comics shakes his head. "Why do I feel like I'm being hustled?"

Julia and I extend our hands in perfect symmetry, then say the word "Deal?" in unison. He smiles begrudgingly and shakes our hands.

"This conversation has cost me two thousand pounds. How did that happen?"

"Welcome to Sheffield," Julia says with a grin.

He gets to his feet and pulls out a business card from his wallet. "Email me on this and I'll send you the details."

We shake hands for the third time and he exits into the night. There's an awkward silence around the table as we all try and figure out what just happened. Then Tariq finally opens his mouth and we all know exactly the word he's going to say.

Park Grange Court, Sheffield
July 18, 2015

"Mum!" I yell, barreling through the front door.

As I enter the house, I hear Radio 2 blaring and I follow the sound of Creedence Clearwater Revival to the kitchen. I'm met with what can best be described as a forest's worth of admin paper covering every inch of the dining table. The family cat, an aged tortoiseshell named Agatha, is sprawled on top of the documents, pawing a packet of pens off the table one at a time.

"I like your new tablecloth," I jest as I enter.

"Oh, Jess, I wasn't expecting you," she says as she hugs me tight, pulling me into the back of her chair from her seated position.

"I was in the neighborhood," I white-lie. "So, what's the sitch?"

"The 'sitch,' my dear, is that Sheffield City Council have deemed our little four feet of extra space a planning permissions violation. They say our only option is to remove it, and that'll end up costing more than the initial build."

My stomach cramps a little at the thought of her dealing with stuff like this alone. Our dad walked out on us when I was four and my little brother, Dominic, was two. I know some cod-psychiatrist would use this (a runaway father) and Olly (a duplicity weasel) to explain my current relationship obstacles, but if they tried to do that to my face, I'd bend them over and shove an entire couch up their rectum.

The truth is my parents were both heavy drinkers, and not in that "we're British and we're fun" way. I suppose it really stopped being fun for him when he had the actual re-sponsibility of two human lives to look after. And so, he ran. Mum's drinking took longer than it should have to stop, but stop it did. I have nothing but admiration for her for getting there in the end.

She did an amazing job with both me and Dom, sacrific-ing everything, because my a-hole of a "biological" father couldn't just suck it up in the trickier times. To me, she's a superhero, and if she needs my support every now and again during episodes like this, she gets it. One hundred percent. Above all else.

I scratch under Agatha's chin and slide a piece of paper out from under her, a BT phone bill from ten years ago. "So, what are you looking for in this tree massacre?" I ask.

"I don't know really," she giggles. I love it when she gig-gles at the ridiculousness of life. "I just assumed I'd magi-cally land on the document that says, 'It's All Fine, Really.'"

I leaf through a few more letters.

"Here it is!"

Mum peers over to see what I've found, and I shield it from her so as not to shatter the illusion that I've just picked up an old mortgage statement. "It says, 'To Whom It May Concern, piss off back to chasing real criminals and leave my brilliant mother alone.' Brew?" I start the tea-making ritual before she responds, because in my twenty-seven years she's never said no to a cup.

She nods and smiles. "What would I do without you?"

"You'll never have to find out," I assure her.

As she turns back to the paperwork, I see the worry on her face and start to visualize the worst. I open each cup-board one by one.

"The tea is where it always is, Jess. Don't think I don't know what you're doing."

Even though I'm the one playing parent here, I hate being rumbled.

"You don't need to check the place for contraband. I'm doing OK. Even my mouthwash is alcohol-free now."

I offer her a sympathetic smile. "I know, Mum. You're doing better than OK. But"—I hold up the paperwork as if it's evidence in a courtroom—"I also know how crap like this can be triggering. I had to do a self-assessment in January and almost turned to smack."

She barks a laugh and a fictional Freud enters the room to tell me how my chosen profession is entirely built around the warm feeling I get from making my mother happy.

"But you won't always be here to look after me. What about the day you meet a nice boy"—she pauses and I know what's coming—"or girl."

As much as I love her, her tendency to think I might be gay, simply because I haven't had a long-term relationship in my twenties, is as offensive as it is infuriating. I'd never let anyone else off with the "different generation" fallacy but, like I say, I cut my mum a huge amount of slack.

"For the hundredth time, Mum," I say with a heavy sigh, "just because I have gay friends, it doesn't make me gay. I had a date last week, in fact. With a man."

"How was that?"

"He was a dick."

"They're not all bad, y'know."

"I know."

"You'll find someone when you're ready."

I love her outlook despite the hard evidence to counter it.

"Nah, Ma. I'm done with all that for a while."

She looks at me with a mix of "I've heard that before" and "You'll be all right." I consider mentioning that I've had several thoughts about "Guy in Café" but realize I'd sound like a total loon for fantasizing about a stranger whose face I can barely remember. I think of a positive note to end on, not wanting my entire identity to be defined by the fact I can't get a date I don't want to club to death and eat. Before mating or after.

"I'm off to Edinburgh next month. To do a show."

"Oh, that's wonderful, Jess. Maybe you'll meet a wee bonny Scottish lad. Or lass?"

I chuck a tea bag at her head.

"It's for work, Mum. No romance allowed."

5

Mr. Pitiful

Tom

Glenlockhart Valley, Edinburgh
August 2, 2015

I sit in one expensive-looking chair and she sits in another. She asks questions and I answer them. I'm offered a glass of water. There are tissues on the table between us. There are long silences. But this, this is where the similarities with a real counseling session end. There is no notepad in her hand because she isn't a real therapist. She will not ask me about my relationship with my parents. Because, along with my father, she's one of them.

"You said you feel unwell?"

I downplay it. "Just a bit of a stomach upset."

She continues, "Have you eaten something strange? You should cut down on the spicy curries. You know they don't do you any favors. Internally or externally."

"Thanks, Mum," I offer drily, more than aware that my own mother just made a fat joke at my expense.

Continuing this line of confidence-boosting questioning, she asks, "Are you getting enough exercise?"

I nibble at my top lip. I'm really only here today because Dad said he was having a clear-out of some stuff. He can bin anything I've accumulated over the years, but I know he has a boxful of my grandfather's stuff that I desperately want. It's mostly annotated notes on his song sheets, a few back-stage passes, and a couple of scrapbooks. But the big item I've been waiting for is his diary. Having to put up with my mum's passive-aggressive health advice is a price worth paying.

I finally retort, "Playing music for two hours straight every day is pretty great exercise. I don't need a gym membership."

In response, she drums her fingers on the chair and I wonder if it's her or me that's more desperate to get up and leave the room. I visit them less and less these days. I have no guilt over this. They've seen less than an entire show of mine, so if we're playing the game of who makes the most effort, I'd still win hands down.

My parents are Conservative with a moderately large C. Money and status and what other people think of them has always meant everything to them. On the money front they have done exceedingly well. Their house is enormous, their bank balances likewise. They have hired help and consider themselves above anyone who doesn't. They offer their wealth to me as a replacement for affection and are still baffled at my refusal. Having continually espoused the idea of those less fortunate being "pulled up by their bootstraps," they offer me handouts to get ahead, blind to the hypocrisy.

If I were being generous, I'd say my father's personality was shaped by having an artistic father. The definition of a free spirit. It's natural to want to revolt against your parents, but I didn't think that revulsion was supposed to be put onto your own kids if they, in turn, turn out like your parents. Maybe this is an unending loop and if I ever have children of my own they'll turn out to be cash-grabbing culture-phobes. But considering the last meaningful conversation I had with a member of the opposite sex was over twelve lunar cycles ago, me having kids is a pretty massive IF.

"How is Scott?" Mum asks.

"He's good."

Our small talk getting smaller by the second.

It's difficult for me not to read everything she says or does as resentment, but not once—*not once*—has she ever asked about the band. I read a quote once that said, "Most of human heartbreak is caused by parents loving the child they imagined rather than the child they have." It stuck.

"I saw his brother has been promoted," she continues. "And bought a new house. They must be very proud of him."

At this I stand and start to pace around the room. "Of him." Proud of the one who has his life together, she means. The one that isn't a screw-up in a band. That I've chosen to follow my grandfather's lifestyle and not my dad's is one of many reasons for the hostilities between us. That both he and my mum refuse to talk about him is another. I can read articles and listen to old interviews (there's even a decent biography about him called *Patrick Delaney: Fret Not*). But when I want to know what he was like as a person, as a family member, they both clam up. It's fair to say his last few years with us, as his illness took over, weren't exactly a great testament to his character. The fact that he became a differ-ent person in his final years has made me desperate to know more about his whole life, not just the bits I already know.

"We've got a gig tonight. Part of the Edinburgh Festival. They say some of it's going to be on TV." I might as well be miming, without hands, in a foreign language, for the reac-tion it gets.

"Are you staying for tea, Thomas? Your dad should be ho—"

She stands as his car pulls up.

"Speak of the devil."

I look down at my hand to see I'm subconsciously mim-icking her finger drumming as her inane phrase plays on loop. "Speak of the devil." He isn't, though. He's not a bad person. Not a great father, but not abusive either. He just didn't notice me as much as I wanted him to. As if to prove my point, he isn't aware of my presence until a good minute after he comes through the door. He and Mum talk about his day, about what he's bought, about the weather. It's only when I pipe up that I won't be staying to eat, that either of them turns their attention to me.

He even looks at Mum a little perplexed, as if to say, *This guy, eh?*

"I didn't know you were popping over. You well?"

"Fine." The monosyllabic nature of my reply is intended to get a rise out of him.

"Good to know you're not starving," he says, patting my gut before he turns his back on me to kiss his wife. The affec-tion they have for each other hasn't lapsed in thirty years. I know I should be grateful to have grown up in a home that had love on show, but in truth it just reminded me of what I missed. What they didn't want to offer me. I was the third wheel throughout my own childhood.

"Are you staying for tea?"

"No. I just wanted to share my news and grab that box of Grandad's stuff?"

They look at each other with something akin to shame and my stomach drops about a meter.

"About that," Mum says as Dad makes his way into the kitchen, unwilling to stay around for the battle. "A man got in touch online. Said he was a collector."

Anger brews. I shake my head in tiny movements at the betrayal as Dad calls out from the other room, "We thought you'd be happy that it's gone to someone who'll really appreciate it."

"*I'd* really appreciate it!" I yell. "You should too! He's your bloody family. How could you do that?"

Dad reenters the room. "It was only a few scraps of paper and some photos."

I take a calming breath. "Fine. Just give me the diary and I'll be off."

"What diary?"

"The one in the box. Tell me you took it out before you handed it over?"

His silence tells me all I need to know. I ball up my fists.

"I told you I wanted that diary," I say quietly. "*I told you!* How could you do that?"

"No need to get melodramatic about it," Mum retorts. "Anyway, what was this news of yours?"

I know I'm not fifteen years old, but it feels like I am. I grab my coat and march for the door, slamming it behind me. I have no idea when I'll come back here. But it feels like any time that passes between now and then won't be nearly long enough.

St. Andrew Square, Edinburgh
Three hours later

I'm still fuming with them when I meet the band for our pre-gig ritual of naans and Neck Oil at the Prince of India. My mood isn't improved by the invitation I obviously didn't receive extending the meal to partners.

This decision was likely taken by Scott, who's been more than a little distracted by the reemergence of Holly. Scott and Holly have been on and off so many times I've lost count. Once, when I thought they were off, I made the questionable move—after overhearing a particularly nasty slanging match between them—of suggesting maybe they were better off apart. When they got back together the next day there were corners of the Antarctic Peninsula warmer than the atmosphere between us. Before this most recent "on" they'd been split for the best part of three months. I didn't say peep in case of what might transpire.

To be clear, this isn't some bullshit Yoko thing. Holly's great. She's funny, warm, understanding. Most importantly, she makes Scott happy—when they don't make each other mad. It's just unfortunate timing with arguably the biggest gig of our lives so far less than five hours away. A gig I'm still struggling to get on board with.

As the day in question got closer and closer, more and

more details started to emerge of just what we'd signed up to. First, the "Showcase" was very much being billed as a "Talent Show." Second, said talent show was being sponsored by a brand of footwear and within our contract was a clause that stipulated we had to wear said footwear. The point isn't that eighty percent of us already do wear those shoes; the point was that we should be able to dress however the hell we want.

The third and biggest problem is one I admit is very much just on my shoulders. The gig is to be televised. Not live. But recorded for a Spotlight on Edinburgh thing. It's why there's not just bands in the lineup, but also comedians and poets. The idea being to represent all the Festival has to offer. We've each been given a ten-minute window to do what we do. The results are announced at midnight and my nerves are shot to shreds.

All of this is swimming around my head as I take the only seat left, between Gretel and Brandon's boyfriend, Carl. They're both good people, but I really wish I was sitting next to Scott so I could try and persuade him we shouldn't go through with the gig.

As the meal goes on and we get closer and closer to gig time, Christian and Scott get buddy-buddy at the other end of the table. I know it's Christian's opinion Scott listened to about the Showcase. That he whispered sweet nothings in his ear. Paranoia creeps in and I start to worry about what new direction Christian might try to take the band in.

Meanwhile, so as not to be the rudest guy at the table, I've been keeping Gretel company. She smells of coconut shampoo and that sweet but sickly mix of Diet Coke and vodka. She is not my type. I am in no way attracted to her. But here

I am struggling to keep my leg from shaking like a dog having a leak.

"D'you know what I mean?" she says for the umpteenth time tonight, like it's her mantra to the world.

I could confess I don't, but instead I smile and nod and wonder if anyone at the table can see through this facade. I'd like to blame her flirtatious manner. Her hand on my arm, my leg, her insistence on eye contact. But it's not her fault I'm incapable of normal human behavior. There's a brief pause in our one-sided conversation and I use it as a window to take a toilet break. As I'm about to step into the loo, I feel a tap on my shoulder. I turn around to see Holly, arms open wide, ready for a hug. I swallow hard and embrace her. For some reason, she seems the apprehensive one.

"You OK?" I ask.

"I was going to ask you the same thing," she replies, a quizzical look on her face which gives away the fact that I'm definitely exhibiting signs of peculiarity. "You don't mind me being here, do you?"

Another familiar downside to acting skittish and losing control is that people project their own insecurities onto you. You see someone start to dry up or get lost to the thousand-yard stare of a panic attack, and the natural human response is to question what you did to cause this.

"Of course not. I'm glad you're here. I am. It's just all a bit overwhelming. Curtain up in what, four hours? Why do you ask?" I still feel like I'm in the fact-finding stage of this problem. The more data I can collect, the better I'll be able to hide.

"Nothing, you just seemed quiet. I thought you might be missing Sarah."

"I am now," I say, trying to make a joke of it. Trying to make my made-up girlfriend sound natural, even to me, the one person who knows how absolutely nuts I am.

"We really can't wait to meet her. Sarah. She sounds brill."

Every time her name is mentioned I get a punch of guilt and a kick of self-disgust. What kind of pathetic man am I? Holly's face falls and my heartbeat rises. This may sound insane, but I feel like I'm letting her down. That every lie I tell is letting everyone down. That guilt in turn leads to nausea, and the nausea turns to panic.

"Everyone will meet her soon. I'm sure."

Her look is one of rejection. Not for her, but more on Scott's behalf. What kind of best friend doesn't introduce his girlfriend to him after more than a year? Raise your hand one more time, Mr. Pitiful.

"Oh, OK," she offers.

"OK," I counter.

These OKs could last awhile and so I point at the little man on the door.

She gives one more "OK" before I smile and enter the bathroom. She returns to the table wounded that her ideal has not been realized. That the dream of her, me, Sarah, and Scott will make a happy little foursome.

I haven't had so much as half a poppadum and my insides have already turned to mush. I take my place on the throne as sweat creeps up my back. It's hard not to think of a vengeful God when you have anxiety that manifests itself in your guts. The few books I've read about it describe the feeling as a churning sensation. Which, without getting too graphic, is exactly what's happening now. There is a liquidizer somewhere in the middle ground between my heart and my feet turning all food and drink to something that could pass through the eye of a needle.

Thoughts of people discovering my secret, coupled with images of us getting booed off stage, collate in my mind's eye. They swirl and collide and then the pain comes. The cramping. If I deny my lungs breath, my eyeballs shake in my skull. I'm doubled over now, face screwed up, caked in sweat, trousers around my ankles. I am such a catch.

Before I even think about wiping, I know I must get out of here. Skip the meal. Get some air. Get ready for the gig. And when the gig comes, just look at the ground. Ignore everyone's presence. Do not make eye contact with anyone.

Once I'm playing, it'll all just fade away.

6

Free Shoes

Jess

Edinburgh, I love you! You wondrous, undulating, warm-hearted, crowded, feral, tourist-ripping-off, deep-frying, Irn-Bru-swilling, dream-killing, hope-thrilling bastard of a city. I! Love! You! Within twelve hours of our arrival I have located the bar in which I will happily die, the greatest chippie in these British Isles and a view that I will forever return to in my mind. I have found home. (Although I did peek into an estate agent's window and rent is *insane,* so maybe I won't be moving here and dying anytime soon.)

Julia's giddy too, but she's doing her professional grounded thing to keep me from exploding in a sea of joy. I am very lucky to have a friend like her—someone who stops me spinning off. I make a mental note to spoil her rotten after the show.

"OK. They've asked that we soundcheck there for five.

It's"—she checks her watch like she's organizing a bank heist—"ten past four now."

"Let's get a curry!" I squeal.

"We had chips like two hours ago!"

"You know me, I always get ravenous before a show."

"Nervousness is not a concept you're familiar with, is it, Jess?"

I adopt my most offensive Scottish accent and wiggle my eyebrows up and down. "I guess you could say . . ."

Julia groans, knowing what's coming.

". . . I'm just not a nervous Nessie?"

She shakes her head as if to say, *Put that material in a bin and then set fire to that bin and then bury the bin in a quarry.* It's a good job I have Julia around, because there's a high chance I might have opened with that. I point to a curry house, The Prince of India, and she shakes her head with a grin.

"Can I check out the menu at least? Maybe just grab some pakora." I make my way over to the board outside. Christ, £9:50 for a veggie balti. You can see the "Festival Prices" stickers plastered over their regular, reasonable charges.

As I make my way back to Julia to tell her the bad news, a guy coming out of the curry house barrels into me, and I mean *barrels* into me. He's a reasonably heavyset dude and he sends me flying onto the pavement, skinning my knee.

Julia runs over to my defense.

"What the shit, pal?" she says as she gives him a shove, and me a hand up.

The guy is white as a sheet, even for someone who gets Scottish levels of sunshine. I can see his hands are shaking and he has the same look in his eyes my brother, Dom, does, when he's having an episode.

"I'm all right," I say, putting my hand in front of her to stop her swinging at the guy, who I can tell is suffering much more than I am with my skinned kneecap. He looks lost in himself, but my God there's a soul screaming out. His eyes are the same color as mine—the color of Coca-Cola—and for a moment mine and his connect.

He half mumbles an apology and starts to walk away.

"Wait here," I say to Julia and I run after him.

"You all right?" I ask.

He doesn't stop walking; instead he quickens his pace.

"Wanna come to a comedy show? It's me and my friend, the one who wanted to punch you for ruining my jeans."

He looks down and clocks that my legs are bleeding through the denim.

"Shit, shite, shit," he offers in a weird mix of Scottish and English.

"It's all right." I wiggle my leg like a cancan dancer to put his mind at ease. "Nothing broken. My name's Jess. What's yours?"

He mumbles again, the name "Tom" barely making its way out of his mouth.

To counter his silence, I start gabbling at a mile a minute. "I know what you're going through, Tom. My brother has panic attacks all the time—he has this phrase he repeats to himself: 'And. That's. OK.' Don't know how or why, but it helps."

Tom suddenly stops walking and looks me in the eye again. I feel like I've seen this guy somewhere before. For some ridiculous reason, I lick my lips, as if he's going to kiss me. That would be weird, right? Maybe I'll kiss him. That'll make him feel better. Wow. Turns out I get hungry *and* horny before a show.

"I'm sorry," he apologizes again. "I really am. But could you . . . *fuck off*?"

As I stand, dumbstruck, he hightails it into the night. Leaving me with a bleeding leg, wet lips, and the weirdest feeling in my stomach I've had in a very, very long time. I return to an impatient Julia.

"What was that all about?" she asks.

"Dunno." I shrug. "I offered him my hand in marriage but he declined. Woe is me."

"His loss," Julia tells me as she links her arm through mine. "Right. Let's go check out this venue."

Hill Street, Edinburgh
Ten minutes later

It quickly becomes clear that we've been had. The venue is gorgeous. Truly high-end. There's a camera-crew setup that would make Spielberg shit his beard, and enough advertising on the stage to make it feel more like the QVC channel than a comedy venue. The idea that David Matthews could only just stretch to two hundred quid per act is laughable.

"What the actual, Julia? I've seen royal weddings with less money."

"And to think we had to barter for anything."

"Dave Matthews is an arsehole."

Her eyes are wide as she takes it all in. She points up at the rigging.

"Those lights are gonna give me a migraine."

She's only half joking. Julia gets these horrid migraines after shows sometimes. The stress of it all takes a high toll on her. Bright lights and eating late are other triggers. In the past I've likened her to Gizmo out of *Gremlins,* but she doesn't seem to like that much.

David bounds across the stage, all smugness and light.

"What do you think? Pretty neat, right?"

"I think you could afford to pay us more than a couple of hundred quid, you tight bass."

His smugness amplifies as he looks up at the giant advertising banners showcasing the latest brand of sneakers that look exactly like these sneakers have looked for the past twenty years.

"You named your price. And don't forget the—"

"The exposure. Yeah, yeah, yeah."

"And these!" David holds out two boxes of box-fresh trainers. He hands them to us. "You get to keep them!"

"A gift. How generous of you. I'd rather have the cash equivalent, though." I smile enough to let him know I might be joking. But this time he isn't laughing.

"Your contract. Remember? The shoes?"

I look at Julia and she's wearing the face of a kid who's been caught eating all her Easter eggs on Good Friday. "Did I not tell you?" she asks, all innocence and light. The facade quickly crumbles and she fills me in on how the corporate sponsor has stipulated that all acts need to be clad in their footwear. She does this while begging my forgiveness.

"It wasn't so much a lie. More an omission of the truth. I

thought you might go all Bill Hicks on me, the righteous angry comic, raging against artists working as salesmen."

"Because I would have!" I holler back.

What Julia has really done is not only instantly forgivable, but also incredibly generous. She's made it so that I get to have the high ground, principles intact, in the knowledge that it would be beyond crazy to travel to Edinburgh and then refuse a gig just because they made you wear a brand of trainers you probably would have worn anyway. Also. Free shoes!

"Well. What can you do?" I shrug. She smiles in a way that suggests we both know her master plan has worked perfectly.

"Still," she counters. "If I'd known there was this kind of money in shoes, I'd have applied for a job in Clarks years ago."

Despite feeling like we've had a number done on us, we're still both in very high spirits. It's easily the most professional setup we've been a part of, and despite that same tiny Bill Hicksian voice telling me I'm a sellout, I'm really quite proud of me and Julia for getting here. After all, Mr. Hicks never had to try to make it in the world of comedy as a woman. His rigid set of principles might just have taken a little bending if he wasn't born with that oh-so-privilege-making thing of testes and a knob.

David returns and offers a hand to each of us in turn, pulling us up onto the stage. He tells us to get used to the space, that tonight we'll be on second to last, and then retreats into the shadows. Julia looks at me and we beam. The space holds at least five hundred people, and with it being televised—on digital, but still—who knows how many earballs and eyeholes will be on us. The same thought seems to flash through Julia's mind, and seconds later we are blasted with the full set of house lights.

"Jesus!" I yell, shielding my own face from the retina-scorching filaments. The lights go off and someone yells an apology from the back of the stage. Julia squints heavily and we both file off the stage to be met by David.

"You all right?" he asks Julia, and I'm suddenly hit with the nauseating thought of her getting sick.

"I'm fine," she offers breezily, but I can see her blinking and slightly wincing with her left eye screwed tight.

"How long until we're on?" I ask David.

"A little over three hours."

Julia looks at her watch and presses some buttons, synchronizing the time. I blink away the big bright light from my eyes.

"Is there somewhere quiet we can go, preferably without a bajillion lumens being shot into our eyeballs?"

David leads us behind the stage and down a small corridor into a green room that's painted blue. In one corner is a sink, a kettle, and a microwave. In the middle of the room, three tatty non-matching sofas are arranged in an almost-U.

"There's a bathroom through there." David points to a door opposite the sink. "It'll get a little crowded in here once the other acts turn up, but you should have some time."

His mobile rings. He pulls it to his ear with the fluid motion of someone who constantly talks on the phone. He whispers to us if we need anything we should shout and then disappears to more important problems. I run Julia a glass of water and sit her down on the middle sofa. Already looking pale, with her left eye pretty much all the way shut, she's exhibiting all the signs of a major migraine.

"Don't look at me like that, Jess," she says and I instantly feel all the frowning muscles in my face doing overtime.

"You'll be fine, mate. Three hours is plenty. What we'll do is . . . you down that water, I'll switch the light off and stand guard outside. You try and sleep it off. Deal?"

She salutes me and I make my way out of the room, leaving her in total darkness. Suddenly my worst fear isn't the two of us standing on stage getting heckled as corporate sellouts. Looking at the state she's in, it's clear there's a fifty-fifty chance she won't be able to go on. Which leaves me with a pretty shitty decision to make. Break our contract and take the two of us back to Sheffield with our tail between our legs, or go on solo and most probably tank. I hear the toilet flush from inside the room, and whatever was in the bowl goes down the pan along with our hopes of a good show.

7

One of Those Mystical Things

Tom

Thistle Street, Edinburgh
August 2, 2015

As I exit the bathroom I am plunged into total darkness. Which is odd because five minutes ago, as I sat in the green room alone, it was definitely fully illuminated.

I scramble about for a light switch immediately outside the loo but to no avail. Unfamiliar with the layout of the room (I think there were some sofas in the middle and the exit is definitely on the other side of that), I begin to paw my way forward. On the second step, my shins hit what I assume is a coffee table. I let loose with a couple of quiet profanities and carry on inching my way to safety. I feel the wall and take the approach that if I just stay left I'll find the way out. Like in a maze. As my head whacks into a shelf about eye level, I start to rethink this plan. Finding nothing else in my brain, I edge my way slowly along the wall until I finally find my salvation. A door handle.

I stumble out into the corridor and immediately trip over.

As my eyes become accustomed to the light, I see a familiar face looking down at me. I look at her knee to make sure it's really her.

"You all right?" she asks upside down, before her face lights up with glee. "It's you! The guy who rugby tackled me outside the curry house. Tom, is it?"

She puts out a hand and I take it, overcome with embarrassment, and clamber to my feet.

"Somebody turned out the lights."

"Huh?"

"In the green room."

"Oh yeah!" she says, full of enthusiasm. "That was me. My friend has a migraine. I say 'friend.' She's my partner, too."

The second she says the word "partner," the wave of discomfort, the overwhelming feeling of discombobulation I usually feel in the presence of someone of the opposite sex, completely evaporates. The idea that there is zero potential for me to let myself down in a romantic sense suddenly allows me to be a normal human being. Well, a normal male at least.

"Yeah, she gets these terrible migraines. Bright lights and late eating usually trigger them."

"Like Gizmo," I suggest.

She lets out a squeal of joy at my reference and punches the air.

"Exactly! That's what I always tell her." She pauses. "She does get wet, though."

As much as I'm strangely comfortable in her presence, the double meaning of this makes me go a shade of red that's off the Dulux chart. Her face when she realizes what she's said is a truly beautiful thing to behold.

"I didn't mean it like that!" she yells, before realizing her loud voice might wake up her partner. She whispers, "Although that is definitely going into the set." It suddenly dawns on me that I'm fraternizing with the competition.

"You're in the show?" I ask.

"I am! Well, if Julia comes round. We both will be. I'm Jess."

"I'm—"

She interrupts. "Tom, right?"

"Yeah."

"It's weird. I swear I know you from somewhere. Other than when you violently stopped me buying Indian food."

It sounds like a line but, knowing I won't be making a fool of myself for saying it, I reply that I feel exactly the same way. She asks me a few questions about where I'm from and we can't pinpoint a single merging of lives.

"Oh, well," she concludes. "Must just be one of those mystical things."

It's a weird sensation to suddenly experience how other people behave. If she were straight, there's no way we'd be having this conversation. Not without me tripping over my tongue, sweating incomprehensibly, and genuinely making a huge tit of myself. That she's incredibly attractive would be the first inhibitor. That she's actively talking to me would be the second. As we continue to jabber away, I almost feel like a regular person.

"What's the name of your band?" she asks.

"Wider Than Pictures."

"Oooh, arty. Do you play old-sad-bastard music? Is that your thing?"

I know she's teasing and I like it. Am I letting my guard down? Is this what that feels like? Oh, happy days!

"No. It's all new-sad-bastard music. You and . . ." I ask, waiting for her partner's name.

". . . Julia."

"Is it all militant-feminist comedy?"

"I don't even have a comeback to that. It really is. We've caused actual riots in Conservative Clubs before."

I throw my fist up as if I'm about to start my own political movement. "Rock on, sister!" I must have nailed the tongue-in-cheek self-deprecation I was aiming for, because Jess laughs and steps closer.

"How long have you and Julia been together?"

She looks up and to the right as if accessing some secret calendar. Counting the days of their union. "Five years, eight months, and three days."

"That's weirdly accurate."

"I just remember our first gig together." She adopts a broad Yorkshire accent. "Like 'twere yesterday."

"So, you dated *before* you were in an act together?"

She looks at me as if I've just announced I'm the King of Uzbekistan. Or as if I've just offered her a half-chewed biscuit. Half confusion, half disgust. She steps away from the little circle of trust we'd made.

"Because I'm in a female double act, I must be gay?" There's genuine rage in her voice and I take another step back.

My stomach drops. The feelings of inadequacy, self-loathing, and uselessness flood my body again.

"I'm so sorry. I really didn't mean to . . . I just . . . when you said 'partner.' I don't know . . . I just . . ."

Brandon's booming voice saves me. "You owe us twenty quid for the curry, mate." I turn to see the band heading toward me.

Jess steps in front of the door, just as Brandon grabs the handle.

"You can't go in there," she instructs him.

Christian steps up. "The guy out front said this was the green room. He said we could hang in here until the show starts."

I decide to step up, to do whatever I can to make up for my stupid error.

"It's rubbish in there. No drink. No atmosphere. Let's just go back out. Watch the competition."

Colin shakes his head. "Some crap comics and a poet. No thanks."

I look over to Jess, who's now in a real rage. She steps up to Colin, almost nose-to-nose.

"Crap comics, yeah? What are you, then, faux-Arctic-Monkey-wannabe-douchebag?"

I try not to grin at this, because I'm one of only a few people who know that Colin once walked into a barber's with a picture of Alex Turner and asked for hair "just like this." We've never stopped ribbing him for it. Instead, I step in and physically drag them away before more words are hurled. Not one of the band has a violent bone in their body, but the look in Jess's eyes leads me to believe she could really throw down. When all's said and done, none of us fancy getting thrown off the bill or kicked in the balls.

As they file away and out into the venue, I fight against the urge to just walk away and cut my losses. My usual modus operandi. You can usually count on me to quit, but not this time.

"Jess. I'm really sorry about my mistake. Earlier. You

know. And for them"— I point to the back of my band's heads as they round the corner—"being a bit knobbish."

At this she cracks a half-smile.

"It's OK. I'm just a bit highly strung. Worried about my"— she flips up the bunny ears—"'partner.'"

I raise her half-smile with a full one.

"Cool."

"Cool."

"Best of luck with the show."

"Yeah. You too."

I begin to walk away before I stop. Then, in the most uncharacteristically Tom Delaney move in the history of moves by Tom Delaney, I add, "Maybe I'll see you after?"

None of the other acts are bad. The first poet is great in fact. She's got this unashamedly honest sexual-awareness thing going on. And she's damn funny to boot. The act before us got the biggest reception by far, just for walking on stage. He's midway through his third and final song. It's just him and a guitar and crooning that might not be out of place on a cruise ship for the over-sixties.

He can sing. Undoubtedly. All the right notes. But there's a question I ask when it comes to other people's music: Do I believe you? And, right now, as he's singing about having his heart broken by an angel, I very much do not.

Jess hasn't been on yet. I haven't gone back to see if her friend is doing better. As the nerves begin to rise, it's our brief encounter outside the curry house that I keep replaying. Those three words she said her brother tells himself. *"And. That's. OK."*

I don't want to be here. *"And. That's. OK."*

I'm scared we're going to bomb. *"And. That's. OK."*

I feel sick. *"And. That's. OK."*

The warbling troubadour who I guaran-bloody-tee hasn't had a problem with women in his whole entire life, finishes up to thunderous applause. He nods to us in a really chummy way as he passes. The emcee takes the stage.

"Another hand for Daniel Reid, ladies and gentlemen. Although maybe more ladies, am I right?"

This guy's schtick seems to be just to say "Am I right?" after every other line. The crowd seems to like him, though. And they certainly liked the last act. Doubt runs through me like a river. This isn't our scene. This isn't our crowd. We've sold out for a swing and a miss.

"Your next act is a local band," the compere announces. "Making a name for themselves last year with a residency in Sneaky Pete's, please give it up for . . . WIDER. THAN. PICTURES."

We step out.

We give him grief, but Christ, Christian has got it.

The audience is eating out of the palm of his incredibly tight jeans. Because I daren't look out into the masses, I need somewhere else to keep my eyes. They've mainly opted for Christian's flowing locks and gyrating hips. Fair play to him. He does good hip work. I don't need to look at the audience to know this is one of the best gigs we've ever played. The response is unbelievable. It's like we are actually bigger than the Beatles even if they had Jesus on tambourine.

I check the time and see we have room for one more song.

I nod to Scott and he telegraphs to the others which track to play. He opts for "Molly," a song I know he wrote about Holly, but people seem to think is about the street slang for MDMA. He's never corrected anyone because, hey kids, drugs are cooler than songs about how you're still madly in love with your ex.

Scott starts things off with a fast, catchy hook, before Brandon comes crashing in with a thumping bass drum. The lead-up to Christian's first vocals is all about atmosphere. It's mostly me playing the ondes martenot, this weird instrument Scott's uncle turned us on to (that's sort of half keyboard, half theremin). It gives Christian time to really play to the crowd before it all coalesces into a beautiful waterfall of melody and rhythm.

Within a blink, it's over. When we're playing, it's like I'm floating above myself. Now I'm back in my body, I can even look out for the first time tonight, toward the two hundred cheering, hollering fans. There's a gender imbalance—skewed female—in those nearest the stage, including some regular faces I know Christian has, let's say, enjoyed the attentions of.

Most importantly, for the next stage of our careers, there are men in suits by the bar. Suits at gigs like this means one thing: industry people looking for the next big thing. I once read an interview with one of my favorite musicians who said, "Execs have absolutely no idea what they're looking for, they have no taste in music, no preference, no internal barometer for why they sign a band. They just go with what the crowd tell them." If that's true, this lot have just helped us nail the best job interview of all time.

I walk to the edge of the stage and throw up an uncharacteristic fist into the air. Scott wraps his arms around me from behind and I turn to see him sporting the goofiest grin imaginable. This is what we've been working for. Fighting for. Dreaming of.

Faced with the faces, my eyes fixate on the woman with the long, sleek brown hair. Her wide mouth, turned up at the corners. The girl with the skinned knee. Jess. She mouths, "That. Was. Amazing," and beams a thousand-kilowatt smile, and I feel even better than when I was playing.

I give her a thumbs-up and her megawatt smile increases in strength. The Matthews guy who's running the event is the only one not smiling and I realize it's because there's another act waiting to come on and we've overrun. The fact that we're soaking up every inch of praise is only putting him further behind.

I round up the others and physically push them off the stage.

"Let's end on a high, lads. Yeah?"

8

Kill or Cure

Jess

Thistle Street, Edinburgh
August 2, 2015

Julia is in a bad way. She's vomited twice and can barely see for the lights. There's no chance that we're going on as planned, which leaves us with two choices.

Choice One: we bail. We explain the situation, maybe even get a little argy about the fact that it was their shoddy stage setup that near-blinded Julia and sent her down a migraine-hole. This leaves us out of pocket and with a pretty major black mark against our names when it comes to Edinburgh and other opportunities.

Choice Two: I go solo. Together we have over an hour's worth of material, with a pretty even fifty–fifty split of Julia content and Jess content. There's enough quality stuff for me to get a more than decent ten minutes out of it. And I don't care about the crowd. I don't. No nerves. If I tank, I tank. My brother's words come back to me. *"And. That's. OK."*

Although now they make me think of that guy outside the curry house. No. My big fear is being away from Julia.

Julia is heavily up for Choice Two. She's constantly pushing me to do solo gigs. If we have one recurring fight it's that she's always telling me how big I'll be one day. I tell her it's *us* that will be big and she just smiles this all-knowing smile. Like she's the Gandalf of comedy and I'm the Frodo. I have to "walk this path alone." Part of me wonders if she's faking the whole headache thing. Unless she's storing minestrone soup in her cheeks and jettisoning it down the toilet every time I hold her hair back, that theory is garbage.

"Let's get out of here," I suggest. "I'll take you back to the hotel."

Julia shakes her head.

"Then what do you want to do?"

She dabs at the corner of her mouth with toilet tissue and wipes the sweat away from her forehead with her sleeve.

"Go out." She steadies herself against the bowl and sits up, her back against the cubicle wall. "Smash it. For us."

"I don't want to do it without you."

She raises her index finger on her right hand and makes it crooked. She points it at my left boob and (considering the state of her) perfectly reenacts the climax of *E.T.*, delivering her line in a croaky, alien voice. "I'll be . . . right . . . here."

With Julia off in a taxi and me with nothing better to do, I decide to watch the other acts in the Showcase. As timing would have it, Tom's band is taking the stage as I join the crowd. There are *a lot* of women in the front few rows and it becomes pretty evident they're there for the lead singer. The skinniness of his jeans would make Olivia Newton-John in *Grease* weep. If he gyrates any more there could be an incident.

Away from Robert Plant by way of Derek Smalls, I see Tom. He's doing his best not to be noticed. Head down, completely absorbed by the equipment around him. And there's a lot of it. Keyboards, a harmonium, some bizarre little box with lights and pulses he keeps stabbing at. It's like he's working in the music section of Cash Converters. But it works.

Fuck me, it works! The music is gorgeous. Ethereal. It pulses through me and I feel this weird mix of dread and complete comfort. Wave after wave. I shut my eyes and am taken to another place. I don't care too much for the singing and I can't make out the words either, because the front man is making love to the mic with such gusto he's become unintelligible. But the music. The ambience and spirit of it all. This really is something.

It takes the entirety of their set for me to remember I'm on that same stage after the act after them. And all alone. As they soak up the well-earned applause, I catch Tom's eye. He grins a big goofy grin and my heart lifts for him. He flashes me a thumbs-up and I clap so hard I feel blisters coming up. I really want to see this guy again as soon as possible. But first . . .

There are many great types of laughter. Contagious is good. Belly is better. Crying actual laughter tears is the best.

And there are also many bad types of laughter. The snort is OK but it makes people too wary of what their body is capable of. The etiquette laugh simply vexes me. It's the "I'm laughing because I should be, not because I want to" laugh. It's the kind you hear in an independent cinema coming out of a pretentious douche in a turtleneck. But nervous laughter, nervous laughter is the worst type of laughter. And that's all the audience has given me for the first three minutes of my set. Here's why I hate nervous laughter above all other forms. It's neither genuine nor involuntary. It's a pity laugh. The audience is pitying me and I can't stand it.

Dying on one's arse is a rite of passage for all comedians. This isn't the first and won't be the last time. But there's something particularly galling when your hopes for a good show go up in smoke. And I had high hopes for this show.

One of the biggest problems is that me and Julia use a fair amount of sound and music cues. Without her to play the music, I have to stop and start the show. I might as well be announcing there's a joke coming every thirty seconds. The fact that we can back and forth is our greatest asset. Solo, our bits are just *too much*. It's time to completely rethink my approach.

"OK, that last bit went down harder than an elderly grandmother on an icy winter's day, overladen with Christmas shopping, running for a bus you just know she won't catch."

From the back of the room, I hear it. A short sharp "HA." I look up with a smile and see Tom hovering at the back of the room.

He's not a small guy, so he stands out. Especially with his full beard, the exact same color hair, and eyes to match his face fuzz. Like a hamburger of brown. He looks down sheepishly as my eyes find him. Now I have a focal point.

Instead of the pre-planned sketches and routines, I decide to freewheel. It's the comedic equivalent of eating a fry-up after a heavy night of booze. Kill or cure. Whatever happens next, it'll be an experience. Something to learn from.

"These shoes," I say, pointing to my bright, shiny foot-wear. "You know they made us wear these. I am contractu-ally obligated to wear these fucking clown shoes." I look over to David in the wings. He's not amused but the audi-ence chuckle. They seem to be going for my mid-set hand-brake turn, so I take the mic from the stand and begin to stroll. "The worst thing is, I signed that paper. Give me that filthy cash and you can have my principles. I am an-other millennial learning that my existence is purely trans-actional."

As I continue my snippy little takedown of the people paying my wages, my confidence grows. As does the laugh-ter. As does the grin on Tom's face. Considering he's part of my critique of being a sellout, the lines coming off the top of my head must be pretty good. I focus my attention on him, as if we're just having a chat after the show. I envision us talking about being financially screwed over by the organiz-ers. And so, the words come out.

"Do you know how much we're getting paid for this?"

I can hear the sound of David Matthews's butthole clenching from the side of the stage as I riff on the size of his marketing budget compared to our wage. Maybe because it's a little peek behind the curtain, but the crowd really go for it. It could also be that most of the audience are in the same demographic as me, most of them in dead-end jobs, getting shat on by their bosses. They can relate. After all, except for the suits at the bar, not a single one of the 18–30 audience is going to be able to afford their own house anytime in the next decade. Not at Edinburgh prices.

"But what are you gonna do?" I ask, glancing down at my watch to see I only have sixty seconds to go. "If time is money, my watch stopped a while ago. The teat of capitalism must be suckled at. So go forth and consume. Join me in bowing down at the altar of things! THINGS! THIIIINGS! Things like thongs! And kitchen tongs! And things like . . . er . . ."

Someone in the crowd yells out, "Those little plastic cases you hold a banana in!"

"Yesssss!" I cry out. "My God, what is the point of them? But tomorrow, my good people of Edinburgh, we'll forget all this rabble-rousing and go back to buying and selling and working and buying. And when we do . . . well . . . at least I've got a really nice pair of shoes to do it in. Thank you and good night!"

I give the emcee a pat on the back as I pass him and he asks the crowd to give it up for me. It's a send-off that lets me know I did good. Which, two minutes in, seemed like an impossible task. I can tell Julia we earned our money tonight.

David Matthews looks less than pleased to see me as I saunter off stage. I give him a wink for good measure. When all is said and done, I don't think my cheap shots are going to keep him up at night. Whoever's cutting the edit together for TV might have a tough job on their hands, though. Someone told me it airs tomorrow night. As for this night, I am sans my best friend in a city I do not know. Once I ask myself what I'll do for tonight's entertainment, Tom appears as if by magic at the side of the stage.

"Hey. That was great," he says.

I mime a little bow. "I mean, the start was godawful, but I think I recovered it."

"Just a bit. That was excellent!"

The way he says it makes my stomach twist and turn like a Slinky in a tumble dryer.

"You really think so?"

He looks back over his shoulder at the room I was just performing to.

"I know so. Every single person in that room loved it. How's your friend?"

"Back at the hotel, sleeping it off."

"Migraine?"

"Yeah."

"Ouch."

There's a pause you could drive a snowplow through as I wait for him to follow up on his earlier offer to "see you after." He shifts from foot to foot and I get the impression he's about to turn on his heel and go. From inside his belly I hear his gut gurgle. It's that loud.

"You hungry?"

He shakes his head and laughs. "Not really."

"Do you . . . do you fancy a beer?" I ask.

"I'd love one," he replies.

The pub he takes us to is wonderfully "Old Man Pub." Despite it being the eve of the Festival proper, there's still only a smattering of tourists. Me being one of them. There's a pool table in the corner, a dartboard, and even an old-style (not-screen) jukebox. The holy trinity is a rare breed in any city these days, so it's nice to see Edinburgh keeping it real.

When Tom returns with our drinks, I commend him on his venue choice and ask if he wants a game of pool. He says yes, and as we search our pockets for fifty-pence coins, he says something I don't hear over the clatter of the red and yellow balls being jettisoned. I ask him to repeat it.

"Oh, I was just saying, you do righteous indignation really well. I thought the organizer was going to pull you off stage. Is that your usual stuff?"

I offer him the chance to break and he declines. "Not at all. We're usually pretty tame. Very light on the vitriol. We don't get the flexibility most male comics do."

"You don't think you could get away with being Bill Hicks with a vagina?"

"I'd *love* to be Bill Hicks with a vagina. But no. Everyone gets put into a bracket, and truthful anger isn't something we're allowed to do. In comedy, as in life, there's the Madonna/Whore box. Right now, 'whore' is where people are being pushed. Even though the 'filthy female comics' have better clean material than any of their male peers."

He stops chalking his cue and looks pensive, suddenly sad for me. I don't read it as pity, more disappointment in the world at large. He shrugs and suddenly looks happy again.

"You did it tonight," he tells me.

"What do you mean?"

"That wasn't tame. Or light on the vitriol. Or in a box."

He's not wrong. I mean, for an off-the-cuff seven minutes of straight stand-up, that was exceptionally good. And unusually fierce. If I do say so myself. But for that one success I could tell Tom about a hundred times where I've been told I must be "on my period" by some jerk punter, because I dared raise my voice on stage. No. We're still put into boxes. Still restricted by what we can say and how we can say it. Two thousand and fifteen years after Jesus came out of his mother's snatch, we still can't be ourselves. I take my frustration out on the cue ball and give it an extra whack. I fluke two reds as Tom fills the gap in my response: "Well. I thought you were great."

I pot another without looking up, and tell him, "Your old-sad-bastard music was good too."

We clink our cues.

"When I was at the bar Scott texted to say that that Daniel Reid fella won," Tom informs me with a hint of bitterness.

"Who? James Blunt's inferior cousin?"

"You mean, Chris de Burgh's understudy?"

"The love child of Mick Hucknall and Celine Dion?"

He physically shudders at the last one.

"Can you imagine?"

Then the image appears in my head and I retch a little.

"Forget him," I tell Tom, as I pot another couple of reds. "Who remembers the winners anyway?"

His megawatt smile is back and there's a look on his face of pure happiness. If I had to guess, I'd say fifty percent of that happiness is because he put on a pretty great show and the rest is a mixture of booze and my company. Whatever the ratio, if he's having half as good a time as I am, I'm doing well.

"Twenty years from now," I continue, "you'll be inducted into the Rock and Roll Hall of Fame and this night and this competition will be but a distant memory." I've just the black ball to go. I line it up and look him in the eye as I pot it and win the game.

"I don't know," he says with a playful grin. "Something tells me I might remember this night for a while."

We take our seats and start to talk again about our chosen paths. This time we go broader, less about the specifics of what we've done and more the how we get to where we want to go. With a dash of the why, too.

"What's success to you?" I ask.

He takes a moment to think before answering, "Making a living from music, I suppose."

"So, if you were offered a gig on a cruise ship, playing piano for some C-list crooner . . ."

"Fair point. Making music that I want to make."

"And does it matter if no one wants to listen to it?"

"This feels like a job interview," he quips before, again, taking time to really think about the answer. "OK. How about . . . I want to be able to play the music I want to play and have an audience that gets it. And to make a comfortable living out of it. You?"

I don't need to think about my answer. I've always known it. But when I've said it in the past, the response I've been given has always been a letdown.

"I want to make people feel better," I tell him.

He doesn't say a word. He just nods.

I fish for clarity. "Aren't you going to tell me to be a nurse instead?"

He looks confused at my slightly combative tone and plays with the last bit of his pint, swirling the drink around in the bottom. He looks up and at me.

"I think your answer is the best answer I've ever heard."

9

Quantum Leap

Tom

George Street, Edinburgh
Two hours later

"This is nuts. I've known you about four hours. But I really, really like you. Maybe it's the booze talking, I don't know. I want to tell you all about myself and find out everything about you."

As the toilet flushes behind me, I jump out of my skin. I genuinely thought I was alone as I practiced my slightly drunken monologue in the mirror above the sink. An old man in a cardigan steps out from the cubicle and starts washing his hands in the bowl next to mine. I offer him a little head nod. He shakes his and mutters something about youth being wasted on the young.

There's no doubt in my mind it's the success of the gig that's letting me be this confident with Jess. This is it. This is the start. If we'd bombed and she'd been watching, I would have turned tail hours ago.

But how do I trust this feeling? It's been such a long time.

Maybe this is how everyone feels when they communicate effectively with someone they're attracted to. Maybe there's nothing special about her. But that's not what my instinct is telling me. I tell my reflection to "just go back out there and see where the night leads. Stop trying to plan it and go with the flow." It feels like the man telling me this is an entirely different person to the one I've lived with lately.

I sit back down and see I have a third pint waiting for me. Jess meanwhile is drinking water, which I start worrying is a bad sign. Does this mean she's drunk and wants to sober up? Is she stopping the booze because she's done for the night and wants to go home? Is she worried she'll make some stupid mistake if she drinks more? The questions swirl and so does my gut. I thought three drinks would be enough to calm me down, but this minor curveball has thrown me. There must be something happening to my face because Jess squints and studies me before concluding, "The water, right? It's freaking you out?"

Not as much as your clairvoyance, I think. Instead of saying this aloud, however, I simply nod and say, "A little, yeah."

I can see the thought process she's going through, deciding whether or not to divulge something. The usual catastrophizing voice shuts up and lets her explain, before jumping to mad conclusions.

"My parents. They drank. Like, a lot."

"Both of them?"

She nods, before letting me know she doesn't just spill like this to random strangers. I make it clear she can tell me as much or as little as she wants. She chooses the former and I feel grateful for her trust.

"My dad left when I was young. Really young. My childhood pictures of unicorns and fairies couldn't quite compete with the lure of a freshly pulled pint or seven."

"Hence the water . . ."

She shrugs. "I don't really enjoy getting drunk. I like being tipsy. Tipsy is good. If I have a pint of water between drinks it helps me stay at a level. I know, right. It goes against all that British people hold dear."

"There's an expectation—when you're in a band—that you should drink morning, noon, and night." I don't say that it's an expectation I've done little to limit over the years. "I have a worrying tolerance to it now. There came a time when four pints felt like three pints and now it's five before I even consider doing anything stupid."

Her eyes widen from behind her glass.

"And what 'stupid' thing might you be considering doing tonight?"

Panic. Panic. Alarm. Alarm. Please Ground Swallow Me.

"I didn't mean that . . . I . . ."

"Chill," she says with a grin. "I'm just teasing you. I'm afraid it's a professional hazard if you get with a comic." I see her eyes flicker at what she's said and suddenly she's the one backpedaling. "I didn't mean 'get with.' I meant— actually I don't know what I meant. This water is rubbish. Can I come sit next to you?"

I nod and shift along the little bench and Jess sits close. My heart begins to beat an unorthodox rhythm. *And. That's. OK. And. That's. OK. And. That's. OK.*

"I like people-watching," she tells me. "Wondering what their lives are like."

We watch the world together as if it's a giant TV in the corner of the room and the two of us are an old married couple, curled up on the sofa. We analyze people's clothes and getups for clues to their personalities, studying their body language and expressions to ascertain the relationships they have with the people around them. What, I wonder, would people make of me and Jess if they did the same?

A random question pops into my head.

"Do you remember that show *Quantum Leap*?" I ask.

With a perfectly straight face and without batting an eyelid, she repeats the opening monologue of the show word for word, including an incredibly spot-on breathiness, beginning with "Theorizing that one could time travel . . ." and ending a full minute later with ". . . hoping each time his next leap . . . pause for emphasis . . . will be the leap home."

My face hurts from the size of my grin.

"That's quite a party trick."

"Why, thank you."

"Sometimes when I'm watching TV or at a gig—"

"You quantum leap yourself into other people?"

I nod, more than a touch freaked out. But as my grin is, if anything, widening, I'm guessing this is a good scared.

"Exactly," I yell, splashing my pint a little as butterflies flap inside me with the kind of intensity that really could cause a typhoon on the other side of the world. "You do that too?"

"No," she delivers in perfect deadpan. "That would be really weird. And I'm not weird. Now, drink up. I want you to show me more of this wonderful city."

We step out into the street and I'm curious as to what "tipsy" constitutes in Jess's head as she yells into the night sky, "I feel invincible tonight. What you were saying earlier, about me being Bill Hicks with a . . ." She mimes genitals with her fingers.

"Vagina?"

"Yeah! That's what I want to do. Forget being pigeon-holed. I'm gonna be me. And *only* me. I'll take on the whole comedy world. Make any agent who's turned me down weep when they see me on TV and billboards. The one that got away."

I don't doubt she will for a second.

"You have to be obsessed," she continues. "And even then it might not be enough. Hard work. Luck. Talent. In that order. Unless, of course, you have some famous relative. Those fuckers get the world handed to them."

I try my best not to show how offended I am. Judging by her naughty-schoolgirl impression, I've failed mightily.

"Whoops! So. Who are they? Rod Stewart? Annie Lennox? The Proclaimers?"

"That's deeply offensive," I reprimand her, with a smile, before explaining my grandad was Patrick Delaney. She rolls the name around in her mouth and brain.

"I know that name. I think my mum's into him. He's a bit 'down' for my tastes. Not exactly happy, funky, party music. I see where you get it from now. Can he get you a record deal?"

I shake my head. "He died."

The jokes suddenly stop and she offers me a genuine apology. I let her know it's OK and she asks me if he's the reason I got into music.

"One hundred percent," I tell her.

"He made it. Having heard you on stage, I'm pretty sure you can too."

Jeffrey Street, Edinburgh
August 3, 2015 (Early hours)

We spend the next couple of hours pub-hopping. It's long gone midnight and there are plenty of places still open. There was a Hibs versus Falkirk football friendly earlier and the streets are only just starting to quieten. On the way to the next pub, The World's End, we talk about our families some more.

I open up about my parents and my grandad. The difficult relationship with the former and the unbreakable connection with the latter. I get deep and talk about a pull of a thread between me and my grandad. How I find all these similarities in the two of us. How it scares me a little. I don't go into how he died, specifically. That's a little heavy for a first night, but I do mention some of the struggles he had. Jess is attentive and compassionate, limiting her inbuilt joke machine as I mention how he was defined by his illness in his later years. When I tell her about the diary my parents sold for money they didn't need, she's as outraged as I am.

"That sucks!" Jess says.

"I know, right?"

"Could you hunt it down?"

"I could try but I doubt I could afford it. If the collector knows what he's got he won't let it go for anything less than five figures."

"Let me guess, those are two figures too many."

"Might be four too many after this weekend. Edinburgh prices, man."

It's Jess's turn to talk all things familial. She tells me about her brother, Dom, taking a gap year and how her mum is in some very minor but annoying legal trouble over some planning permission snafu.

"I know a guy who might be able to help her," I offer.

Jess stops and asks me to elaborate.

I explain how I studied law at uni for half a term before dropping out, and that while there I met a guy who stuck with it and who now has his own practice. This little info dump gets the expected jokes and jibes from Jess, mostly rooted around how much better off I'd be if I'd not quit.

"You sound like my parents. Anyway, he does stuff for free."

"Pro bono?"

"The U2 guy?"

"What?"

"Huh? Anyway, his parents are rich. We're talking Richie Rich rich. So rich he'll never need to earn a penny in his life. He takes on cases he thinks will cleanse his soul. I could get you his number if you like."

"I like."

She bites her lip and skips a couple of steps. Suddenly childlike and playful.

"I could give you my number. Now. If you want?"

"I do. Very much."

"I mean, I probably should have asked this earlier in the evening, but you aren't seeing anyone, are you?"

I think about my fake girlfriend and wonder if I told Jess about her what she'd think. I honestly believe I could and she'd just laugh it off. But then I have had about five beers and Five-Beer Tom isn't the smartest guy in the room. Probably best to keep it to my chest that I've an imaginary girl-friend who I've told all my friends and family about.

"I'm not. I am not seeing anyone," I reply.

She narrows her eyes and studies my face. "Definitely? You took a little while to answer there, Tom. You're not a scumbag guy who pretends to be all nice and shy but is in fact banging half of the Hebrides?"

I feel like correcting her on her appalling geography knowledge, but all I can do is be mildly ecstatic at the thought that she could see me as someone confident enough to be a complete and utter arsehole. Then I repeat as clearly as I can, "Jess. I am not seeing anyone. I am the dictionary definition of a single man."

"Good," she says. "I believe some of the high-numbered circles of hell are reserved for people who cheat on their partners. If I find out you're lying I will send you there my-self."

"Not to put too fine a point on it, but that sounds like you've been—"

"Burnt in the past. Correctamundo. His name was Olly. He was a comedy promoter."

The way she admits this last bit tells me most of what I need to know. Stories in the industry of promoters taking advantage of people are rife.

All I offer is an "Oh."

"You can probably fill in your own blanks, but yes, this industry is full of snakes and worms and other slippery, slimy, spineless scumbags. With apologies to actual snakes and worms."

I offer her an apology I hope means something.

We stop walking and she dips into her bag and pulls out a

piece of makeup. Maybe something for the eyes. I have no idea.

"Roll up your sleeve," Jess says.

I do as instructed and she writes the eleven digits of her number on my arm in black. The few seconds in which she's doing this might be the happiest few seconds I've had since I stood next to the founder of Mogwai after a show at the Leith.

"When can I transfer that to my phone?" I ask.

"Let's say . . . in the morning. If it's still there." She delivers the line with a cryptic look on her face and puts her makeup stick back in her bag. Neither of us moves for a moment.

I get the sudden urge to compliment her, to make her feel good. Because despite *me,* and all that is *me,* I think I'm about to kiss this girl in front of me.

"You know your comedy?" I ask.

"I am aware of it," she replies, smiling.

"You should be *you.*" I emphasize the *you.* "I like you."

"I like you too," she repeats.

Up ahead, I hear a couple of drunk Hibs fans singing some offensive song about Hearts. The football season kicks off in a couple of weeks and with it flows the pent-up testosterone of a summer off from chanting and insulting people. I decide to wait to kiss Jess until they're safely past. I'd prefer this moment not to be ruined by some pissed-up jeering. As they come alongside us, I see just how wasted they are. If I had to guess I'd say it's more than just booze. They're jittery and their eyes are wide. I don't mean to look at one directly, but it's already too late.

"All right, pal?" one spits at me. "Ya got a light?"

I shake my head and take a tiny step in front of Jess, not enough to feel like I'm shutting her out—I just want her not to be the focus.

"What about yer bird?"

Jess shakes her head too.

"Well, what have ya got?"

"What do you mean?"

He looks at his mate and laughs before parroting my accent. "'What do you mean?' What sort of accent is that?"

Jess tugs on my arm and I hold my hands up defensively to the two men.

"Sorry. Guys, we've got nothing for you."

As we walk away, I hear them taunting me. Mimicking my voice again and calling me a soft southern prick. Despite Jess seeming to be wholly unaffected by the encounter, I rapidly start tormenting myself that I should have done more, said more, stood up to them. Replicated what it is to be a man in any way possible.

"Well, they seemed nice," Jess jests as we head in the opposite direction.

I try to monitor my pace, desperate to put some distance between them and us. I hear them singing their song again, the sound getting closer and closer. As I turn around, I don't have enough time to react to the fist being thrown into the side of my head.

10

2 Become 1

Jess

Jeffrey Street, Edinburgh
August 3, 2015

"Police. And ambulance. Please. We've just been jumped. Two guys in football shirts. They just ran up and smashed my friend on the back of the head. He's fallen really badly. I think his arm might be broken. Where am I?"

I look down at Tom, sitting on the curb, clutching his right shoulder, which sits at a jaunty angle. He looks up and mouths "Jeffrey Street."

"Jeffrey Street," I repeat into the phone. "Outside The World's End." The operator asks for more information and tells me they'll try and get someone to us as soon as possible. I relay the message to Tom. Every time he moves even an inch, he howls in pain.

"Is it your head?"

"No," he whispers. "My shoulder."

"Can you wiggle your hand?"

He does. "Yeah, it's just . . ." He lets out a deep, searing cry, like he's in labor and they've just told him to push. "Christ. It's every time I move my arm."

"Is there anyone you want me to call? Anyone in the band?"

He nods and instructs me to call Scott and tell him to meet us at the Royal Infirmary. The circumstances might be less than ideal, but I really liked him using "us" in that sentence. Focus, Jess. Your amorosity is not the priority right now. I call Scott and tell him everything that's happened, then hang up as the ambulance arrives. A heavily tattooed paramedic steps out, and his colleague joins him to stand beside Tom. Tattoo Man shakes his head as he instantly diagnoses Tom.

"Tom, is it? You OK?"

"Not really." Tom winces.

"My name's Marv. Do you know why you're not OK, Tom?" The paramedic's riddle-me-this doesn't seem to be helping Tom's agony.

"Not a clue," Tom replies.

"It's because you've dislocated your shoulder." He places his arm on top of Tom's and Tom howls again. "Yep. That's dislocated."

"Can you just pop it back in?" I ask, using all the expert medical knowledge I've gleaned from multiple viewings of *Lethal Weapon*.

"You really don't want me to do that, love. Between where your fella's arm is out of its socket, there's a ton of nerve endings. The more he moves, the more they tear and, well, nerves being shredded isn't the nicest feeling, is it, Tom?"

Tom shakes his head.

"Can you get to your feet for me?"

With the driver and Marv on either side of him, Tom gingerly makes his way to the back of the ambulance, a banshee cry leaving his lips every step of the way.

"You coming with?" Marv asks me.

I look to Tom and he looks back with a very eager *Yes*. I'm glad he does, because this is definitely not how I wanted this evening to end. I climb in the back as Marv fiddles with an oxygen tank.

"Have you had Entonox before, Tom?" Marv asks.

Tom shakes his head again.

"It's a mix of nitrous oxide and oxygen. Should help with the pain. Until we get you to the hospital, then you can have something a little stronger." He hands a mouthpiece to Tom and Tom inhales heavily, sucking the oxygen into his lungs.

"Just go easy on it. It can make some people feel a little funny."

It's virtually impossible not to laugh at Tom high as a kite on nitrous gas.

For one, it's done such a number on him, the agony of his arm seems almost inconsequential now. But mostly it's because he's currently banging out the entire songbook of the Spice Girls, word for word. He's already serenaded Marv and me with a perfect rendition of "Wannabe" and "Stop," and is now a chorus and a verse into a very sultry rendition of "2 Become 1," informing anyone who'll listen how he needs love like he's never needed love before.

He switches out from being Mel C for a moment when he notices Marv's tattoos. He giggles to himself, not for the first time, and whispers far too loudly.

"That man has got drawings on his arm and on his face."

I try to shush him but it's no good, he's already turned to Marv to repeat himself.

"You've got drawings on your arm and on your face."

Marv, big guy that he is, has probably seen this a million times before and reacts with a simple shake of his head. I, on the other hand, wish I had a video camera and a notepad. This is comedy gold. Tom takes another hit of gas.

"Easy there, Sporty Spice. Not too much. We're nearly there."

Tom looks floaty as the ambulance pulls up to the hospital. Like he's sitting on a giant fluffy cloud of marshmallows and puppies, not a care in the world. I wonder if they'll let me have a go on the air once we get inside. It looks mega fun.

Just as he seems out of the woods, the ambulance goes over a speed bump, causing him to scream again. I look at Marv to see if there's anything more he can give Tom for the pain. I have the craziest urge to stroke Tom's face. To let him know it'll all be OK.

"They'll probably give him some morphine. With a dislocation, the pain, unfortunately, only gets worse from here on out. I know someone who's both given birth *and* dislocated their shoulder. She said the shoulder was worse, and who am I to argue? He'll have to have X-rays before they put his shoulder back in. Stick about for that, though, if you can. Once it's back in"—Marv mimes the international sign for mind-blowing—"the euphoria! He'll be hugging the doctors and all sorts."

The ambulance stops, Marv opens the doors, and we get Tom to his feet. He's still taking tiny steps. What little blood he had in his cheeks has well and truly left his face. A guy about Tom's age, but with a slightly smaller frame and about fifty percent less hairy, comes running over to him from the entrance. I'm guessing this is Scott.

"All right, mate?" he asks, with a mix of curiosity and affection. Tom rather comically gives him a thumbs-up with his other arm as Marv leads him to the reception area and away from us. Scott uses the opportunity to introduce himself properly, before he registers me as one of the acts from the Showcase.

"So, you're the person he sacked off our post-gig drinks for." He gives me a little once-over out of the corner of his eye. "Very un-Tom-like."

"Oh yeah?" I ask, fishing for more about this wonderful man who I very much intend to spend some time with over the next few days. A brief fantasy of me nursing him back to health runs through my head, until it's roadblocked by feelings of feminist guilt.

Before Scott can answer, Tom is back with us, plopped down on the seat next to me by Marv, having filled in his information at the desk.

Marv says, "Very nice to meet you, Jess. Make sure our little troubadour looks after himself in the next couple of days. And get ready for the euphoria of the arm going back in. You'll never feel a hug quite like it."

Tom, still whacked off his bonce on Entonox, cozies up next to me. Scott eyes us both with a fat dollop of suspicion. As much as the gas is helping, every now and then Tom moves an inch and the pain returns with a vengeance. He grabs my hand and squeezes, waiting for the moment to pass.

Scott leans forward and asks, "You OK, Tom?"

Tom lets out the longest "Yeah" known to man as the wave of discomfort crescendoes.

"You want me to call Sarah for you? Tell her where you are?"

My ears prick up and alarm bells start ringing in my mind and gut at the exact time Tom is called through for his X-ray. He completely ignores Scott's question, stands, and turns to me with hope in his eyes. "You're still gonna be here when I come back, yeah?"

I nod while silently screaming, IT REALLY DEPENDS WHO SARAH IS, TOM! Once Tom is far enough down the corridor, I turn to Scott and ask the question that's been screeching in my head for the last thirty seconds.

"Who's Sarah?"

I can see Scott wrestling with the dilemma of telling me the truth or lying.

"Please," I say. "Don't lie."

Scott shakes his head in semi-disbelief before answering with conviction. "Sarah is Tom's girlfriend. They've been together just over a year now. She lives in Sheffield. I wanted to say something the second I saw you two together. All cuddly. It's not like him to do something like this. Like, at all."

The qualifier at the end of Scott's sentence does nothing to sate my absolute fury at Tom's duplicity. I wasn't going out tonight looking for something. I came here to work. I came here to do a show and then he turns up all fake humble and shyness. The absolute bullshit of it.

I get to my feet in search of Tom. It doesn't take me long to find him, outside the X-ray unit waiting to go in. He's on his own.

"Who the FUCK is Sarah?"

He says nothing, just shrugs.

"You bastard!" I yell.

Whether it's the drugs or not, he doesn't react the way I expect him to. I was anticipating a defense, excuses, guilt and shame. Perversely, he lets out a little giggle. The same one I found adorable on the journey here. A giggle that makes me want to tear his other arm from his socket.

"Sarah isn't real, silly-pants," he tells me, his pupils wider than saucers.

He reaches to take my hand, but I pull it back as quick as I can.

"You're real, though," he says, his eyes dopey.

There's a lot you could forgive a man in Tom's current state. But the lies, the goddamn lies, after I asked him point-blank if he was seeing someone . . . And this girlfriend? I know he's off his face, but saying she isn't real? Who does that to someone? Especially given she should be the one here, holding his hand. The betrayal is infuriating. I get flashbacks to my friends telling me about Olly, and me not believing it until I saw it with my own eyes. Words cannot describe the anger I feel in this moment.

"You absolute piece of shit."

There's genuine sadness on his face, fighting to get out from behind the drugs. I have zero sympathy. I want to kick him in the crotch or stamp on his shoulder for good measure. Instead, I simply stand and look at him with utter scorn. In one quick motion I rub at my phone number on his good arm, smearing it to an unintelligible mess. Before I leave, I let him know . . .

"I hope it hurts, Tom. I really hope it hurts."

Eglinton Crescent, Edinburgh
August 3, 2015 (Morning now)

Back at the hotel, the lights are off. I make the assumption that Julia is still dozing. I sneak in as quietly as I can, but when I fill a glass of water for some much-needed hydration she whispers, "Is that you?"

Under normal circumstances I'd tease her for asking a question that can only have one answer: *yes*. I mean, even if it was a horrible murderer, the answer is still yes. Everybody can only ever be them. As—more's the pity—tonight has expertly illustrated.

She asks how the show was and I say great. She asks how my night was and I say awful. I don't elaborate on the Man of my Dreams turned Cheating Little Shit for fear of stressing her out and triggering another migraine. I don't mention how "he's just another Olly." I'll fill her in in the morning. In the harsh light of day. I strip down to nothing, throw on an old T-shirt and shorts and crawl into bed next to her.

"Can we get out of this city as soon as possible tomorrow?"

She murmurs something I can't quite make out and I take it as a yes. Goodbye, Edinburgh. Goodbye, Tom. What a crushing disappointment you turned out to be.

Part Two

OPPORTUNITIES

11

—

Justin Fucking Bieber

Tom

Cliftonhall Yards, Edinburgh
May 15, 2016

There are three ways I've considered getting in touch with
Jess and three reasons why I've talked myself out of it. The
reasons all boil down to lack of nerve, insecurity, and an exceptionally low opinion of myself. I can find facts and figures
to back me up on all counts. The ways of reaching her, however, all have their own drawbacks.

1. Social media. Her pages are for friends only. Putting in
a request for said status would almost certainly be shot down
in a hail of bullets so large it would make King Kong's execu-
tion look like a single pop from a BB gun. I can see bits on
her Twitter and Instagram (probably more than is healthy),
but sliding into her DMs is just a big, fat, simple NO.

2. One of her gigs. I bought tickets. Twice. And bottled it
on both occasions. The second time I even made it to the
venue before turning tail and running. My main excuse for
this is . . . it's her job. Turning up unannounced at some-

one's place of work is a stalker move right out of the *How to Be the Best Stalker You Can Be* stalker handbook. I'm a few bad things, but this I'm not.

3. Ringing the smudged number. In her haste to erase herself from my life, Jess didn't do the greatest job of deleting her number from my arm. But she did do just enough to make it a lengthy and potentially futile endeavor. I have about seven of the eleven digits, scribbled down on a piece of paper after I was released from the hospital. On one particularly low and lonely evening I did try and fill in the gaps, but all I received for my troubles was angry strangers telling me I had the wrong number.

This last method of contact reminds me why I shouldn't be doing any of the above. She doesn't want to see me. She made that clear. While her decision to leave the hospital was based on a lie (my lie), there's no earthly reason why she wouldn't fight that lie. "Oh, sorry!" I hear her saying, sarcasm dialed up to eleven. "You didn't lie to *me,* you lied to everyone you've ever known. You sound like a top bloke, then! Let's get married!"

Another truth I've wrestled with since we parted ways is, well, I'm embarrassed. Embarrassed of the lie, for sure, but also the incident itself that led to the lie being uncovered. I'm a big guy. If two people jumped me, shouldn't I have defended myself a little better? This experiment in masculinity is failing at every point.

And so I go on, alone.

While I think of her at least twice a day, it's Christian's face I see everywhere.

Looking like Marlon Brando and James Dean, on the

cover of every music magazine. He's ubiquitous. Which I believe is Latin for all over the sodding place. In some photos he's smiling—or smizing, to be more accurate. But mostly he's doing the sultry "two too many buttons open on a designer shirt" thing. He almost always has scantily clad women draped across his torso, like they're the window dressing and he's the center of the universe. Men want to be him. Women want to screw him. And vice versa, I'm sure.

Because Prince Charmless is the next big thing. The beneficiary of a solo—repeat *solo*—album deal that will see him make hundreds of thousands of pounds, that will see him tour the world, that will see him live the life we intended for ourselves.

And where are we? Still gigging in bars and halls within a two-mile radius of our houses, playing to a handful of people, under a brand-new band name. Is it simply jealousy that makes me hate his very existence? Pride? A feeling of betrayal? A feeling that, without us, he'd be modeling turtlenecks in some door-drop clothes magazine which offers three tops for twenty-five quid?

The answer is, it isn't any of those things. Christian may have taken the money and run on that night at the Showcase (when it was clear to the suits that *he* was the main attraction), but it's the night in question that I can't stand to think about. His face is simply a reminder of my mistake, and what it cost me. The old self-loathing comes back with a vengeance and instinctively I reach out to touch the top of my arm. Some of the nerve endings in it are dead, never to return. Another reminder of the repercussions of my lie. A lie I was convinced couldn't hurt someone. But it did. It hurt a couple of people, actually. Scott's a pretty moral guy and since that day I've dive-bombed in his estimation. I'm sure I have. One quick reveal of the truth would set him straight, but I still don't have the courage for that. I wonder if I ever will.

That night, after my arm was set right, the doctor told me he'd never seen anyone look so forlorn when their shoulder was put back into place. He said he'd been kissed by big hairy bikers and once had a pregnant woman so overcome with emotion she promised to name the baby after him, simply because he was the one who made the pain stop. The disappointment of me just sitting there, when I was supposed to feel such euphoria, was, he said, one of the strangest things he'd ever experienced.

I didn't tell him why. I didn't tell Scott either. In fact, we've never mentioned the night in any detail. Some friend I am. One positive thing I did do was "break up" with Sarah a month later. As much as Scott wanted to talk about it, I just kept repeating that it was "one of those things" and that we were "just gonna be mates now." He asked, only once, if it was something to do with the "girl at the hospital." I lied again and said it wasn't.

Here, in the same rehearsal space we've been in for three years now, it's back to the music. It's the music that will save me. It's the same setup. Just minus a lead singer. There's one notable addition to the room. We've put up a dartboard on one wall. A picture of Christian's face is on it. Nobody else is here yet and so I'm filling the time by hammering arrows into his forehead. Pulling them out and doing it again. When

Scott arrives and sees my borderline psychotic ritual, he shakes his head in disbelief.

"You really have to let it go," he tells me, with the patience of a saint who's been stuck on the M8 for two hours and cares not a jot. "It's been ten months."

He picks up his guitar and tunes up, as I throw another three darts into the board and Christian's forehead. Brandon enters and sits down with barely a nod, puts his headphones on and starts drumming, oblivious to our conversation.

"It's been nine," I tetchily correct him, remembering that day in August like it was the most monumental of my life. The gig. The glory. And above all that, the girl. Jess. Then the descent and disappointment of reality.

"That night should have been everything for us," I complain.

"We got a manager out of it," he counters.

"A band manager who works part-time at his dad's accountancy firm."

"A band manager who helped us get an EP out next month."

"On a shitty label."

"On a decent indie. You've been glass-half-empty for almost a year now. Can't you just be happy with what we've got?"

"It's not exactly EMI and private jets, is it, Scott?"

He forgets tuning for a second and throws his arms in the air.

"Sorry, Tom, I didn't realize you wanted to be Justin Fucking Bieber."

He stares me down and I stop chewing on the inside of

my cheek long enough to realize I'm being the biggest prick this side of a needle factory. I start to laugh. He starts to laugh. And we're back to where we should be.

"Look," he continues. "Forget Prince Charmless and his twenty-album deal and his pool parties and supermodel GFs. That was never what we wanted."

"It wasn't?" I ask half ironically. Scott arches his eyebrow. I accept his point. "OK, it wasn't what we wanted. But I wanted to be the one to say it wasn't. I wanted to be the one who'd say, screw you and your money and your sellout lifestyle. Not them. Picking him over the rest of us. D'yae ken?"

"I ken, Ken," Scott replies.

And I understand his point too. I really do. But again, I'm reminded of what might be available to me if we can just turn this little band into a success. If I can be "That Guy in That Band," I can hide behind the artifice of celebrity and not have to worry about my failings as a human being. Then maybe someday I'll be worthy of someone like Jess.

I want so desperately to tell Scott the truth about my anger. The reason behind my rage. His oblivious role in it. I want to ask for his advice and see if he knows a way to make it right. Because even after nine months of constant thinking about her, I haven't come up with a single explanation for Jess that doesn't make me sound like a lunatic. Or a liar. Or a lying lunatic.

He sees my sadness and reminds me that today is the day Alan—our manager—is coming over with the newly pressed EP. He also reminds me that if we had signed with the same label as Christian, we'd be doing things their way, releasing their music, standing behind him in blurry press releases. What we're doing now, he smartly tells me, is creating music we actually care about. Music we can proudly own as ours. As if summoned by our talking about him, Alan knocks on the door of our rehearsal space and pokes his head into the room.

"Is now a good time?" he asks, dripping with civility.

Today, like every day, he's wearing his brown suit and tie. The brown suit that looks like—and probably was—his dad's, two sizes too big for his tiny, skinny, size-0 frame. He's the kind of absolutely-bloody-lovely person who when he orders food sounds like he's genuinely asking if it's OK for him to have it. Whereas everyone else just barks instructions of what they want to people earning minimum wage.

"Yes, Alan. Now's a great time. Please come on in." Scott has an almost paternal way with Alan, talking to him in clear, comforting sentences. Whenever anyone in the band so much as thinks of a joke to denigrate him, Scott flies to Alan's defense.

"I have something for you," Alan announces, bursting with pride. He enters with a small cardboard box, about the size of an open laptop.

Brandon takes off his headphones and asks, "What's in the box? What's in the box?"—adopting a pretty spot-on impression of Brad Pitt at the ending of *Se7en*.

I ask, with my tongue firmly in its cheek, "Is it the severed head of Gwyneth Paltrow, Alan? Because we've talked about this."

"Oh, heavens, no," Alan replies, I assume completely unaware of any film that has a higher certificate rating than PG.

Like clockwork, Scott shoots me the "Don't be mean to Alan" look.

"It's your EP!" Alan tugs ineffectually at the parcel tape before clawing at the flaps and leaving the box a mess. "Ta-da!" he says, handing out copies like he's delivering welfare parcels in the Sudan.

The EP is a joy to behold. Exactly how I wanted it to be. The artwork on the front is three simple blocks of color—brown, purple, and green—lying on top of each other like a trio of concrete slabs. There's no pictures of us, no T-shirt, jeans, and haircuts, just the artwork. On the back are the four tracks, all without a name—there aren't any lyrics after all—just numbers: 1., 2., 3., and 4. It is anti-marketing at its finest and, as Scott would no doubt point out, is something we'd never be able to do within the confines of a big-money record label.

"What do you think?" Alan asks nervously, bracing himself for a negative response.

"Well . . ." I pause for dramatic effect. Scott sees what I'm doing and kicks me in the shin.

"We love it," he says to Alan, but Alan is still eagerly looking for my confirmation.

"Alan," I say, "we do."

The relief that washes over him could drown a city.

"Thank goodness," he says, "because I've already sent it out to a dozen radio stations."

Brandon, Scott, and I look at each other, dumbfounded at the new cojones on Alan. That he would even have an idea about something without checking and triple-checking with us first is unheard of; that he'd actually follow through on that idea without telling us is completely mind-blowing.

"And?" Scott asks.

Something about Alan's huge grin makes me pretty sure this isn't the last bit of good news he has for us today. I turn the CD over in my hand and smile at the name of the EP—an in-joke for just me and one other person in the whole world.

12

Truth to Power

Jess

The seated audience is fairly big. A sea of smiley, attentive faces. But not one person is here for me. Not a single soul thought, "Today, I'm looking forward to the comedy stylings of one Jessica Henson." No. Instead, they're all here to see a pre-record of *Numbers and Letters,* a TV quiz show that's half crossword, half Sudoku. The host is a light-entertainment legend, so popular in the eighties he's probably dined with Diana. Now, he's relegated to half an hour at three thirty in the afternoon on a digital cable television channel. Still, I don't feel too sorry for him, considering he earns at the very least thirty times more than me an episode. But then, my sorry mug will never even make it onto the screen.

I'm a warm-up act. A fluffer. My job is to get the audience in the mood for the recording, get them gee'd up for when the "talent" comes out. The audience is ninety-nine percent gray army with one percent accompanying relative, and so, I've been told repeatedly, the material must cater to such a demographic. Even as I walk out, I register how they view me—young, female, bags of energy—with the sort of skepticism usually reserved for political figures attending high-profile football matches.

I manage to get them onside by opening with a very safe routine about how "bus replacement services" should really be called "train replacement services," but as soon as I get any momentum, Gloria, the set manager, throws me the Time Out sign.

"Alrighty!" I say, in the most enthusiastic way I can muster. "Please welcome, the man you've come to see, the host of *Numbers and Letters,* Mr. Kenny Davis!"

I like to think I've done my job properly as they erupt into applause. There's even a few whoops, which I worry might be too energetic for the attending masses. It wouldn't be the first time we've had a defibrillator incident this week.

It's Thursday and they've filmed four episodes a day since I started on Monday. Any novelty or thrill I had at being surrounded by camera crew, grips, and live studio audiences vanished sometime around Tuesday morning. Now it's just another job where I'm completely bored and thoroughly unappreciated. It does, however, pay the rent.

"All right?" a voice asks me from behind.

I turn to see a rather round, ruby-faced guy in his midfifties, with something of a seaside entertainer vibe about him. Judging by his lanyards, he's clearly wandered over from the studio next door. He extends a hand for shaking and looks me up and down as if I'm the enemy.

"I'm Billy. Billy Hopkins. Fellow warm-up artiste."

"Jess," I reply, "Jess Henson."

"Like the Muppets."

I bob my head from side to side as if to suggest it doesn't bother me that I've heard that a thousand times before, and usually from men about his age and complexion.

"Your first week?" Billy asks.

"It is."

"Tough crowd?"

"A little."

"I used to do this show. Nice little earner it was too. Till the powers that be decided they needed to 'diversify.'" He sneers and makes bunny ears around the word; I grin dispassionately back. "Anyway," he continues. "You want to know the secret. These aren't old fuddy-duddies. You can be a bit blue with them. Make a few gags below the belt. They can take it. And anything at the expense of Lord Kenny Davis"—he points at the show's host, who has the audience lapping up every word—"is always guaranteed to be a hit."

"I'm not sure if I—"

"Truth to power. Thought your generation was all about that." His condescension is reaching Olympian levels. "Comedy's about risk, love."

Seconds after I've finished visualizing dropping a lighting rig on Billy Hopkins's head, Gloria calls me back on to rouse the crowd.

"All right. All right," I try in my most exuberant and cheerful voice. "A hand for Mr. Kenny Davis, please." They do as they're told, but their collective disappointment that he's no longer on stage is visceral. I want to win them over.

"He's like the grandfather I never had."

This lame aside gets the biggest laugh I've had all week and I start to think maybe Billy was right. After all, they're all here to see Kenny Davis. Maybe I do make him the gentle target of my material. I see Kenny handed a coffee offstage; he raises it to me as if to say, *You're all right*.

"Kenny Davis. The Man. The Myth. The Legend." The audience is grinning. All I can see is a sea of white dentures. "Messy, though, isn't he? I know he looks all neat and quaffed on stage, but I'll let you into a secret. Kenny's dressing room . . ."

The mass of septua- and octogenarians titter and nudge each other.

I carry on. "Filthy. Absolutely filthy. I mean . . . you would not believe the amount of letters he gets from the Inland Revenue. Not one of them opened. Not like the bank statements he gets from the Cayman Islands."

There's a hush over the audience. And not a good one. I can hear each individual cough. The cameraman's mouth is literally wide open in a way I thought only happened in the movies. Billy, the old pro who gave me such stellar career advice, stayed to watch and is beaming. His ruby-red cheeks positively aglow. I fell for the hook, the line, and the sinker. Gloria beckons me over and I feel like I'm in primary school.

As I approach, Billy waltzes past and blithely says, "That's where quotas gets ya."

"Oh, you total piece of sh—"

Gloria's face is super stern. "A word, please, Jessica."

———

When I met her, I'd have envisioned her office on the top floor of a skyscraper. In reality, Gloria's workspace is basically a Portakabin in the car park of the studios. The glamour of TV. She sits in her thousand-pound suit, her hair and makeup so meticulous, and so at odds with her environment.

She opens with a compliment. "Your show reel was good. It's why I hired you. There's a great range of stuff on it, and the thing I liked the most, is how capable you were of being clean. Family friendly. Safe."

"What wasn't clean about what I said?" I protest. "I even edited myself. What I wanted to say was, 'His dressing room is filthy. Hookers and cocaine all over the place.'"

She's unimpressed, but I continue to fight my corner.

"How was I supposed to know he's under investigation for tax evasion?" She raises an eyebrow as if to say, *We both know you knew,* and I try a different tack. "Maybe it's good, what I said. Y'know, a little truth to power."

She shakes her head, exasperated. "It's daytime TV, Jess! Get down the docks if you want to start a revolution."

"I'm sorry. Give me another chance."

"You want my advice?" she asks, answering before I can. "Figure out who you want to be. It'll make things a lot easier."

As I slope out of the office a nine-month-old memory pops up. The last thing Tom said to me, before he was drugged up to the eyeballs, flashes into my head. "You should be you. I like you." It hurts every time I think of it. It felt like such a genuine thing to say. Until I found out there was no truth to him, that it was just another line to get into my pants behind his girlfriend's back.

Cemetery Road, Sheffield
May 19, 2016

After what should have been a thirty-nine-minute train journey turned into a two-hour journey, I stomp back into our flat and throw my bag down on the chair opposite the sofa. That's pretty much it for the contents of our living room, except the desk that Julia is trying to beaver away at.

I huff.

She doesn't look up.

I huff with added gusto.

Julia sighs and takes her headphones off.

"What happened?" she asks, head tilted to one side.

"Got sacked."

"Why did you get sacked?"

"Because stupid, old, rich men can't take a joke."

She shakes her head but doesn't seem the least bit surprised. Since Edinburgh, I've struggled to hold down a job for longer than a week. So far, I've been in a writers' room for a shit sitcom which was so painfully unfunny I called it a shitcom and the showrunner overheard. I've been banned from three open-mic nights for "inciting violence." (This really was an overreaction because all three times the bachelorette parties were quite obviously pissed past the point of no return. It wasn't me that kept serving them, and it's certainly not my fault if they find some of my material about the female uprising to be highly motivating.)

And that's just the comedy jobs I've lost, saying nothing of the temp ones Julia has begged me to take to keep a roof above our heads.

"I love you, Jess, but we do need to pay the rent."

"I know. Sorry. I'll go see Dean tomorrow."

Dean is our agent. He books us as a double act but also finds work for us individually. Although Julia is adamant she'll only perform with me. She believes writing is her strength and that's where her future lies. From the amount of commissions she's got lately, I wouldn't argue. For me, though, I need the stage. Without an audience at least once a week I'd go loco.

"Let's get out of here," she says. "Pub or café?"

It's a test from Julia. I know it is. I'm desperate to have a drink (maybe even two) and get buzzy, especially after the misery of the day. The problem is, if we write at the pub we'll get about an hour's worth of work done and once I get tipsy I'll start to write down everything we say, believing it to be groundbreaking comedy gold. In the morning, we'll look at our notes and see it's a pile of utter tosh. And we'll also end up spending money we don't have.

The café on the other hand is run by a guy who loathes me. Julia knows this. I dig deep.

"I think the café would be best."

The volume of the radio in the café is way above an acceptable level for Julia. Her preference is for complete silence. Silence makes me want to smash things. I want to smash things mostly because then there will be the wonderful sound of things going smashy-smashy, thus breaking the awful, soul-crushing sound of silence. It's win-win. Except, of course, for the things that get smashed and for the people those things belong to.

"I can ask them to turn it down if you like?" I offer.

Julia shakes her head. "You're good. I'd rather not draw too much attention to our presence. Especially since all we've ordered over the past three hours is tap water."

"Do you think that's why the owner hates me?"

"I reckon that's one of fifty reasons," she says with a wink.

Feeling combative since my dismissal earlier today, I stand and skip over to the man behind the counter, doing my duty for my comedy wife. "Would you mind popping the music down a touch?"

Man-behind-counter sneers and fixes the volume to a more Julia setting. Then, for no reason other than wanting to show off, I add, "We're writing."

I wait. I'm not sure what for.

"We're comedy writers."

This provokes a look I can best describe as "Who gives a damn, love?"—which pisses me off considerably. I mean, how dare his eyebrows and facial muscles be so condescending!

"Don't you think women are funny?" I attack.

"What's that?" he asks in an American accent I hadn't noticed when ordering, which infuriates me even more.

"Women?" I continue. "You don't think we're funny?"

"I think some women are funny," he replies, treading on thin ice. He pauses and with incredible speed reels off, "Lucille Ball, Carol Burnett, Phyllis Diller, Lily Tomlin. I think they're all funny. Joan Rivers, Whoopi Goldberg, Mary Tyler Moore. But you? I have no idea."

I should be apologizing or at the very least introducing a new argument that lets me debate with this clearly pretty cool sixty-year-old café owner, but I'm distracted by Tom. That Tom. The Tom of last August. I have not been pining for him. Or his music. Or the fjords. Or anything. This woman does not pine, especially not for lying bum-cracks. But. But. But.

"Turn it up," I tell Mr. Comedy Encyclopedia.

"What?"

"The music."

"Turn it down? Turn it up? Make your mind up."

I turn to Julia and yell, "This is his band!"

She rolls her eyes.

I turn back to the café owner as if it's his fault. "This guy, this guy whose music you're playing, is a cheating, manipulative scumbag of a person."

"It's the radio," he reminds me, slightly affronted.

"Still! You should be ashamed, sir."

Julia instructs me to sit down and leave the nice man alone. I do as I'm told, despite the fact I'm absolutely seething. She moves in time to the music and I offer her a death stare.

"Sorry," she says. "It is quite good, though."

She's right. It's annoyingly good. I don't understand how his music can be so peaceful yet so completely unsettling at the same time. Then it hits me. Maybe it has something to do with him being a duplicitous, two-faced slimeball. I let out a small rage grunt. What was it I'd said to Julia after I finally filled her in on the awfulness of that night? I'm done with the opposite sex. Jokes before Blokes. I start writing, the music spurring me on. Sets before Sex. Land Jobs before Hand Jobs. Julia stares at my waggling pen and the paper underneath it, then up at me with a look that suggests I might need to be sectioned. Her expression is part disgust, part awe.

"Why have you just written 'Charlie Mingus before Cunnilingus'?"

"Do you think 'Jazz before Jizz' works better?"

"Why is your mind always in the gutter, Jess?"

"But, Julia," I say, affecting the poshest voice imaginable, "I'm looking at the stars!"

I drumroll in perfect synchronicity to the end of the song and I feel a little freaked out considering I've literally only ever heard it once before. The DJ on the radio starts to applaud, before announcing, "That was The Friedmann Equation with 'Three'—the third track on their new EP, due for release on Kayak Records next Friday. Look out for that one. It's called *Nitrous Oxide Makes Me Wannabe Your Lover*. Good title."

My heart skips a beat and a tidal wave of guilt crashes into me as I feel the thrill of hearing the title. It's so weirdly specific. Like something only me and that paramedic would have any memory of. Why has he done that?

"Bastard!" I yell and the whole café turns to look at me.

Julia offers a nervous smile to our fellow diners and whispers through gritted teeth, "You're going to get us chucked out of here."

"That title, *Nitrous Oxide Makes Me Wannabe Your Lover*!"

Julia offers a look that says "And?"

"It's a joke from our night together. He sang the Spice Girls while high on Entonox. It's like a weird, flirty message over the airwaves."

She puts her hand on top of mine, but I pull it away, too angry for comforting.

"Jess. You need to calm down, mate. It's been nine months. I know this guy hurt you, but you've got to let it go. There are millions of arseholes out there. They don't deserve your time and neither does he. It's a little more important that you think about your work right now. Your career. Ever since that night you've had this massive distraction weighing over you. Talking about him. Moaning about him."

I stand, grab my notepad and coat. "I've gotta go," I tell her. "I'll see you tonight."

Her face is the picture of baffled. "Where are you going?"

"To confront him."

"What?"

"Someone needs to look out for this girl he's with. I'm gonna be the one to tell him you can't send the music equivalent of dick pics behind your girlfriend's back."

Julia blusters, unable to conjure up a response that might get through to me. She doesn't attempt to stop me as I run out into the street. A second later, I pop back into the café and point to the owner with a wink. "You're all right, Mr. Café Owner. You're all right!"

13

Columbo

Tom

Elliot Street, Edinburgh
May 20, 2016

On the bus to Scott's, I listen to the record for the hundredth time. It's out and getting plenty of play on the radio. With this moderate success, invitations have followed to play in locations with unfamiliar postcodes and more than a few interviews. They seem to like the idea of us having a former singer who's gone on to be a pop star while we've been doing our thing. I can't say I'm not a little in love with the picture it paints of us fighting the good fight. All of this is great, but what I really want is for the record to reach one particular person. And so far, it hasn't.

Granted, naming a record after a shared moment might not be the best way to seek forgiveness, but surely there's no harm in letting someone know you're thinking about them? There's a slim outside chance Jess will pick up on it . . . isn't there?

Truthfully, what am I really hoping for with this strategy?

That she'll hear me on the radio and forget the whole *Do you have a girlfriend? / No, of course not / Oh wait, that's not what your best friend said* teen angst of it all? That she'll track me down and come running, arms outstretched, because I named an EP after a moment in a night we had nine months ago? Ultimately, in the cold, harsh light of day I can see what this really is. Just more avoidance. Pine after someone who probably won't ever forgive you and then you never have to worry about making an emotional attachment to anyone ever again. Classic Tom.

When Scott's dad left his mum, his mum got this house. A tiny two-up, two-down terrace. After Scott's mum hooked up with Scott's "Uncle" Steve (in name only, thank God) and she moved out, the house pretty much became Scott's.

When you're in your late teens and early twenties, a house to yourself is pretty much the greatest thing of all time. We'd have parties. We'd drink. We'd lie about all day watching movies. The doorbell still lets out that same ice-cream-van jingle it always has. I'm here today because Scott sent a text saying that he and Holly have "something really cool to share."

He opens the front door and greets me with the same winning smile that's been written on all of our faces since the EP got its first radio play. He wraps his arms around me—not easy when I'm almost twice his size—and pulls me in close.

Inside, the scene is set up like an IKEA catalog come to life. Holly made this place theirs, as opposed to just his, after a couple of months of moving in. Out went the moldy, hot-rocked recliners. In came a duck-egg-blue sofa and a city's worth of cushions. And while they still have the framed poster of the Death in Vegas gig we went to in 2011, said poster sits next to a rather arty transit map and a far bigger than necessary canvas picture of their tabby cat, Skittles. A canvas picture I happen to know Scott detests. Compromise has been a bedrock of their "new" relationship after years of antagonism endlessly pulled them apart and back together. Truth be told, he's a stronger man than me.

"So. What's the rumpus? Is this about the band?" I ask.

"Nope," is Scott's quick reply as Holly shakes her head next to him.

I ignore their weird beaming as I notice their bookshelf, overflowing with titles I know I should have read but haven't.

"Well, we asked you here—" Scott begins before I cut him off.

"That book I lent you, Holly, the one about the tiger and the boat. Have you finished it? I promised it to a friend."

They look at each other, buzzing. Scott rises and takes the book I asked for off the shelf and another one too. He presents me with both and says, "We've only been reading this one lately." He theatrically points to the cover showing a couple of baby feet poking out from a blanket. Holly laughs.

I want in on their little joke and so I scan the title. *YOUR BABY, DAY-BY-DAY*.

I still don't get it.

"I don't get it," I say.

"Wow," says Holly. "I didn't realize we were being that subtle."

"We're having a baby, Tom," Scott explains. "Not a Baby Tom, although who knows, right?" Holly shakes her head at the thought of naming her first child after me, as it finally hits me like a truck what this means.

"This is a wind-up, right?" I ask. "An April Fool's joke one month too late?"

"Congratulations is usually what people say in this situation," Holly offers drily.

"What about the band?" I squeal, reaching a pitch reserved for very upset dogs and dolphins.

"I. Told. You," Holly lets out in a singsong manner, evoking a prime look of hostility from Scott.

The illusion of the dream couple with the dream house and the dream setup is shattered in a moment, and I wonder if I'm about to play a crucial role in another of their ups and downs.

"It's fine," Scott attempts to remedy. "There are loads of musicians with children. In fact, I can't think of many who don't."

"Not at twenty-five!"

"I'm twenty-six. And yes, quite a few people, in many, many occupations, have kids when they're in their mid-twenties!"

My head begins to hurt and I start to tap my left foot. I was not ready for this news today. Not by a long shot. Can I dig deep enough to not be a total arsehole? Can I think of my two friends and their feelings first? As my next utterance slips from my loose lips the answer to those questions is clearly a pretty hefty no.

"Will the baby be coming on tour with us, Scott? Maybe it could be our roadie, Holly?"

They roll their eyes in synchronicity.

"You're being a dick, Tom," Scott tells me, matter-of-fact.

"Am I a dick?" I ask. "Am I a dick? Am I a dick? Am I dick? Am I dick?" The phrase repeats, stuck on a loop, my silly little mantra echoing around until both Scott and the lovely mother of his unborn baby are suddenly doubled over with laughter. Their laughter snaps me out of it and I utter, "I am. Aren't I? I am a dick."

The reply is two nodding heads. I let out a loud, cleansing profanity that makes Skittles shoot across the floor.

"I'm sorry. I just. I can't get my head around it."

"We could draw you a picture?" Holly offers, playing the room perfectly.

A nervous gurgle comes from deep within the pit of my stomach.

"Hungry?" Scott jokes, unaware that through no fault of his, my insides are turning to mush as the plans we made are scattered to the winds.

Touring. That's the big one that I can't see him doing. Not when the baby is due. Not when it's sick with measles or whatever. Not when it means going to Europe for weeks on end. But then there's the time-swallower this thing will be. Rehearsals every other day will become rehearsals every other week. Money that he would spend on demos and new instruments and transport will now go on nappies and one-sies and chew toys. Shit. Shit. Shit. Keep positive, I tell my-self as Scott leads us into the kitchen. Don't crumble under this.

"Cheese *and* ham?" Scott offers in a faux-Welsh accent, repeating a joke from a stand-up routine we'd first heard half a decade ago. Back when we were young and carefree. Is that an oxymoron? Didn't we care more than anything when we were younger? I'd argue the older I get the more I stop giving a damn. Except about this. This was supposed to be our dream and now . . . now it feels over.

As this last thought enters my head, my knees begin to buckle. All the blood rushes out of my head and ends up God knows where. It's fine, I tell myself. I'm fine. And I almost believe what I'm saying as—on my way down to Scott and Holly's kitchen floor—I take a loaf of Kingsmill and the bread board with me.

I don't quite know if I made it to the sofa myself or if Scott dragged me. But here I am. Looking up at two very concerned parental types.

"You all right, mate?" Scott asks, wary of the reply, as Holly passes me a glass of water.

I sit up a little. "Yeah. That was weird."

"You just blacked out."

"Really?"

"That ever happened before?"

"Errr. No," I lie. "Don't think so."

The dishonesty is back between us for the first time since the "Sarah" fiasco. Holly, smarter than most, eyes my last remark with the appropriate amount of suspicion. She glances at Scott and makes an excuse to get out of the house. To leave us alone. Before she goes, I repeat as honestly and passionately as I can how happy I am for them and their news.

After she's gone, Scott and I sit in silence for a while. He lets out a big sigh and stands.

"You want another water?"

I shake my head. "I'm good."

"I tell you what, it'll be a relief to be able to tell other people about the baby now."

Not being the brightest bulb, I ask him to elaborate. Once he does, I immediately wish he hadn't. He tells me how he wanted his best friend to be one of the first to know and I feel an overwhelming urge to start crying. It's partly because he's never said anything like that to me before and partly because I feel so much guilt for not reciprocating his friendship with actions. Or words. But now—now I feel ready. Finally. I feel like I can say it.

"Scott," I say, pretty dramatically. "I need to tell you something. It's about Sarah . . ."

Scott goes quiet and his entire forehead wrinkles. Before I can say it, he finishes my sentence for me.

"She never existed, did she? You made her up?"

The stomach-falling-through-my-arse moment I was expecting doesn't occur. It's replaced by a fascination with how he knew. And for how long.

"When you were going out, I didn't have a clue. But when you broke up and said so nonchalantly you were still gonna be mates, alarm bells started ringing."

I don't fully get his Columbo deduction. "Huh?"

"You wear your heart on your sleeve, Tom. Like right on it. That this breakup, from a woman you seemed pretty keen on, hardly affected you, was just . . . nah, mate. I wasn't having it."

He elaborates. "At first I just took you at your word. Like, why would you lie about being with someone? Then I started to think back to other moments. That time at the hospital with . . ."

"Jess." Saying her name physically hurts.

"Yeah. I could never believe my mate would be with someone the way you were with her—drugs or no drugs—behind his partner's back. It's just not you."

I manage to fight back the tears. Fainting, admitting you made up a girlfriend, and having a good cry, all on the same day, might just be a step too far. Instead, I start telling Scott things I never have before. Why I made up Sarah. Who Jess was and what she meant to me, even after just one night. I don't have it in me to talk about some other stuff. The panic I feel. The way I get so lonely sometimes. The fact that I've been using alcohol a bit too often to fight all of the above. He's gonna be a dad soon. He doesn't need some man-baby bothering him now. I don't need to burden him with any of that. I just need him to know that I'll be honest with him from now on.

"So," he announces, after I'm done with the telling of my tales. "What are you gonna do about this random funny lady, then?"

"Aside from obscurely naming records in the hope she might hear one and think of me?"

"Yeah, Tom, aside from that awful, awful plan. Have you got a number?"

"I did. She wrote it on my arm in eye makeup, before SarahGate. Then in one fairly violent move she smudged it off. I've looked her up online, obviously."

"Obviously," Scott says. "Can't you just send her an

email? Say sorry. Explain the situation, without the plans and schemes."

I want to tell him it's the plans and schemes that protect me. As long as I have them, I can keep myself locked up, away from the possibility of pain. But he's my best friend. And he knows this already.

14

Lather. Rinse. Repeat.

Jess

Cemetery Road, Sheffield
May 19, 2016

Back at the flat, I switch my laptop on, mimicking the famil-iar *bing-bong*. I type in *The Friedmann Equation* and their website comes up. Part of me has decided the whole thing is a mix-up, that the song just sounds like one I've heard before and the "Wannabe . . . Nitrous Oxide" thing is a massive co-incidence brought on by the headfuck of that night. The complete confusion of thinking you know someone, only to have the rug yanked from under your feet.

Despite it being 2016, they've purposefully designed their website to look like a relic from the past. Nineties-era dial-up screeches from the speakers as the screen "loads," aping an old printer, creating the homepage line by line, pixel by pixel. It triggers a flashback to a time before high-speed broadband, when things seemed slower. When life was—cliché alert—simpler. As the website fully loads, I think how many people they'll have lost with this gimmick and am even more convinced I'm in the right place. It has Tom's finger-prints all over it. From our very brief encounter, Tom struck me as someone who'd rather have ten fans that "got it" than a million who didn't. As with everything Tom-related, I have to fight the urge not to like it. Remember he's a rat. Remember he's a rat. Remember he's a rat.

The site is minimal, a few bars of color with four drop-down menus at the top. MUSIC. TOUR. ABOUT. CON-TACT. I click TOUR and see there's a handful of upcoming gigs. When I see he's coming to Sheffield in two weeks' time, a plan begins to form.

I click on CONTACT and begin to draft the strangest email I've ever written. In it, I say I'm a freelance journalist from a pretty well-known music website looking to write a piece on bands and relationships. *It's a think-piece,* I write, *speaking to people within the music industry about how they make a relationship work when their other half is tour-ing.* I say we'd like to interview both the band and their part-ners to ask what they make of the "sex, drugs, and rock and roll lifestyle" in the twenty-first century. Is it harder for the one left at home or the one being tempted on the road? I have no idea if he'll bite, but it's all I have.

As my finger hovers over the SEND button, I ask myself, is this the behavior of a crazy person? Or is it me doing my bit for a woman who needs help? I genuinely do not know the answer to this as I hear Julia's key in the lock.

Once I've finished explaining my plan to Julia, she looks at me like I've lost it.

"This is weird, Jess. Like, next-level weird."

I try for breezy. "It's fine. I'm FINE! If you were seeing someone and someone else knew they were being unfaithful, you'd want to know, right?"

"Sorry, how does pretending to be a journalist help her?"

"Because!" I have to make sense of my not-too-well-thought-out plan. "Once I have proof that he's with someone, I can ask more questions and track her down and let her know her boyfriend is an arse."

"I think you may have lost the plot, Jess . . ."

"Maybe. Maybe not. I just think she has a right to know."

"This whole Tom mission is a major distraction from your work."

I let out a *pfft* and she volleys it back with a matronly look that would put hairs on your chest. She has a point. Since Edinburgh, I've been losing more than I've been winning when it comes to my career. As if reading my mind, she dips into my brain and offers a way out.

"My advice, for what it's worth, is that you should forget about all of this. Maybe get away for a couple of days. Throw yourself into your work. Perform. Write. Perform. Lather. Rinse. Repeat."

"I told you, I'm seeing Dean tomorrow. Maybe get off my back when it comes to the work, yeah?" Using the prearranged meeting with our agent gives me the upper hand. Julia and I don't really fight. We argue, about a great many things, but we don't fight. Yet for some reason, tonight I'm pushing for it. I'm not seeing it from her point of view. I'm questioning her motives and it's riling her.

"Look. All I'm offering is my advice. You'll do you, Jess. As you should."

"I'm not doing it for me. I'm doing it for her. This girl who's being screwed over. I thought you'd be supportive."

She grabs the book she's been reading and tucks it under her arm. Ready to depart.

"Stop kidding yourself, Jess. This whole plan isn't to see her. It's to see him. At least be honest with yourself about that."

She doesn't mean it as cold as it comes out. I've just used up all the goodwill I have on this subject and she's reached breaking point. I have no comeback to the truth. As soon as she leaves the room, I open up the email window again and read through the absolute bucket of crazy I've written. Without knowing why, I hit SEND.

May 20, 2016

Dean's proposal has everything Julia recommended, just to the nth degree. It will mean absolutely throwing myself into work and it gets me away for more than a couple of days. I'd have to write new material on a deadline—something that weirdly benefits my work—and there'd be nine thousand miles between me and all of this Tom idiocy. My hot shame for actually sending the email had me up most of the night.

"You don't have to give me an answer now," Dean tells me.

I repeat the offer back to him. "Australia? Four weeks?"

He nods. "Sleep on it. It's a big ask. You wouldn't be earning mega-money either, but it's a great place to make a name for yourself. The comedy scene there's phenomenal."

"And Julia?"

He shakes his head. "They only want straight stand-up. No double acts. No experimental stuff."

I genuinely don't know what he means by that. But then Dean's only been to our show once. I don't think it would be a huge leap to suggest he selected us for representation from our headshots alone. He's young, early thirties, but his dad was a big-time agent before him. Mainly film stars. Rumor has it, he repped David Niven and Deborah Kerr at the end of their careers. Little Dean wanted to step out from under his father's wing, but only so far. He went for comedy. He's OK, as far as agents go—let's face it, he's all we've ever known—but he's absolutely about the commerce and not the art.

"If you do say yes," he says tentatively, "we should have a chat about the direction you want to go."

"What do you mean?"

"Well, no one really knows who you are right now. A four-week tour is a pretty good opportunity to try on some new faces. See what sticks."

My face, I think to myself. Mine is the one that sticks. He reads my reaction and tries to clarify his take.

"I'm just saying, the silly songs, the impressions, they're all great, but is that what you want to be known for? Without Julia to bounce off, some of the sketches will have to be dropped anyway."

"What about the Edinburgh stuff I did?"

He shakes his head, like an exasperated parent who's had the same argument about lending his seventeen-year-old his car a million times before. "We've been over this."

I protest. "It worked in the room."

"And it didn't make it to the edit. You had an opportunity to do some decent material and get it on national TV."

"Digital."

"Whatever! Instead of getting five minutes of fame and exposure you made fifty people laugh and got less than thirty seconds' air time."

I don't regret a thing about that night. I was more me on that stage than I've ever been before or since. And it worked. If I'd carried on with the material that wasn't working, the rest of the night wouldn't have panned out the way it did. Until it went wrong, that night was right and it started there. With me being me.

Tom's words again. "You should be you. I like you."

Dean leans back in his chair for the conclusion of his argument. "You're funny, Jess. But if you don't play the game, you'll be funny to fifty people for the rest of your life."

Back at home, Julia is ecstatic at the news of my possible Antipodean excursion. She jumps around the room like I've been invited to open for Beyoncé. When I tell her I'm not sure whether I want to go, she dismisses the idea as ridiculous, telling me this is the sort of opportunity that makes people's careers. Having had one fight with her last night, I don't fancy round two and so I simply nod and smile. Borrowing her enthusiasm to get me through. She squeals with joy for me, before announcing she's off to get some cheap fizz to help us celebrate.

As she closes the door behind her, I grab my laptop and open up the fake account I made to send the message to Tom. VeronicaFreelance all one word with a Yahoo address. I type in the password. L0ve_R@t. There's one unopened email.

Re: Article on Bands and Relationships

To Veronica,
    Scott is in a long-term relationship. As is Brandon. Colin and myself have been single since the band's inception. Nobody would like to talk about their partners (or lack thereof) as it's nobody's business. The music should speak for itself.
    Tom Delaney

I don't know what to make of this. But I do know that this obsession has to stop. I sign out of the account and delete it. Either he lied that night or he's lying now. I'll never know because I'm not going to follow it up. Even if he'd responded in the affirmative, I really don't think I'd have had the balls to go through with it. After all, the truth will out. It always does. Good luck to Sarah is all I can say.

I put my laptop to one side and slope off to the kitchen to make myself a drink. All that's in the fridge is Foster's from a house party we had months ago. Maybe it's a sign about the Australia offer. I crack it open and return to my computer, switching *Grand Designs* on in the background. I open my real email account and see that there too I have one unopened message sent around the same time.

It reads.

Subject: The Friedmann Equation

Hey.

I hope you don't mind, I got your email address from an open reply you sent someone on Twitter. Weirdly stalkerish, I know. I totally understand if you want to delete this message before reading it. But me and the band are playing Sheffield soon. If you're about (and would like to) I'd really like to meet up and explain a few things.

It's Tom, by the way, from Edinburgh.

15

Everything to Tell

Tom

Manse Road, Edinburgh
May 20, 2016

Who would have thought it? My original sophisticated plan to name a record after a joke we shared had yielded nothing, but then simply emailing her and asking if she'd be willing to see me had immediately brought a positive response.

OK, so, "positive" might be too strong a word, but a channel of communication has been opened. Jess has sent me a message. A one-word, abstract "Maybe" message, but a maybe is a million times better than a no. It offers possibility. It offers hope.

I email back immediately.

I can get you a backstage pass if you like?

As soon as I've sent it I realize how creepy it sounds and desperately want to hit the UNSEND button. But what if she's already seen it, which she almost definitely has? What if

she's half-seen and then I undo it and, oh, here's another
message.

Smooth.

I deserve her ridicule and take it. I am a ridiculous person,
sometimes.

That wasn't supposed to sound so douchebaggy. So, do you
think you can make it? This Wednesday, we're playing the Leadmill. We could grab a drink in the Rutland Arms after, if you
like?

I press SEND and wait. And I wait. I conjure up a billion
replies from her. The ratio of no's to maybe's I invent is
heavily geared to the former. There are no definitive yesses in
my mind.
Five minutes later, her next missive arrives.

You know Sheffield pretty well, I take it? Your friend did say
that's where Sarah was from. Got a thing for Yorkshire girls,
have you?

Whatever tone I choose to read this in, it's a reminder of
my up-mountain battle. Again, hope rears its tricky head
and I think there's a way through this. A way out.

If you come for a drink with me, I'll explain the entirety of the
Sarah thing. I promise.

I can't say (or type) fairer than that. A more manipulative
part of me thinks it's a perfect setup. Who can refuse such a

tantalizing piece of bait as an "explanation"? It clearly works because the next thing she types are words to the effect of *Sod it, I'll be there.*

On a roll, I risk it for a biscuit.

Can I get your phone number? Again.

The pause is longer than the message Jess sends back.

No.

A quicker one appears.

But I will be there. I am a lady of my word. Unlike some people. See you on the 25th, Mr. Delaney. And this "explanation" you have better be bloody spectacular.

It's rare I get to switch off my computer with a sense of hope. A sense of excitement. Usually it's turned off after spending hours down rabbit holes, mindlessly scrolling through social media feeds, reading depressing news articles and opinion pieces. But today—today there's hope. The 25th can't come soon enough.

Cemetery Road, Sheffield
May 25, 2016

Our first two shows go great. The little underground venue in Manchester was tailor-made for our new type of heavier guitar sound. Where once there was melody and lyrics, now we specialize in the purity of beautiful noise. To have the cavern to literally bounce the sound off was glorious. Next was Newcastle and again, despite some early technical glitches, things went better than we could have hoped for. Brandon went to uni there, so, for him and his boyfriend, that was a real memorable one to tick off.

But for me, it's all been about Sheffield. In the city of steel, with the connections I have, there's something special in the air and someone very special I'll be meeting after the show. Before that, though, I've come to see the other person in my life who means so much to me.

The cemetery is pretty empty. It's an overcast day and threatening to chuck it down. I find Grandad and place a plectrum on his grave. When I first came here by myself, a year after he died, there were dozens of these triangular pieces of plastic. Fans would make the pilgrimage here from all over the world to place these little markers. I just sort of got sucked into the ritual. There are fewer of them these days.

Despite managing it last time I was here (and there being no soul around to hear me), I still can't speak out loud. Instead I think of what he might say to the news that I'm touring, actually touring in venues that he might have once played. It's usually easy to conjure his voice but today it isn't working. I want to hear him say he's "chuffed to bits" for me, to hear the word "proud," even if it's from my own head. But I can't. I'm too distracted by her.

"Of course you are," the voice interrupts, "as you should be."

"All right, Grandad," I reply. "We're playing the Leadmill tonight."

"Forget that, tell me more about this girl."

"What's there to tell?" I kick at a patch of mud by my foot, like a twelve-year-old with a crush.

"Everything, Tom. There's everything to tell."

I'm about to open my mouth and embrace the crazy when a couple I've seen before turn up. Bad weather be damned. Like always, they're holding each other tight.

"That could be you one day soon," the voice tells me, "minus the lost loved one, though."

I allow him the morbid humor. In life he was pretty dark. And I guess he was in death, too. Racing along to the final post the way he did. The darkness becoming too much for him.

"Less of that," he reprimands me. "Today is supposed to be a happy day."

"A gig to come."

"A girl to see."

I can see him smiling.

"I know which I think is more important," he tells me from beyond the grave.

Leadmill Road, Sheffield
Hours later

I don't see her before the show and while we're on stage I can't even consider looking around. Our lighting setup is such that it really does feel as if we're by ourselves until the last song. We don't do encores, never have, never will, and so the only bit of crowd interaction is before and after we've played. I didn't see her at the start.

But in the last email she sent, she said she was coming. I'm glad she declined the backstage pass. After all, backstage is basically a box room with some tatty seating and a crate of piss-warm beer. Meeting at the pub across the road after the show makes much more sense. During the set, Scott keeps telling me to slow down between numbers. Brandon's sweating to keep up. It's unprofessional, I know, but I just want to get to the last song as soon as I can. We're halfway through the penultimate number.

I've told Scott about my after-show plans. And for the first time I told him about going to see my grandad too. How I'd visit him when I said I was seeing Sarah. The full extent of my "conversations" with him is still a secret and best kept so. After the fabricated girlfriend, I don't need to tell him I fantasize conversations with dead people too. My fears that he'd see the visits as unmanly or weird were as ill-founded as I probably always knew, deep down, they would be.

We finish up to rousing applause and a few hollers. The knowledge that when we walk offstage we won't be coming back has yet to filter down from our Edinburgh days. But today, more than ever, I'm glad our final number is our final number.

"Great stuff, everyone," I say as I hurriedly put my coat on behind the curtain.

"In a rush, mate?" Colin asks.

I can't shift the grin from my face. It's been nine months and I'm finally going to see her again. To tell her the truth. To put things right and, with any luck, make up for lost time.

Shoreham Street, Sheffield
Two hours later

The staff in the pub have started to give me the pity look. The "he's been stood up" sideways stare. Every time I glance up and see their lips moving, I convince myself they're talking about me. Solipsistic arsehole that I am. One looks over her shoulder. She must be looking at me. They're giggling now. That's about me.

After another fifteen minutes of this—fifteen minutes of checking my phone, its signal, turning it off and on again—I want to scream the words "I'M JUST MEETING A FRIEND" but there's something very untrue about that. I'm sure she'll be here any minute. It's only after the twelfth time of checking my phone that I remember she only has my email. And that I turned notifications off on my emails years ago.

I open the mail app and there's a message from her. Sent two hours ago. It reads:

I promise. I wasn't trying to stand you up. I was going to be there. I really did want to hear what you have to say. I'm so sorry. Can you call me in the morning and we'll arrange a time and a place. I really am sorry—Jess x

Reading her apology to me certainly isn't the way I thought this evening would go. And then something else I really wasn't expecting happens. A face walks through the door that I recognize. It's one half of the double act I bumped into outside a curry house in Edinburgh nine months ago. One half of Jess and Julia. But for a reason I don't fully understand, it's the wrong half. Julia waves a half-hello and takes a seat across from me. I wonder what the joke is. But she doesn't appear to be laughing.

16

Distractions

Jess

I pinball between hate and hope. I don't know how Tom is going to explain himself, but I'm starting to believe he can. I want him to, desperately. Even after close to a year of feeling such contempt for the man, I want to believe there's a reason behind it all.

I typically tell Mum everything that's going on in my life but she doesn't seem in a great place at the moment and I don't want to rock her boat. My little brother Dom's gap year has lasted over twenty months now. Last we heard he was somewhere near Fiji. I get why he'd want to be as far away from here as possible. Life wasn't what you'd call easy for us growing up. Dom had it harder. I don't think he could see that Mum gave us love. As John, George, Paul, and Ringo said, it's all you need.

When I'm spending time in my fantasy world—the one in which there are posters of my shows on Tube stations in

London—there's always a moment where I buy her the house she deserves. To let her know that, despite everything, we made it. That she did all right.

Dom being gone is tough on Mum. She sees it as a form of rejection. I keep telling her it's a gap year, not a gap lifetime, but each new month gives her more reason to fret. She's told herself the reason he's gone is because of her. I remind her she's been sober for a decade and, if that really was the case, he would have left years ago. She's not convinced. Once you tell yourself a story, especially one about your own life, it's pretty hard to ever see another version of events. I worry she's lonely and I *really* worry my swanning off to the other side of the world for a month isn't going to help. To do my bit, I put the kettle on and make some not-so-subtle inquiries into her social life. Something is eating away at her and I want to find out what it is.

"How's Janet?" I call to Mum, from the kitchen into the living room.

"She's fine," Mum yells back, as I enter with two builder's teas. "Or at least she was last time I saw her. It's been a little while."

I hand her the mug I bought her for Christmas a few years ago. It reads QUEEN OF THE MUMS on one side and tells her she deserves all the biscuits on the other. It's true. She does.

"Do you still swim on a Thursday?"

"No. I got a bit bored of just going up and down and up and down."

"They wouldn't let you on the water slide?"

She fakes a laugh and I ask another question: "Do you see much of Michael these days? I always thought he was nice."

"What's this, the Jessica Inquisition?"

I turn my back on her and fiddle with some books on her bookshelf. She's always known when I'm up to something. She says she can see it in the corners of my mouth.

"Just asking," I say, picking up some Agatha Christie novel I want to pinch for the plane.

"You've never got anything past me in twenty-eight years of trying—what makes you think you will now. Is it Australia? Are you worried about your trip?"

I sigh and face her.

"No! I'm worried about you, that's all."

Her face warms into one of adoration and she throws her arms around me.

"Oh, petal. You're a good egg. But, please, you've got to live your life. You can't spend all your time worrying about others. This time next week you'll be neck-deep in Hemsworths."

"That was clean for you," I jibe.

Her face goes serious, a rare look on her. And one that gives me cause for concern.

"As callous as it sounds," she tells me, "worry about yourself a bit more."

A pang of guilt rises up my spine as I realize I'm meeting a guy whose relationship status is still very much undefined. It will be defined in the first five minutes of seeing him, though, that's for damn sure. No more of this *are-you-aren't-you, were-you-weren't-you* crap.

"And you definitely need to stop worrying about my love life," she says, with a maternal huff. "When are you gonna bring someone home so I can get out your naked-baby photos?"

It's too much of an opening not to share a little, especially when I'm sharing it with one of the best people in my life.

"There is . . . was . . . someone . . . sort of. The problem is there's a good chance he's"—I play up for Mum's amusement—"a cad. A bounder. A rogue. A good-for-nothing ne'er-do-well. But aren't they all?"

"They're not all bad, Jess."

"You mean, they're not all like Frank, Mum?"

"You can't call him Dad?"

I shake my head.

"Nope. Because he isn't. A dad is someone who's there for you. So that man you once knew called Frank is not, and never will be, my quote-unquote dad."

My reluctance to acknowledge the man she must have loved once brings a sadness to her, the past writ large on her face. There's no hiding our emotions, me and Mum. We know too much about each other. Straightforward and true is the only way we can be. Which makes the fact that she's hiding something now tough to take.

"Jess?" The simple syllable carries plenty of weight.

"Mum?"

"Sit down, love."

I do as I'm told and in the few seconds before she explains things, my mind races with alternative realities. It's only when she opens her mouth that this timeline begins to form.

"Your dad . . . Frank . . . he's been in touch."

I can't form a whole word to exit my mouth. The best I can do is a vowel.

"Oh."

"You remember that newspaper thing you and Julia did a few months back?"

I nod. It was just a little piece in a local paper profiling our comedy night. Julia thought it might get us a bit of an audience. And it looks like one person in particular took note.

Mum continues, "Frank read it, saw your name. He took a chance that we'd still be at the same address and, well, he sent me a letter, I'll get it if you—"

"No." I cut her off quickly, before she's had the chance to get out of her seat.

"I understand."

As awful as this is for me, I know she has chasms of sadness that I deny his existence.

"You're gonna be OK, yeah, Mum?" I ask, hoping I'll get the truth.

She grabs my face between her hands and repeats her new catchphrase. "Worry about yourself, love."

It isn't the answer I needed.

Anger, fear, disgust, sadness: they're all jostling for control of the console in my mind.

My focus should be on tonight. Meeting Tom. But distractions are nothing if they're not distracting. I try and play them at their own game.

"Are you sure you won't come to the gig?" I ask Julia, as I put on and remove makeup in equal measure, unsure as to what "look" I'm supposed to be presenting. "Moral support?"

Julia, head down in her laptop, looks up and shakes her head. "Sorry, buddy. The fact I'll be on the other side of the pub for your 'date' is weird enough. Watching you watch him on stage for ninety minutes is just a step too far."

I'm grateful that she's going to be there for Act Two of the evening at least. Usually going to a gig solo would not faze me one jot, but there's something different about this. The idea, as Julia says, of watching him for an hour just feels . . . intimate?

And so I don't blame her. I went against her smart advice and sent that stupid email. That it ended up having little effect, beyond lessoning her view of me, is irrelevant. Sometimes friends say it best by not saying anything at all. She's not an "I told you so" sort of person. But something is telling me that by the end of tonight, she'll have every right to be.

I told her about Tom's email, how it had nothing to do with the fake journalist plan. I told her about my response and our subsequent exchange of emails, and the more I told her the less I could see she wanted to be involved in any of it. She thinks the whole situation is crackers and I don't blame her. She's also extremely worried that this might have an effect on my imminent career plans. It's all very bad timing.

I *do not* mention my mum and Frank for many reasons, but the main one is that I want nothing to do with him, so he's not worth mentioning. Instead, I try once more to elicit some solidarity, waving the spare ticket I have in front of her.

"Final answer. Standing room only to the hottest show in town?"

She shakes her head. "But I will be there for beers in the Rutland Arms after. I will watch from a distance as you tear a man's insides out."

"Depending on the way things go," I remind her.

She proffers her trademark look of unromantic skepticism. I let it go and ask if she's seen my hair clip, the one with the moon on it. Without looking up she says, "Bathroom."

I fiddle with my phone, scrolling through my contacts to see if there's anyone else I can ask for gig support. Someone who can stay for the fireworks after, if they so choose. Once my spleen is fully vented. As I enter the bathroom my phone rings. It's Mum.

"Hey, Mum. Whatcha doing?"

There's no answer. Just silence.

"Mum. Mum." I try one last time, a little louder. "Muuuum." Still nothing. I hang up and try to call her. It rings with no response until voicemail cuts in. I don't leave a message, and just as I hang up, my phone rings again. Mum's number.

"Mum?" I start to panic, fear rising through me along with an avalanche of possibilities. What's happened? Is she OK? Is it him? "Mum?" Still nothing.

"Julia!" I yell and Julia comes running into the bathroom to be met with my panic-stricken face.

"What's wrong?"

I hand her the handset. "Can you hear anything?"

"Some heavy breathing. Urgh. Is that the guy you're meeting?"

I take the handset back.

"It's my mum. Something bad has happened."

"You don't know that."

"I do!" I tell her, even though she's one hundred percent right. I don't know. But I feel it.

"Jess." She places her hands on both shoulders. "I'm sure it'll be OK."

I call my mum's number again. Still no answer. It just rings and rings.

"I've got to go," I tell her. She nods. She knows that this is my worst fear come to life.

Then it hits me. Tom, the gig. Our meet-up. I won't make it to Mum's on the other side of town and then back. Even spending what little money I have left for the month on two taxis. That's if Mum is in any state to be left.

"If there's anything I can do . . ." Julia offers.

"Will you still go to the pub? If he's there, if you see Tom just sitting on his own, tell him I really am sorry. That I meant to be there. I'll email him anyway, but I don't have his number and . . ."

Julia looks like she wishes she never said "if there's anything I can do." Her mind is looking for a way out of something she really doesn't want to do. But she digs deep. Like the true friend she is.

"Sure. I will. Just go see your mum."

I hug her and sprint out the door.

17

Macho Bullshit

Tom

Shoreham Street, Sheffield
May 25, 2016

She doesn't seem happy to be here. Like there are a million places she'd rather be than sitting opposite me in a dark corner of a dingy pub as I try not to pout or fidget too much at being stood up by her best friend.

"She's sorry," Julia tells me. "It's her mum, she's . . ." Julia stops herself, unsure as to how much information she should be divulging. I feel for her. It's an awkward one for sure. Go meet a guy her friend has met once before, because he's told her he has something important to say. She finally comes up with a diplomatic response. "Jess is worried about her. That's all."

"This is a bit weird," I say. In doing so I crack her necessary defenses.

"It is."

"You're a good friend for coming all this way to deliver a message."

Julia shrugs. "Going to the pub isn't exactly the biggest sacrifice anyone has ever made." There's something she's not telling me, and a small squint is enough to get it out of her. "I was going to come anyway, sit in the corner and check up on you both, to make sure you weren't a complete psycho."

I can't help but chuckle at her honesty. She smiles and my foot stops bouncing. My usual fears of being seated opposite a stranger start to abate.

Julia continues, "I should have been here earlier but I've been debating whether or not coming at all was best for Jess. She's usually a very good judge of character. Doesn't suffer arseholes, as the saying goes. When she told me about you, I was quite surprised."

"Why, what *has* she told you about me?" I ask. This question causes Julia to shift in her seat and I realize I've just put the wall back up between us. She lets out a lengthy "Err."

"That bad, huh?"

She shrugs again. "It's not my business. I'm just here because she didn't want you thinking she'd stood you up."

"Did she tell you about Sarah?" I say, before instantly hiding behind my pint.

Julia nods. "It may have come up that you told her you didn't have a girlfriend before your friend came in with the truth."

"I never had a girlfriend."

She sits forward, suddenly intrigued. "So . . . your friend lied to Jess?"

"Nope." I take another swig for courage from the Dutch. "I lied to my friend."

I'm unsure as to whether Julia is suppressing a laugh, but she's definitely tickled by the whole mess. As a comedian,

I'm guessing she knows a thing or two about funny, and, well, once the hideous personal embarrassment of it fades away, I suppose it is pretty absurd.

"Why?" she asks, now genuinely curious about my tale. It takes me a moment to find the best, most honest expression of my thought process at the time.

"Macho bullshit, I think."

At this, Julia really does let out a laugh. I think about what she said about Jess being a good judge of character. Judging by her best friend, that judgment is spot-on.

"It's true," I tell her. "All my friends were seeing someone, and I was incapable—and still struggle, if I'm honest—to not trip over my tongue when I talk to people I like. Just seemed easier to invent someone."

"Well, that really backfired."

Her laughter dissipates and she's suddenly sad again.

"If Jess had known at the time . . ."

She doesn't finish her sentence and I'm glad. The thought of missed months over something that's so fundamentally my mistake has been tearing me up since August.

"Why didn't you get in touch with her sooner? Come clean about the mix-up?"

"Vomit-worthy embarrassment."

Julia makes a face as if to say she gets it. I decide she's a very understanding person and find myself opening up more than I usually would.

"I only confessed to my friend last week. Once I did, it dawned on me pretty quickly how stupid I'd been to—one, start the lie in the first place, and two, keep it up. He didn't care. He thought I was a bit of a knob . . ."

"He sounds like a good friend."

"He is."

But Scott isn't who I want to talk to Julia about. I want to talk to her about Jess. I want to use this chance to get to know Jess through the person who knows her best.

"Can I get you a drink?"

I'm surprised and delighted by her reply. She says she's parched from the journey and could do with a pint. Once I've ordered her a drink and me a fresh one, I sit back down opposite her, full of a rare confidence.

"Tell me about her."

Julia half chokes on her drink at the forwardness of my question. I'm more than a little surprised myself.

"What, like her favorite color?"

"No. Like, what she's like. We only had a few hours but she left a mark . . ."

Julia takes a proper drink and thinks carefully about the question.

"She's brilliant. And infuriating. She's brilliantly infuriating. The way her mind works, when we write together, she's able to think in the abstract with virtually no effort." Julia is on a roll now. "She's highly principled. As you've already had a taste of. Infidelity is rage-inducing for her, but it's also small things. Like littering, or talking in a cinema. She does not suffer fools. But then she's pretty foolish herself. Impulsive. Quick to get excited over new shiny things. Quick to anger too. Very easily distracted. Like, right now, her mind should completely be on Australia, but—"

"Australia?" I ask, unable to mask the fear in my voice.

"She leaves in a couple of days. Or at least she should. Depends on the mum situation, I reckon."

"A couple of days?"

She nods.

"For how long?"

She grimaces at revealing too much. "Just a few weeks."

"Oh," I say, unable to hide my despondency. "We've got to drive down to Nottingham tonight."

"Another gig?"

A dash of pride runs through my veins. "Yeah. Things are finally going well for us. We even sold out our first four nights."

"Jess played me some of your music. It was good. Hard to listen to with Jess calling you every name under the sun over the top of it . . ."

I look at my pint to see I'm already close to the bottom of it. While Julia's open and talkative, I know I have a finite amount of time to say what I want to say. The problem is, I'm no longer sure *what* I want to say. The Australia thing is a bit of a curveball. Especially if there's now no way I'll see her tonight. My phone buzzes, a message from Scott. It tells me not to forget our bus leaves at midnight. It's now 11:21.

"I'm glad she disliked me so much," I tell Julia. "I like that she has a code."

Julia's expression is one of acceptance. She's still slightly guarded, but that wall is coming down, brick by brick. Then, in one strike of the wrecking ball, it's decimated.

"She likes you. I mean, she really does. Even despite the fact her evidence suggests you're a total scoundrel. If she didn't like you, she'd have chalked you off straightaway. Like I say, she's a good judge of character and she's clearly felt, and still feels, something for you."

I can't read what I should do and so I ask her flat-out. "Do you believe me? About making up Sarah?"

"I didn't realize I was here to vet you for Jess." My silence makes her fill in the blank. "Honestly? Yes. You come across as genuine."

This seems like a compliment somehow, but her shift to the edge of her seat isn't inspiring me with hope. I can see how carefully she's considering what to say next. Reluctant to say what's on her mind for fear of sticking her nose in where it doesn't belong. I try to remove any guilt she may be feeling and home in on the truth as she sees it.

"I'm just looking for advice."

"OK," she says directly. "I'd say . . . I'd say wait."

I screw up my face like she's suggested I throw myself in front of a train to prove my feelings for Jess. She reads me like a novel.

"Is that so hard?"

"Until when?"

She offers me a look of sympathy and I can tell there's no malice behind it. "I have absolute faith that Jess is going to be huge. She's smart, hardworking—when she wants to be— and without making this too much about aesthetics, she's got a face that looks pretty damn great on camera. She's gonna make it. If she doesn't get distracted. Just wait until she's where she needs to be."

"But then she won't want to be with me."

Julia lets out a laugh with a weird amount of anger in it.

"If you believe that, then you're basically saying you want to keep her at your level."

"I'm not saying that!"

I sort of realize I was saying that and hang my head in shame. Once again, Julia's compassion and empathy are fully on display.

"Those early days of a relationship—and I'm guessing a relationship is the thing you want out of this . . ."

I nod, realizing this is my first opportunity for a real relationship in eons.

"Those early days are tough. I'm not sure if pinging each other messages across the world, both of you waiting for the other to wake up and respond, is the best start to it all."

She paints a pessimistic picture, but it's one that I can see clearly. Would I be able to cope with that distance? Or would I be second-guessing every message she sent? Every pause in every phone call? Julia tries to lift the mood.

"Look, what do I know? This is just my advice. Jess is strong-willed. If she wants to start something she will. I'm guessing once she learns the truth about you and your made-up girlfriend, she will. Nothing I suggest will deter her." She pauses here and I feel a "but" coming that will undo all the nice words she's just uttered. Sure enough—"But . . . from where I'm sitting, it sounds like things are going pretty great with the band. Things could go great for Jess down under too, given some space, without the distraction of everything a new relationship's saddled with. It's only four weeks."

I don't want to see her point but I do.

"So what do I do?" I ask.

She shakes her head. "I shouldn't have said anything."

"No." I try to convince her it's OK. That she's right. "I'm glad you did. It makes sense. Like you say, it's only a few weeks. Then we can go for drinks like normal people do."

Julia's glass is empty, as is mine, so we both stand and make our way out of the pub. It's pretty clear what I have to do. Even if I don't want to. Eat your veg before you get your pudding. I instruct Julia not to tell Jess right away about the

Sarah thing. I made a promise to myself, I'd do it in person. I can do it at the same time I tell her that we should put a pin in this.

Julia doesn't say anything more as we step out into the street. The rain is getting worse and it comes with the wet chill of life in Northern England. Just before she says good-bye, a thought hits me. A surprise for Jess, something to show her how I feel when she gets back. Something to look forward to down the road. Long after I have to tell her that now is the wrong time for us.

"This is a weird one," I tell Julia. "But do you have Jess's mum's address?"

Julia's expression is one of horror and incredulity. If I had to guess what she's thinking it would probably be "Why the hell has this guy not listened to a single word I've said?" I work quickly to quell her fears.

"I'm not going to go there, I promise. It's for a favor I promised her a while back. Something for when she gets back. A gesture, if you will."

I pass Julia my phone and she writes the address in a message I send to myself. Then she leaves.

Tonight did not go as I hoped it would. But the future? The future might.

18

A Little Fun

Jess

Heathrow, Terminal Two
May 27, 2016

Looking at myself in the mirror, it's like I'm playing fancy dress and my character is "a backpacker." Hair tied up beneath a baseball cap, sunglasses on, backpack bigger than I am.

This look isn't exactly the one I'd go for on a second date—is this a second date?—but this was all our schedules would allow. And there's something romantic about it. The airport scene. I have a couple of hours before my flight. And about five minutes before I meet Tom at the Costa. In the airport bathroom, I glance at my reflection and pull a couple of strands of hair out to fall on my face just so. It would be impossible to look great right now, but I'd like to aim for good at least.

I find him waiting in the corner of the chain bean dispensary, his leg bouncing up and down as he pours black coffee into his mouth. There's a drink for me, sitting opposite him.

I take off the sunglasses and swing the giant luggage down to my side. He rises and tries to help me with it, to stop me crushing an old lady under the weight of my clothes and a month's supply of suntan lotion.

Once the bag is under control, I take a seat and grin at him.

"So, you made Sarah up, right?" I say it with a shit-eating grin, proud of my detective work.

He shakes his head but smiles. "I told Julia not to tell you."

"It wasn't easy, I'll be honest. But I have my ways."

"Do tell."

"Mornings are her weakness. I played Metallica loud and jumped on her bed at five a.m. until she blabbed. It didn't really take long. Impressed?" I ask.

"Very," he replies.

"I've spent a long time not liking you very much . . ."

"Rightly so, given the information at hand."

I say the next bit softly, because he's been through enough. "Julia also told me you didn't get in touch earlier because you were too embarrassed." I wasn't quite soft enough, because his cheeks still go red.

"It's a pretty humiliating thing to confess."

"I don't get humiliation."

"Lucky you."

"The way I see it, everyone is equally useless as human beings. I'm not going to judge anyone for their mistakes in the hope they'll let mine slide."

"And do they?" he asks.

"No. The bastards!"

We take a sip of our coffee at the same time and both end

up with burnt lips. It's a shared moment for sure, and as the drink hits my stomach, I feel the rare joy of happiness inside. The happiness you only really get from being with a person you're beginning to feel something for. In the light of the revelation about Sarah, I'm reminded again that my radar was right about him. This one's a good one. As if to back this up, he asks a caring question.

"How's your mum?"

"Oh, right. Yeah. It turned out she was just watching TV and butt-dialed me. Her phone was on silent. She was pretty shocked when I kicked the front door in like a SWAT team member."

Tom laughs and then frowns. I can guess what's going through his head. The frustration of little things getting in the way. I attempt to remedy it, but his hangdog expression seems here to stay.

"Did you have to run to the airport?" I ask. "Like in the last act of a romantic movie?"

He shakes his head and downplays it. "No. Thankfully, I'm very well organized. No mad dash to leave me covered in sweat."

He cringes a little and I have to remind myself that while he's a good one, he does have a habit of saying the absolute worst thing. I don't know him well, but I do feel like I know him. And I know I have to give him time to say what he wants to say. No pressure.

"The EP title was a good one, though, yeah?"

"Was it?" he asks.

"I think so. I mean, you could have called it, 'Sarah isn't real. I made her up. Jess, please get in touch,' but . . ."

"It probably wouldn't have fit on the spine."

I let out a bark of a laugh and feel a little self-conscious. Which is not like me at all, but being in his presence is doing weird things to me. He looks a little sad again, like there's too much on his mind. I want to reach out for his hand and tell him it's OK, but let's face it, we're not there yet.

"I just wish . . ." he says, pushing each word out like it's a car that won't start. "I just wish I'd got in touch earlier."

Sod it, I think, a hand touch is fine right now. I reach out and put mine next to his.

"We're here now, though."

He pulls his hand away.

"About that."

The look on his face is all I need to know that this isn't going the way I want it to. It amazes me how quickly I can go from happy to hurt. The speed at which anger can take over from elation. I withdraw my hand and place it in my lap, my shoulders hunched. A protective little ball for what's to come.

He continues, "I like you, I want to make that clear. I just . . ." He hides behind his coffee cup again, as if the answers are written on the rim. "I don't think the timing is right. Like, right now, I mean."

"Why's that?" I ask.

"Distractions?" he says, as a question. When what I could really do with right now are answers. I try to remind myself to be patient. That whatever this is, probably isn't easy for him.

"Are you saying, I don't need the distraction?"

"No," he tries. "I mean, yes."

"Or *you* don't need the distraction?"

"Yes! I mean, no. What I'm trying to say is the band is

going really well at the moment. Nothing should really get in the way of our careers, right?"

I seethe. There's nothing like being told you're "getting in the way" to make a woman feel special.

He carries on, oblivious. "We're super busy and we're meeting new people every day. And you will too. In Australia."

An alarm rings in my head. Loud and clear. Nah, mate. You got this wrong again, Jess. He's basically telling you he doesn't want you. He doesn't want you distracting him from what he's now being offered. He wants a month—at least—of dicking around. Before he settles with you. If he even wants to.

I ask him flat-out. "So, you want a little fun, do you?"

"Exactly!" he says, happily crushing my heart. "You should have fun. Enjoy yourself. Then when you come back . . . I mean, four weeks is nothing really."

I stand and grab my stuff. He looks confused, somehow unaware of what he's done. Self-doubt creeps in and I start to question whether I have any right to be getting upset about this. He hasn't promised me anything. But I know my worth. I'm worth more than this. Aren't I?

"What even is this, then?" I ask, trying to keep the anger out of my words. Instead, I sound pathetic. "Why did you even come here?"

Tom looks around, down at the floor. "To see you. I really, really wanted to see you. And I desperately wanted to tell you about Sarah. I'm a bit gutted Julia got there first, to be honest."

The anger boils over. "Forget about your bloody made-up girlfriend for a second. This, me getting on a plane now, us not exchanging numbers, you not calling me when I land . . . that's really what you think is best?"

He breathes a weird sigh of relief.

"Yes. Exactly."

I can feel my face suddenly fall expressionless. A light inside me has just gone out. He opens his mouth to speak but no more words come out. I look over at the Departure Board and my gate number is flashing. There's a different Jess waiting for me when that plane touches down. I can leave all this baggage on the conveyor belt.

I punch Tom on the shoulder.

"See you around, then, Mr. Delaney."

And with that, I'm gone.

Part Three

CHANGES

19

—

Bulldust

Jess

Brynmaer Road, London
December 6, 2016

Something happened at the airport. A new Jess was born. And her mantra was *I do not give a fuck*. She takes no prisoners and suffers no morons. My routines became darker, edgier. Less earnest, less sincere. While I always wanted to do some of the stuff I was doing at Edinburgh, Dean was right. If I keep doing that, I'll play to fifty people. It turns out not caring about what you say makes people laugh. Quite a lot, actually.

When I took the stage for my first gig I had the trifecta of rage coursing through my veins: lack of sleep from jet lag after twenty-four hours on a plane; angry thoughts about Frank's sudden and unwanted reappearance into my life; and Tom. Bloody Tom. I couldn't shake him and that car crash of a "whatever" at the airport. And so I channeled it. I wore the anger on my sleeve and ranted and raved about all the things that piss me off.

And it worked. People laughed. Ultimately that's all the feedback I need, and when I started to vent and didn't hold back, audiences lapped it up. And so I did it more. And more. And the high of the applause was unlike any I'd had in comedy before. There were nights when I said things I didn't believe. There were nights when after I felt guilt for overstepping the mark. There were nights when I was cruel. But none of that mattered. Because . . . people laughed.

And my new boyfriend laughed.

Even at the age of twenty-eight, I like saying it. "He's My Boyfriend." "Yep, that's him. My Boyfriend." "Just waiting for My Boyfriend." I especially like saying it when "My Boyfriend" is this mega. I like walking down the street with him and watching other people check him out. That probably sounds shallow, but meh, I get a buzz out of it. He's fit. Like, he-can-actually-run fit. It's rare to meet someone who lives their life on stage who doesn't get out of breath climbing stairs. He's charming. Ruggedly good-looking. And yeah, every time he opens his mouth and an Australian voice comes out, I find it absolutely ridiculous—like I'm dating someone from Ramsay Street—but that will fade in time. I'm sure it will.

And Chris is also, let's not beat around the bush here, a great shag, I mean it. I'm not being cute. It's almost like he's actually taken the time to read a book on it. Or asked a living, breathing woman what she actually wants and likes. None of the usual poking and prodding that we all thought would run its course after secondary school. The roles—captain of the football team, head boy—turned into job titles—project managers, chartered accountants—but the one thing that never changed, the one constant, was the old bad moves. But Chris . . . Well, I'm not going to go into graphic detail (I'll save that for my next stand-up set); all I'll say is, Yes, Chris. Very, very good, Chris.

Which is pretty much verbatim what came out of my mouth thirty seconds ago. As we lie here on my bed, a tangled mass of limbs and sweaty hair, I think back to five months ago when he asked me out. After what had come before, it was nice to find someone who actually wanted to be with me and said so in no uncertain terms. Someone who didn't think of me as a roadblock to their career. Someone who saw me as more than a distraction.

Our hookup story is a pretty simple "funny boy meets funny girl." We met in a club in Sydney celebrating the end of my tour. Four weeks done and dusted. I'd taken my agent's advice and not been me for thirty-one days. I was not me on stage and I was certainly not me off it. It felt good not being me. I was getting sick of her anyway. And Chris evidently got the new material. Which is why when he invited me for a post-show drink, I said yes.

"I REALLY LIKED YOUR BIT ABOUT THE QUEEN ON THE THRONE?" he yelled. His voice was so loud in my ear, I could feel my eardrums dying.

"THANKS!" I shouted in reply. "IT'S THE SORT OF THING I'D GET CRUCIFIED FOR IN ENGLAND."

For some reason I was spitting on him. It might have been that I had to raise my voice to levels usually reserved for family arguments or alerting the authorities that a crime is currently in progress. Or it might have just been that I was mega squiffy. My two-drink limit was also a thing that New Jess had jettisoned.

The club—and the volume of music within it—seemed

designed specifically to prevent effective communication. Like an Orwellian experiment to curb all conversation. Despite the repeating beats and thumping bass, we were doing a fine job of flirting.

"I LIKED YOUR SET TOO. TAKING OFF YOUR SHIRT WAS A GOOD BIT."

"THANKS."

"ALTHOUGH YOU'VE RUINED A THEORY I HAVE ABOUT HOW GOOD-LOOKING PEOPLE AREN'T FUNNY!"

Chris laughed with all his body.

"HAVE I NOW?" he called out, swishing his beer in time to the music. "I'D SAY THAT THEORY IS BULL-DUST."

"I BET YOU WOULD," I replied, nailing the last of my pint.

He cupped his hands over my ear and said, "I wasn't talking about me. Fancy another drink somewhere quieter?"

The "somewhere quieter" was his camper van. He told me he didn't like being tied down, that he liked to go where the wind took him. I'll be honest, I was never entirely sure in those first few days how much of Chris was intentionally funny. But I laughed a lot.

And when I started to bore on about how lonely I was out there, and how I was starting to doubt who I was, he listened. He actually listened, and at the right times he did the sympathetic head tilt and offered me a cigarette. I don't usually smoke but I was at an invincible stage of drunkenness. Where cancer and falling downstairs couldn't hurt me.

"I've always felt like me on stage," I told him. "But this new stuff, there's all this distance between who I thought I was and who I'm presenting as. Christ, this is all sounding self-obsessed."

Despite his gin-soaked state, Chris took it all in. I could see the cogs whirring as he considered his response.

"I get it. I'm always sure I'm gonna cark it on stage and so I do this thing where I detach from my body. Like, I'm watching myself from up here." He held his hand up to the roof of the van.

"So," I continued as if he'd never spoken. "What you're saying is, I am self-obsessed?"

He smiled in a way that I was very comfortable with. He got my sense of humor. He knew when my tongue was firmly in my cheek and because of that I wanted mine to be firmly in his.

"All right, Doctor. What's the remedy?"

He raised his eyebrows suggestively. "Do you like sambuca?"

The next day my head was fuzzy, but my memory was clear. Despite being presented with someone who—judging by the "talking and the necking and the inviting back to his van" part of the night that I do remember—made it clear she liked him, still had the wherewithal to stop himself overstepping a line. We had not had sex that first night. This was one of the first things I really liked about Chris. That he wasn't the type of guy who would push the boundaries of consent. That I actually gave him points for this shows just how low the bar has been set.

Weeks after our first night together, we started talking about me returning to the UK. My four weeks in Australia had turned into three months, but my time on the other side of the world was coming to an end.

Chris talked about how he'd planned to visit England soon and that there was "no time like the present." He carried my bags to the airport and boarded the plane with me. Two months home and here we are.

Turns out it isn't that hard to start a relationship after all.

20

No Biggie

Tom

The last message Jess sent me was four and a half months ago. I still have it on my phone, for no reason other than to torture myself with it. The reply was a simple rejection to the offer (my third) of our meeting for a drink. I breezily followed it up with one that said it was "no biggie"—a phrase I've never used before or since—and that she should text me when she's free. A hundred days later and it would appear she's still busy. Then again, her career's taken off in a way I don't think either me or Julia expected.

Watching bits of her shows online used to be fun. Painful because it was a four-inch-tall, 2D Jess, and not an in-the-flesh Jess, but I loved the stuff she did. Now? Now her new routines are just . . . they've got this real mean streak to them.

One clip that's had over a hundred thousand views has her laying into a woman in the front row for the sole crime of wearing a T-shirt of a band Jess doesn't like. She's punching down in a way that I wouldn't have expected. And people are lapping it up. I know you should NEVER READ THE COMMENTS, so me scrolling down is a form of masochism worthy of the Marquis de Sade, but she is equally loved and loathed for what she's doing now. Both the praisers and the haters are hard to read. When you care about someone (and despite her shutting me out, I do still care about her), people saying nasty things about them is the worst.

This needs to stop. I switch off my laptop and get ready for the band meeting with the record label. Alan warned us on the phone, they have good news for us. And they have bad news for us.

As they deliver both I know my mind will still be on Jess.

Dyott Street, London
That afternoon

"That's the way the industry is now. Record sales mean next to shit. You got great reviews, you're the new critics' darlings, but you've sold bupkes." Mick delivers all this in a flat monotone. He's probably repeated these sentences to every young band that's entered his office, looking to understand why they're not instant millionaires now they have sellout shows and a devoted fanbase.

Alan sits next to the four of us, more than a little out of his depth. We'll never lose him, though. It's just not in our blood. He was there at the start, and he'll take ten percent until we're done.

Mick continues, "While you're not making money from

the record, you are earning on the road. My advice, and it's the same advice I'd give to anyone from the Rolling Stones to Johnny and Jane up-and-comer, is get touring. Europe. The US. Canada. Your streaming numbers in Japan are big enough to get you slots there."

There's a baby-shaped snafu in this plan. Scott's partner, Holly, is ready to drop any day now and we've been gigging nonstop since the record came out. I promised Scott that he'd get a month off, no matter what, when the baby came. Their due date is Christmas Day and so I incorrectly assumed we'd all be off anyway. It's a promise that, in hindsight, I shouldn't have made. We share a look unseen by Mick, who appears to be coming to the end of his monologue.

"And I know how media shy you are—that it adds to your mystique—but it doesn't hurt to get a few interviews out there. Appear on a few radio shows. A podcast or two. Take a look at this and see if any would fit your sensibilities."

There's derision in his voice as he says the word "sensibilities"—like we're some spoiled brats, playing a role. He tosses a piece of paper to me with a host of different titles on it, next to names of presenters I've never heard of. I pocket it for reading later. Mick's the sort of guy who doesn't stand or acknowledge you as you leave. But he has a reputation for getting bands on bills that can't be matched, so we just smile and nod as we slink out of his office.

Ten minutes later, in a classic London pub, in the city we're briefly calling home, we try and fail to dissect Mick's words. Instead, we stare into our pints, unsure what to say next. Five months ago, we'd be chomping at the bit at the talk of a world tour. But after months on the road, I know the three of them are tired, homesick, and ready for a break. I go first.

"Look, the priority remains making sure everyone gets some downtime over Christmas. We've earned it, and I know that Scott and Brandon want to get back to Holly and Carl."

Brandon and Scott both nod, appreciating the sentiment. Considering how I reacted to the pregnancy—what everyone is now, due to the due date, calling the Second Coming of Jesus—it's the least I can do.

"As for publicity, I'll take a look at this list and see what we can set up before Christmas. I'm happy to go on some regional radio shows and offer monosyllabic answers to questions until they play our record. Then in the New Year, once our Lord and Savior has arrived, we'll look at touring further afield."

I get more appreciative nods and with that a semblance of a plan is confirmed. Conversation quickly turns to what we're most looking forward to when we get home. Family seems to be the top of everyone's list. A sadness overtakes me as I realize every one of the people I care about—every one that cares about me, anyway—is already sitting around this table.

Back in the flat I pour myself a drink and reflect on the feeling of loneliness that swamped me in the pub. I've met one person over the past two years who has made me feel anything like the level of comfort I feel with my friends. And somehow, in a five-minute conversation in an airport, I screwed it up beyond repair.

So, what next? Pine and hide away, or face the world. You can start, I direct myself, with that list of radio shows and interview requests. No matter how painful they may be, it's time to put yourself out there. And then I see it. Of all the podcasts, in all the world. At the bottom of Mick's list, beneath a show about someone's dad writing erotica, I see her name.

"Funny Stuff" with Jess Henson. Contact Julia Borne for details.

21

Puppy Dog Eyes

Jess

Mortimer Street, London
December 17, 2016

The podcast was Julia's idea. About a month after I got back from Australia, she forcefully suggested I start one of my own. She'd come to a few of my shows and—while she didn't turn her nose up at my new material as such—she wasn't super enthusiastic about it either. I think the podcast was her not-so-subtle way of steering me away from my new direction.

I'd explained how Chris and Dean both thought the "Give No Fucks" content was a good way forward, and she made some crack about how a new boyfriend and an agent's judgment probably triumphs over an old best friend. I told her in no uncertain terms that it definitely did not. But then she just shrugged and said "You'll figure it out" in a sort of Zen masterpiece of life advice.

A little while later she bought me a microphone and some recording equipment and offered her services as a producer.

"A podcast?" I asked with a little sass, believing—as its core is to sit in a room giving people unasked-for opinions about nothing in particular—that it was something mostly white men do.

"To paraphrase the Cranberries, everyone else is doing it, so why can't you? Patty has one. Melanie too." She told me all this by way of a convincer.

"But why do you think I should do one?"

"You're getting booked now. A lot. I think it'd be a good idea if you had a place where you could be more *you*. Y'know?"

I did know. But I wasn't in a mood to challenge it. And after all, she seemed really enthusiastic about learning how to produce and market it. As is Julia's way, she managed to convince me that it was me doing her a favor and not the other way around.

"You reckon people will listen to it?"

"Hell, yeah. It might be slow going at first, but you know how much I believe you're going to be the future Queen of Comedy. This is my way of coining in early."

If I wanted to be a world-class arsehole I could actually blame her for Tom coming on the show, but everyone in the room knows this is my doing. So I said *Yes* when his management asked. Despite Chris now being in my life. Despite the anger I still feel toward Tom—an anger which comes from so many places I don't know where to start. But I'll try anyway: that he made me feel I'd always be second fiddle to his career, that he convinced me he really liked me . . . Then there was that line about "having a little fun," his stupid big coat . . .

Goddammit, I hate this side of me.

Because, despite all this, I wanted to see him again and so I helped orchestrate this farce. And now here he is, waiting on the other side of the clear door. In that fucking coat.

He knocks on the glass and Julia opens it for him. As he enters the room, she looks for my reaction. I give nothing away, but I notice something shift in her. An uncomfortableness.

"Hi," Tom says meekly.

Julia greets him pleasantly but apprehensively. "It's good to see you again."

It takes me a second to remember that, yes, they have met. And no doubt talked about me. Is that the cause of this awkward air? I don't have time to answer as his attention fixes squarely on me. His puppy dog eyes at their most baby canine, he asks how I'm doing.

"I'm good," I reply, busying myself with buttons and cables the purposes of which I will never know. Julia takes them off me and I smartly nip in the bud this idea of me and Tom having a quick catch-up. "Sorry, can we chat after? There's just a fair bit to do to set it all up."

What is this I'm feeling? A mix of irritable and sad. Why do I want to punch his lights out? Am I hungry? I'm probably just hungry. Flashes of our final interaction at the airport come to mind and I know it isn't the lack of food in my stomach that has me tetchy. I want to scream expletives in his face. Urgh. I've become the cliché of a woman scorned.

As he sits down and puts his headphones on, sipping at the tiny glass of water we've left him, it dawns on me that inviting him here was a really, really, *really* bad idea.

22

Funny Stuff

Jess and Tom

Subject line: Transcript of "Funny Stuff" Episode 8—Guest Tom Delaney. Notes by Julia Borne. To be aired before Christmas.

I just want to prefix this by saying we really don't have to release this one, Jess. After all, I think we can both agree this is not your finest hour. Hope you're OK. I'm here if you need me. J x

Transcript not for distribution.

JESS: We don't do ads for Squarespace or for, for ads for . . . Shit . . . Sorry. Can we go again? From the top. We don't do ads for Squarespace or for that weird food-delivery service where they send you the ingredients but you have to cook it yourself. I mean, what is the point of that? But if you like what you hear and you want to chuck us a few quid for this wonderful free content there'll be a link in the show notes. OK. On with the show.

Insert "Funny Stuff" podcast jingle. A mix of jazz piano and drums, culminating in a drumroll and a cymbal crash.

JESS: Welcome. Welcome. Welcome to this, the eighth episode in our quite probably short-lived podcast "Funny Stuff" in which I talk to . . . relatively . . . famous people about things they find funny. I've run out of comedians who are willing to talk to me, so please welcome musician Tom Delaney of The Friedmann Equation.

TOM: Hi.

JESS: Good start, Tom. Hope you'll be this eloquent throughout. Some background on The Friedmann Equation if you haven't heard of them. They're sort of old-sad-bastard music, but with an up-tempo thing. Is that a fair description, Tom?

TOM: I don't think you have to be an old sad bastard to listen to our music—

JESS: But it helps, right. So, your first full album, *Sarah Isn't Real*, is out now. And you're touring to promote it?

TOM: That's right. We're playing the KOKO tomorrow and the day after. Then we head back up north for a few dates at the end of the month.

JESS: Busy, busy. I'm glad you're not letting anything get in the way of your music.

TOM: Sorry?

JESS: Don't mention it. First up, we've got to talk about these names. The Friedmann Equation? What the holy hell balloon is that all about?

TOM: Erm. Yeah. So. Alexander Friedmann was a Soviet mathematician and physicist who—

JESS: Sounds boring. No, I'm kidding. Carry on.

TOM: So, he was one of the first people to consider the possibility that the universe might be both expanding and contracting. His equation—

JESS: Sorry, got to stop you there. Turns out I was right. That is incredibly boring. Let's move on to the album title, *Sarah Isn't Real*. You're going to give a lot of girls called Sarah an identity complex.

TOM: I didn't think about that. The title was a recommendation—

JESS: By a friend? A lover? Your mum?

TOM: Somebody I used to know.

JESS: He's so mysterious, isn't he? I heard the album was named after a girlfriend you invented. Who does that?

TOM: It was a long time ago.

JESS: I'm teasing, Tom, and, dear listener, he is blushing now. Should I tell them you and I have a history?

TOM: Do we? Er, yes. I suppose we do. But is it something either of us wants to talk about on a podcast?

JESS: I don't mind. I'm in a relationship now—

TOM: You're seeing someone?

JESS: That's what I meant by "in a relationship." And if he has an issue with me discussing my past, I'll happily consign him to mine. Anyway, the reason Tom is blushing now is because I used to fancy him. I say used to, because, like we just mentioned, I have a boyfriend now. Depending on when this airs. Am I right?

TOM: Did you just make a joke about splitting with your boyfriend and then say "Am I right?"

JESS: Says the man who invents women. When did you become catty?

TOM: I wasn't meaning to be catty. It's just I've never heard you say "Am I right?" before. It's like I'm on a shock-jock radio station.

JESS: Please continue (*far too long a pause, edit point JB*). Great dead airtime, Tom. It's like the end of one of your gigs, where everyone slopes off to kill themselves. Let's talk about how we know each other?

TOM: Like I said, I don't really want to discuss that here and now.

JESS: Ah, come on, wee laddie. What better way to fill an hour of chat?

TOM: Seriously, though. Can we stop this for a second and just talk?

JESS: No way! This doesn't have a pause. Think of it as live radio. If I start stopping and starting, my producer will have to edit it and I can't be buggered to put up with her grief. Only about twenty people listen to this show anyway. And they're all contractually obligated to as relatives and friends.

TOM: In that case, why are we bothering to do this at all?

JESS: Well, this took a sour turn pretty quickly, didn't it? Let's dip into our Bucketful of Klostermans and see if we can't make things a little more fun. For those new to the show, Chuck Klosterman is an American writer who has a line in hypotheticals. In this bit—A Bucketful of Klostermans—we ask listeners to write in with their own. So, Tom Delaney of The Friedmann Equation, this one is from Rob in Norfolk. Rob asks, would you rather have fingers as long as your legs, or legs as long as your fingers?

TOM: What?

JESS: Pretty simple question, Tom. Fingers as long as legs, or legs as long as fingers?

TOM: Erm. Well. I suppose if my fingers were as long as my legs I could . . . I could play keyboards that were further away. Which has some benefits. In the legs-as-long-as-fingers scenario, where's the knee joint?

JESS: I'd say where your knuckle is.

TOM: *(laughs)*

JESS: Did you hear that, dear listener? He laughs. We'll have another one of those when the conversation dries up in about five minutes.

TOM: Touché.

JESS: Let's talk a little about your band. You're the drummer, right?

TOM: No. That's Brandon. I play keyboards and a few other things.

JESS: But you sometimes play the drums?

TOM: Well, yes, but mainly it's Brandon.

JESS: Do you want to hear some drummer jokes?

TOM: Not particularly.

JESS: Good. What do you call a drummer who breaks up with his girlfriend?

TOM: I don't know.

JESS: Homeless!

TOM: Very good.

JESS: What does a drummer use for contraception?

TOM: No idea.

JESS: His personality!

TOM: Any more?

JESS: Maybe later. Is it true you don't allow phones into your gigs?

TOM: It's not like we ban them. We politely request that people don't take pictures or videos, that's all.

JESS: Sounds a bit pretentious.

TOM: We just don't see the point of watching a gig through a six-inch screen. It's a barrier between us and the audience.

JESS: I'll refer you to my previous statement. So, when you and the other old sad bastards are sitting around your garage playing with your instruments—

TOM: It's a converted warehouse, but yep, so far so good.

JESS: Do you ever think up ways to make yourselves millionaires? Because this isn't it, surely.

TOM: I'm not sure being a millionaire is top of my list of priorities really. As long as I get to keep doing what I'm doing.

JESS: Oh! That's a surprise, considering you once told me you wouldn't let anything get in the way of your own success.

TOM: I don't remember saying that.

JESS: The "I don't remember saying that" defense. Loved by white guys since the dawn of time. But anyway, I reckon you could get to that million quid. What you need is some controversy. Or a suicide! Nirvana made a packet after Kurt lived fast, died young, and left a good-looking corpse. Yeah, draw straws to see which one of you should off yourselves. The remaining members get the windfall. Side note: the best thing to happen to Dave Grohl's career was a single shotgun blast, discuss.

TOM: With comedy like that I can see why you're so successful of late.

JESS: It's just a joke.

TOM: Of course. You can say what you like if that's your mantra. That being the second suicide reference you've made today, I'm guessing they've both been intentional. But this is the new Jess, isn't it?

JESS: Someone's got their gloves on today.

TOM: I just didn't have you down as one of those comics willing to say anything to get a rise out of someone.

JESS: What's that supposed to mean?

TOM: Nothing. Forget about it.

JESS: It's getting awkward again. Time for another dip into our Bucketful of Klostermans . . .

TOM: Do we have to?

JESS: No, fine. Let's end it there. The shortest podcast in history. Before you run off, let's get to the central conceit of this show, the one that sets it apart from the thousands of other podcasts in which people blather on as if they've got something important to say. That conceit is "What tickles your funny bone, Tom Delaney?"

TOM: I don't know.

JESS: Come on. Quit sulking and answer the question. What makes you laugh?

TOM: Well, once I saw this stand-up in Edinburgh. She was passionate and smart.

JESS: Go on.

TOM: And she seemed to care. She wasn't going for the easy laugh. She was sincere. And she wasn't pretending to be someone she wasn't.

JESS: How do you know?

TOM: You're right. I suppose I don't.

JESS: Tom Delaney of The Friedmann Equation. That's some Funny Stuff.

End of Transcription

23

Happy Christmas

Tom

Mortimer Street, London
December 17, 2016

I throw off my headphones and rage, "What was that?"

"Bloody good radio," she replies with barely a blink.

From the second I walked in I knew she was out for blood. Like those in the front row at her gigs, I was a victim of the new Jess Henson. I try to justify that they pay to be there, and I was a hapless participant, but it's a hard line to stick to. I wanted to be in this room. Just not like this.

I put on my coat, ready for round two.

"You're not fooling anyone."

"With what?"

"Playing the b—"

"Don't you dare call me a bitch."

"I didn't. But I was gonna say you're pretending to be one."

I'm not good with confrontation, but there's only so far I can be pushed. Neither of us seems to mind that we have an audience of two for this, as Julia and the intern, Vin, do their best to keep their distance by acting busy.

"How do you know that isn't me? We've had two conversations. In the second of which you made it abundantly clear that you weren't interested."

I look at Julia and she looks down at the ground. Jess looks to Julia for an explanation. Her forehead couldn't look more furrowed if a plow were rolling through it.

"I clearly don't. The hateful crap you've been spewing lately, that stuff about suicide . . . What was that? Done your research, have you?"

"I didn't realize you were a Nirvana superfan. A suicide joke about a guy who died thirty years ago? Too soon, is it, precious?"

"Precious?!" My voice has reached a pitch only Flipper could hear. "You gonna call me a snowflake next?"

The intern slowly backs out of the room to safety, complete with a great show-business story to tell his partner when he gets home, as me and Jess continue to trade insults. She accuses me of calling her alt-right because I dare to disagree with her style of comedy and I make accusations back about how her new direction is the definition of being a sellout. There's just enough room for her to tear into me about my white male privilege before Julia, unwilling to leave her friend, finally steps in.

"Guys. Can you both just take a deep breath?"

I spit it out before I even have time to think about what I'm saying: "Gonna offer some more great advice, are you?"

Julia shrinks and the angry air turns to something worse, something even more toxic. It might appear to an outsider that I'm ganging up on both of them. Maybe I am.

"What's that supposed to mean?" Jess asks, genuinely perplexed. "What's he talking about?"

"It doesn't matter," I reply in a subdued tone. I point at the recording equipment. "Please don't release that."

As I'm halfway down the corridor all my thoughts go to finding the nearest pub and not so much drowning my sorrows as waterboarding them. I want to hurt myself with booze to make up for the absolute idiot I've been. I replay our last meeting before Australia, looking for signs to see what I did wrong. How I dropped the ball so badly. What a fool I've been.

I hear the studio booth open and hear Jess hurl one final insult, which I return in kind.

"Happy Christmas, Tom!"

"Happy Christmas, Jess!"

24

Red Flag Number One

Jess

Brynmaer Road, London
December 24, 2016

For Christmas this year I've been given the gift of intractable guilt by the UK's worst comedy website. The headline reads:

FEMALE COMIC'S SUICIDE JOKE DIES ON ITS ARSE

One. They can piss off with the "female" comic part. It's the twenty-first century—the only reason for putting gender before a job title is if you're trying to make a wider point. Two. Did they really just make a death pun while simultaneously calling me out for my mistake? Third, and most importantly, I had absolutely no idea. Of course I didn't.

The article goes into greater depth, detailing who Tom is and how his grandfather, a music legend of his era, took his own life at the age of seventy-one. I didn't know much about him, except what Tom told me on that first night and about how Tom's parents sold a diary Tom wanted. I certainly didn't know how he'd died until I opened my social media the day after the podcast aired and was met with a raft of death and rape threats. I called Tom immediately to apologize. But he wouldn't answer. I've tried him three more times today and nothing. As I hang up, Chris shrugs and tells me it's good publicity.

"That's not the point," I reply. "Tom thinks I was saying all that to wind him up, to hurt him. When I didn't have a clue."

Chris hovers behind me and my laptop, reading over my shoulder. "I'd chill out if I was you. It's not like it's the front page of one of your tabloids. It's a comedy website fishing for content." He looks like he's had a bright idea, but (after a few months of him being my live-in boyfriend) I've got used to what follows being anything but. "You should get your agent to leak this to some of those right-wing papers you're always raging about. Young female comic lays into dead beloved hero, they'd go mad for it. Make you a pariah in a week."

"Why would I want to be a pariah?"

He shrugs again. "For the clicks?"

As I reread the article for the five hundredth time, Chris announces he's off to meet someone about some "bonza opportunity." I'm left alone with my guilt and my brain and the replay of the whole horrible episode. What was I really hoping to achieve, inviting him onto the podcast? Was my anger justified in the first place? Isn't it just time I moved on? Like, actually moved on.

My phone rings. It's Tom's number.

"You rang?"

"Tom. I had no idea. I promise."

There's an awful pause as he weighs up my words. "If you didn't know, then you've got nothing to feel bad about." He hangs up before I can say anything more. Tomorrow, Chris and me are off to my mum's for Christmas. I need to see my mum. I need to be home. It can't come soon enough.

M1, Between Junction 23a and Junction 24
December 25, 2016

"Are we there yet? Are we there yet? Are we there yet?"

Chris's current impersonation of a six-year-old is not what I need as I navigate the M1's fifty-seven lanes of traffic, helplessly searching for the one that stops me driving through Nottingham and adding two hours onto our four-hour road trip. The mix of sleet and rain and a nonexistent car heater doesn't help matters either. Or the fact that I'm driving because he's "arguably still over the limit" from last night. He opened his first can about fifty miles back, with the comforting words of "no harm in making sure."

I should be feeling good about this. This is a journey of firsts. My first Christmas with a boyfriend. My first time bringing a man home to meet Mum. What she thinks of him matters almost as much as what I think of him. The jury, as far as I'm concerned, is still out.

But I can't feel good because my head is full of Tom, and the hurt I've caused him.

"Watch out for that lorry," Chris jokes. Or at least I think he's joking, as he opens can #3. I start wondering about relationship red flags. Red flag number one, he's commenting on my driving in a way that I'm not sure is as funny as he wants me to think it is. Like he's trying to make it light but he's still making a rather unsubtle point. The other is how he's crossing the line from tipsy to drunk an hour and a half before we meet my mum, even though his original plan hinged on him doing the driving. I make a point of staring at his empties and the three unopened Carlings.

"Are you planning on polishing all those off before we get to Sheffield?"

"'Course not. I was saving the other three for you. Want one now?"

I put on my best fake laugh and he grins back like a loon.

"You don't mind, do you?" he asks, with what seems like genuine enough concern. I shake my head, providing him with the answer he wanted.

"Good. Because I didn't want to invoke the Noddy Holder defense."

"I'm going to regret asking what the Noddy Holder defense is, aren't I?"

"It's Chriiiiiiiiiistmas!!!"

His Slade scream is enough to see me swerving into the middle lane and getting a mighty honk from behind for my troubles. I shake my damned head.

"Put on some music, you massive dolt."

Chris picks up my iPod and I brace myself for what's coming next.

"Oh, what a surprise. Last played, The Fried Toast Equilibrium."

"Why have you got to be a dick about them? They're just a band I like."

He pulls a face and makes a *pfft* sound I find both annoying and annoyingly distracting. And when a distraction might see us underneath an articulated lorry, my earlier feelings of warmth for this man are being left somewhere on the hard shoulder.

"I've just never met a grown woman with such an unhealthy obsession with a boy band."

"Boy band? They're four talented musician *men* who don't sing or dance, you absolute dillweed."

"Maybe, but your devotion to them is like my nine-year-old niece's with Wand Erection, ooooh." That "ooooh" means he likes his own joke and he's going to write it down somewhere. He pulls out a pen from his pocket and scribbles on the back of a receipt he finds on the floor.

"My devotion? I've seen them live once. I can't write to music with lyrics. I just like listening to them when I work."

"And in the car. And in the shower."

A red mist is forming in my eyes, just below the actual mist of unsettled snow on the car's engine.

"Is this going to be our first proper fight? About how you're jealous of a band I like?"

Another *pfft* flies forth followed by the mouthing of the word "jealous" multiple times. We sit in angry silence for half a mile. Until Chris eventually pipes up with, "This isn't our first fight."

Curiosity breaks my silence.

"What was?"

"The toilet-roll thing."

My heart warms at this. That he thinks our minor disagreement over which way a toilet roll should be placed on the holder could, on any planet, constitute "a fight" tells me more about his naivete and optimism than a thousand therapists could.

"The toilet-roll incident was *not* a fight."

"OK, then," he seethes. "Which way should it go?"

The rage in his face right now is hysterical to me. I have a strong urge to pull over onto the hard shoulder and push him out into a bush full of wee from bladders that couldn't make it to the next services.

"It doesn't matter!" I laugh.

"It does! Otherwise why would hotels uniformly do it a certain way? It has to be facing out to stop you having to reach around to find the next sheet."

"Ha! You are a ridiculous human being. You're arguing over how best to give a reach-around to bog roll." I throw a packet of jelly babies to him from the door of the car. "Eat something, will you? You're being hangry-stupid. Stupid."

Chris opens the bag, shoves three confectionery infants into his gob at once, and chews loudly, before finishing off the third can and opening the fourth. He puts his hand on my leg and I swat it away. He picks out two jelly babies and plays out a scene with squeaky voices, one stereotypically Aussie and one offensively British:

JELLY BABY CHRIS: Strewth, don't be like that, babe.

JELLY BABY JESS: Like what?

JELLY BABY CHRIS: All pissed off with me. It's Christmas.

JELLY BABY JESS: But you're an idiot and I hate you.

"True and true," I confirm.

JELLY BABY CHRIS: What can I do to make it up to you?

"I swear to Holy Jesus I'll crash this car into the nearest petrol station if you start to make those sweets hump."

JELLY BABY CHRIS: You know I love you, right?

He makes the two jelly babies kiss but stops short of full bonbon-on-bonbon action. I stick out my tongue at him and contemplate what just happened. My boyfriend just told me that he loved me. I mean, he didn't say it properly. But he did say it. Does that count?

More importantly, do I want it to?

Park Grange Court, Sheffield
December 25, 2016

Chris is nothing if he's not charming. And so far, since we arrived, he's been absolutely nothing. I can't figure out why, but he's being so rude—actually being rude—to my mum. It's like he's negging her into liking him.

He opened with a couple of "you must be her sister" and "I can see where she gets her looks" jokes that went down as well as Santa in a synagogue. He was trying for ironic, tongue-in-cheek, purposefully bad humor. But it just came out so accidentally bad, Mum gave him a half-hug and walked off to check on the chicken. Things went from bad to worse when Mum revealed that we were indeed having a dry Christmas. I'd warned Chris this might happen. That I'd told her if she needed to jettison all alcohol it wouldn't be a problem. Maybe that was why he mainlined all six cans before we arrived. By the time of the last one it seemed churlish not to let him finish them.

I'm not sure if it's paranoia but he seems weirdly snooty about the house, too. Like his nose has been turned all the way up to eleven. We are not well-off. Never have been. With a disappearing dad and two kids to raise, Mum had bigger and better priorities than trying to kit the house out in Laura Ashley. She stopped her drinking, kept us out of poverty, and made our childhood fun. No parent has ever done better. Chris, on the other hand, has previously described his parents as "comfortable." Which can loosely be translated to mean "rich enough to ski." It goes some way to explaining his nomadic, you-can't-tie-me-down ethos. Those that really have to struggle can't wait to get the security of a roof over their heads.

After lunch it's present time and we settle onto the sofa, all three of us in a line. Me the piggy in the middle. From a carrier bag by my feet I take out two parcels. One for my mum and one for Chris. Mum opens hers first to find a new draft excluder shaped like a snake. She shrieks in glee.

"A boyfriend for Henry! And what a fine boyfriend he is too."

She throws her arms around me and I can feel Chris staring at me waiting for the joke to be explained. I get off the sofa and pick up Henry, at least three decades old, multicolored and moth-eaten—a snake draft excluder with crossed eyes and a little red tongue poking out. I wave him in Chris's face and he recoils.

"You see, Henry here is super gay. Always has been. But there's not a lot of male snake action for him in the house. So, each night he sneaks out and tries to find—"

"Some cock," Mum offers proudly.

"Yes, Mum. Thanks. Some snake cock. We never know if he's managed to find some or not. Mum thinks he has but

I'm not sure. Now, as Henry enters his twilight years, I thought it would be easier if I brought a partner into the house for him."

"I love him!" shrieks Mum. "What shall we call him?"

"Percival?" I suggest.

"Quentin?" Mum puts forward.

"He looks like a Sebastian to me," offers Chris. To include him in the merriment—and to try to make up for the fact that his beer buzz from the journey is probably wearing off—I take his hand and say, "Perfect."

"Can I open mine now?" Chris asks with childlike enthusiasm. On my nod he rips into the snowmen wrapping-paper with glee. Inside is a shoebox marked "Homesickness kit." Inside the box is some Vegemite, three packets of Tim Tams, a bottle labeled "99ml of Golden Circle Lime Cordial" (I point out that he can still take this through customs), and assorted other down-under items. He grins at each element and pulls me in for a thank-you kiss. My mum's proximity makes him pull away quicker than he usually does. In fact, if we were at home I'd be partially undressed by now. He reaches into a bag by his feet.

"And for you."

Chris hands me a card and my heart sinks a little. I thought we were at least at the present phase, hence my well-thought-out care package. He sees my disappointment and smiles knowingly. I surmise there might be something inside. When I tear open the envelope a thin sheet of card falls out. It's a voucher, scribbled in his writing, that says GOOD FOR ONE HOUR OF THE GOOD STUFF.

He beams. "Sorry, I forgot I put that in there! If I'd known you were gonna open it in front of your mum . . ."

"You'd have bought me an actual present?" I offer through gritted teeth.

In a hushed voice he says, "I thought we were doing jokey presents. I mean, yours ain't exactly a Rolex . . ." We all face forward in silence, until Chris reaches into the bag next to him, suddenly animated again.

"I got you something too, Linda."

I immediately recognize the shape of the present as a DVD and hope to God he hasn't done what I'm pretty sure I know he has. She unwraps it and offers the weakest of smiles as she looks down at his girning face from the cover.

"It's my DVD. Some of the stuff is a bit raunchy. But you've seen and heard it all before, am I right?" She rolls her eyes as he leans across to nudge her shoulder and then looks about the room, his snootiness returned.

"You do own a DVD player, right?"

Park Grange Court, Sheffield
December 26, 2016

Chris usually sleeps for Australia and so Boxing Day morning seems like as good a time as any to grill my mum on her first impressions of him. I'm nervous because, halfway through his ill-advised Director's Commentary of his own stand-up material, Mum looked ready to throw herself under a herd of stampeding reindeer.

"So?" I ask, a two-letter word for a much bigger question.

Her body language isn't exactly screaming "I can't wait to be his mother-in-law." When I press her she tries a series of diplomatic platitudes, including crowd favorites "He seems fine," "It's early days yet," and "As long as he makes you happy."

The final one gets me thinking. Does he? He hasn't made me sad yet.

"Jess."

The face that comes with my name being uttered means I know this is about Frank. She hands me a card, my name scrawled on the front.

"This came for you. You don't have to read it."

I grin and put it straight in the bin. The grin masks pain I don't really want to get into today. Thankfully, Mum is the Queen of Subject Changing.

"Oh," she says brightly and suddenly. "The council are finally dropping their challenge over the extension. I got the letter through the other day."

It takes me a while to remember what she's talking about and when I finally do, I feel like the worst daughter on earth.

"I completely forgot about that!"

"Don't worry, it's all sorted," she says breezily, sipping on her tea. "A young man rang up and said he does legal cases for free. I thought it was a scam at first, but he never asked for any money. He wrote off to the council explaining the situation and they said it was all fine."

"When was this?" I ask, trying to construct a timeline.

"Oh. Let me think . . . I know, he got in touch the week after you went to Australia. I remember saying to myself I'd tell you about it on the phone. But then I clean forgot."

As I hypothesize on how this might have happened, whether Tom is involved or if it's all just a huge coincidence, my face must look like it's working out the square root of a million, because Mum immediately asks what the matter is.

"It's probably nothing, Mum, but do you remember his name?"

"The lawyer? A Mr. Patel."

I brush it off and get on with making three teas.

"Said the case was recommended to him by a Tim Dolaney, or something."

My legs go weak under the weight of my brain swimming with questions.

"Oh," is all I can manage.

She repeats my "Oh," adding a question mark and a head tilt. I shake mine and say, "It's nothing. I met a guy a little while ago and mentioned your problem to him. He said he knew someone who could help. We lost touch."

"Well, this is a great reason to reach out to him."

I raise an eyebrow at the fact that she's already matchmaking, even though my very-much-current boyfriend is less than twenty feet away. She perseveres. "At the very least you should say thank you."

Old feelings return and say hello. Feelings I thought I was done with. Feelings I thought were long gone. I should say thank you, I tell myself. I definitely should. But first I need to find out why the hell he did it.

25

Quite a Bash

Tom

Glenlockhart Valley, Edinburgh
Christmas Day 2016

I'm as baffled as the next man why I'm here today. The next man being my dad. He passes me the gravy with a look of befuddlement that's been writ large on his face since I arrived.

Their invitation for me to spend Christmas Day with them was part of a group email. Canapés and champagne for friends at quarter past three. They like to do the Queen's Speech alone, before guests arrive. For some reason, I asked if I could join them earlier in the day and have Christmas lunch with them. That was the first time they said they were "surprised." It's been nearly a decade since we last sat around a table together, decorated with the placemats of a Dickensian yuletide scene.

As I finish off the food, and drink the wine like it's water, I'm aware that even with the band doing well this is absolutely the finest and most expensive meal I've had in years. I watch them exchange a look. It's hard to read, but I think they're impressed I'm here. I know I am. Despite the bin fire that is me and Jess, I'm feeling better about myself. More confident. The band is exactly where we hoped to be by the end of the year. Touring. Getting acclaim. If I could shake Jess from my head, I might actually describe myself as happy.

"Thanks," I say, pushing my clean plate away. "That was delicious."

Not much has been said since I arrived. Mum was busy in the kitchen and Dad was playing with his latest piece of expensive tech. Now the food has been eaten, it seems like conversation is called for. But nobody's budging.

"Are you both OK?" I ask, addressing my father.

"We're fine, Thomas. Just . . ." He exchanges the exact same look with Mum. "I'm very surprised you came."

"We are," Mum adds. "We're just very . . . surprised you came."

The word "surprised" has many different meanings in this sentence.

"You know, quite a few people will be coming after three?"

The message behind the words is clear. *You can't cope in company, so why have you bothered to come?* It riles me. I feel fifteen again. But I can't blame them. I take another swig of wine and feel its calming effects.

"I did live in this house, you know. I remember your parties. I'm sure I'll be fine."

Another look between them. This one is a "get him" look, almost with a smile. This was a classic "look" when I was a kid. Dad repeats what seems like his mantra today. "We just really didn't expect you to turn up. That's all."

"Yeah," I say. "You said that."

Sensing the mood turning sour, Mum changes course, reminding me of their financial support, even when it's not been asked for. "And we already sent your card, too. To London."

"I know. I got it."

"And what was inside?"

"Yes. Thanks. It was very generous."

Mum picks up a cracker and offers it to her husband. He pulls it and "pretends" to read the joke, but whispers a different one in her ear. They roar with laughter. I stand and tidy the plates, taking them through to the kitchen. Dad calls after me, "Just bung that in the dishwasher. The cleaner will sort it tonight, after the party."

I carry on regardless until it hits me what day it is and I return to the dining room. "You're having the cleaner come on Christmas Day?"

Another withering look between the two people who brought me into the world.

He puts on a woe-is-us voice. "Yes, Thomas, I know—the bourgeois trampling on the common man. The terrible Scrooges we are."

"We're paying them time and a half," Mum explains, hoping for justification.

While things started off well, the closer we get to the guests arriving, the more I can sense going south. I pour another glass of red. I'm trying to keep them onside, him especially, but, as usual in their presence, the words I say aren't coming out the way I want them to. Is it my fear turning the day? Or theirs?

My motive for being here today—despite not having any

alternative—is to find out more about Grandad. Since Jess's error of judgment, he's been on my mind a lot. I want to know the similarities we share. For better or worse. Who better to ask than his only son?

I know I have to be careful with the fact-finding as getting Dad to open up about anything is a Herculean task; to get him to speak about Patrick Delaney will be tantamount to getting blood from a landslide. I collect a couple more dishes and say, "If the cleaner's not coming until the guests turn up, we might as well wash these bits now."

My logic works on him and he reluctantly gets to his feet. He kisses his wife as he passes and I see another shared glance between them. "Fine," he says. "But you can wash. I'll dry."

In the kitchen, I ask if I can connect my phone to his Sonos. He shrugs and I put it on a Daily Mix playlist. It's underhand, I suppose, but I know it'll kick out a song by his dad soon enough and I can use it as a segue. As he looks for anything to dry the plates with—the kitchen something of a foreign land to him—I subtly open my line of questioning.

"How's work?"

He looks at me like I've just shat in the sink, before replying that work is fine.

"Off anywhere nice in the New Year?" I try, sounding more like a barber than a son.

He puts down the tea towel with a huff. "This is pitiful. Even for you, Thomas."

"What?"

"This. You suddenly turning into Michael bloody Parkinson. There's only ever been one topic of conversation you want to have with me, so just ask."

In a case of unfortunate timing, a Patrick Delaney song comes on just as he finishes his sentence, the opening chords familiar to us both.

"*Quelle surprise*," he says, before giving in with a hand gesture that says "go on."

"I've just been thinking about him a bit lately. Especially how he was towards the end. I suppose I wanted to know if he was like that when he was younger."

The vein on the side of my father's head is raised and beating. His scowl is etched in marble. His expression of contempt for me is fine art.

"Like what?"

"Depressed. Was he lonely? Before . . ."

"Before what?"

"Before he ended it all?"

He sneers at me.

"What kind of bloody question is that? On Christmas Day?"

He grabs my phone and switches the music off. Near silence fills the house. The only sound left is the dripping of the tap into a half-empty sink.

He doesn't say anything to me until a minute before the guests arrive, when he suggests less than kindly that I don't ruin the day for my mother by pouting all through her party. I tell myself I won't run like a coward straightaway. I'll wait for an hour, tops, before I make an escape.

Like me, my mum and dad were both only children, so we have no extended family to speak of. Yet after the Queen's been beamed into houses across the nation, ours fills up with people wanting to spend one of the biggest days of the year in my parents' presence. They come with gifts, they come with bottles, they come with hugs and air kisses. I could say they're all phony but I don't think it's true. They all fit. It's me that's the odd dog out.

I make my way over to the drinks table and pour myself one more for the road. As I do, a hand reaches for the same bottle as me and quickly retracts with an apology. I look up to see an attractive twenty-something with a nose piercing and a leather jacket. Her hair is as black as her coat, her skin light dark. I look across the room and surmise that her parents are the ones talking to mine. These events have historically been quite monochromatic affairs.

"No, you go for it," I say, letting her take her drink of choice.

"It's Tom, right?" she says. I can't exactly place the accent—Canadian or American?

"It is," I reply, with a look that tells her I'd like to know how she knows.

"Your dad told my mum you might be here. I'm a big fan of your band."

Because I'm shallow and crave affirmation, I get a prickle of excitement that this beautiful person knows something positive about me. It gives me a boost and keeps the nerves at bay. I may be in a loser's body but professionally I'm doing OK. I offer a thank-you for her compliment and it dawns on me that I've seen her somewhere before. I know it's a line but I say it anyway.

"Did you see a film called *Long Term Parking*?" she replies.

"I love that movie," I say, taking a second to realize that

she was the girl who played Abigail, the artist whose tragic death sparks the heroine's journey. "You're Abigail!" I shout, loud enough for her to look embarrassed and other guests to wonder what's going on.

"I was."

"So, you're an actress?"

"Good deduction."

"What the hell are you doing in my parents' house?"

She laughs and shrugs.

"A person's gotta be somewhere, I suppose."

As we take our drinks to a quieter corner of the room, I learn the real reason. It's less cool than her previous answer and boils down to her mum dating some friend of my dad's.

"They met on a cruise for singles over fifty," Cara tells me. "I'm filming in London, so she invited me up here for Christmas. In an appalling Scottish accent. She told me this is 'quite a bash.'"

"That is an appalling Scottish accent. And quite a lie."

We look around the room and see that we're by far the youngest here. Neither of us fits in the surroundings and so we have an instant connection. It allows me comfort and I manage to apply small talk reasonably confidently.

"You're filming something over here now?"

"I am. Six weeks in London. I'm about for a while."

The way she says "about" confirms her Canadian lineage and offers me a chance to show off that I know the difference between her accent and an American one.

"So, where in Canada are you from?"

"Most people go straight for thinking I'm a Yankee. I'm impressed, Tom." I get another buzz from her saying my name, but I start to doubt everything as her face turns into a frown. "No, wait . . . it was me saying 'aboot,' wasn't it?"

I smile and laugh and she mirrors both. We talk about her acting and my music and being on the road, and for the first time since Jess, I manage to jettison my hang-ups for long enough to present not too intolerable a picture of myself.

One huge problem, however, is the furtive glances from my parents. I know that if they come over I'll turn into teen-age Tom, and that's the worst first impression I could leave anyone with. I decide to quit while I'm ahead and make my excuses.

"Shame on you," she says. "Leaving me here with these stiffs. And you didn't even ask my name." Her smile suggests she's aiming for friendly tease, but the dropped ball of it spirals my gut.

"I am so sorry."

"It's Cara."

"It was really nice to meet you, Cara. When you're in London . . ."

"I'll be there next week. For New Year's, in fact."

"Any plans?" I ask, trying not to fish, trying to judge the mood.

"Still waiting for someone to ask me out."

And then, in another "first since Jess" moment, I make actual plans to meet up with someone of the opposite sex.

26

Not-of-This-Planet Beautiful

Jess

Brynmaer Road, London
January 1, 2017

Be honest with yourself, Jess. If you can't with anyone else, at least be truthful with yourself. You liked him the day you met him, and even when you hated him (wrongly, might we add) you still liked him.

Tom's ridiculously nice gesture blew the roof off a few of my assumptions. That he remembered something as boring as a conversation about planning permission from a drunken night means something. That the week I left for Australia he was making plans to help my mum out of a tight spot, it means something.

The couch in our London flat moves and grunts, causing me to jump twenty feet in the air.

"Don't do that!" I yell at the mass of pillows—and Julia, who I hadn't noticed was there for the last ten minutes. She'd clearly passed out after our late-night "tequila and talking" and hadn't managed to drag herself to bed.

Last night Julia and I had a heart-to-heart like we haven't had in years. I told her how I was having reservations about Chris and then I discovered how Tom had done this amazing thing for my mum and how she seemed to loathe Chris and how I couldn't stop thinking about Tom and then she told me to stop talking at a hundred words a minute and to breathe and so I did and then I started to talk about Tom more and what he said at the airport and she almost burst into tears. It might have been the tequila, but she was saying that she'd ruined my life because she, yes, she may have, actually no, she definitely did, strongly suggest to Tom that if he had feelings for me pre-Australia, they'd wait until I returned. And while I'm not blaming her for his car crash of a performance at the airport, there's no way he wouldn't have thought her best friend's advice might be worth taking.

I talked her off the ledge by telling her it was just bad timing and I plan on rectifying all the mess right away. Starting with some very deserved apologies. Just before I leave, she tells me that she's rooting for me. "Like I said," she clarifies, "he seems like a good egg."

Before my epic plan could take full effect, I needed two things. The first was Mr. Tom Delaney's home address. Luckily for me, Julia is a stickler for details. When she was booking him on the podcast she asked for all his contact details, including his London address. I kissed her when she told me.

The second item on my "Let's Begin Again" checklist was harder to track down. I'm not sure that without Tom's initial gesture I'd have come up with something quite so heartwarming, but he seems to be having that effect on me. I thought back to that first night we had, replayed every line I could, and found the perfect belated Christmas present.

It wasn't cheap. The person I bought it from wanted a small fortune for it. If it wasn't for me earning a bit with some nice TV spots, I'd be turning up with just a box of chocolates. But this, this belongs with Tom.

It's a wildly romantic gesture to just turn up at someone's door on the first day of a new year, but that's exactly how I'm feeling. No texts to be misinterpreted. No awkward phone call. I want to make an effort to make up for the clusterfrig of the podcast and what is, in hindsight, turning out to be a pretty badly interpreted airport conversation. He's a crap communicator. I knew this from the moment I met him. But that's OK, right? The stupidly inarticulate and the problematically defensive. That can work. That can be a thing.

Ringing the doorbell, I get a taste of what his life must be like. The knot in my gut. The way my stomach is trying to escape through my mouth. I have sweaty palms and it's zero freaking degrees. Then I see his face. He looks more than a little surprised to see me. But that's OK. I have my speech ready.

"Jess?" he says, as much a question as an address.

"Tom. Right, first I need to offer you a massive apology. Two, actually. One for the podcast and one for the airport. Then I can get on with telling you why I'm really here. So first the airport. I should have cut you some slack, instead of biting your head off. Maybe I was nervous about the flight? Still on edge over your made-up girlfriend? I don't know.

Anyway, I'm not blaming you, it was my mess-up. As was the podcast. Please know that I had no idea about your grandad. Please. So, I came here today to—"

"Tom!" a soft Canadian voice calls. "Do you want to jump in with me?"

"Just a minute," he calls back.

I feel like I'm in an episode of *Looney Tunes*. I'm Wile E. Coyote and a grand piano has just landed on my head. She comes tiptoeing around the corner in just a towel. She is beautiful. I mean, movie-star beautiful. Not-of-this-planet beautiful.

"Hey," she says.

"Hi," I say.

"This is Cara," he says.

"I'm Jess," I say.

Kill me now, I think.

"I know you!" I madly shriek, my voice no longer one I recognize as human. "*Long Term Parking*!"

She nods, humbly. Even though nothing about her needs to be humble.

"I've seen your stuff. You're good, man." I poke her on her bare arm as I say this. Actual finger on her actual naked skin, jabbing away. She looks to Tom for support that this is weird. I try to lighten the moment with a joke.

"You know he's a drummer, right?"

Tom doesn't correct me, lets the punch land and smiles through it.

"Sorry. Couldn't resist." Keep it together, Jess. "Anyway. Forgiveness? Yeah?"

He nods. "Sure. Do you want to come in for a drink? I mean . . ."

Both me and Cara look at him like he's off his rocker, but this is Tom, the king of saying the wrong thing.

"No. I think it would be weird if I came in and had a drink while you're both showering. Together."

He looks at the floor. "Right."

Realizing she doesn't need to be here for any of this, Cara pretends it was nice to meet me and heads off back into what I can only assume is his bedroom. Tom spots the carefully wrapped present in my hands.

"Is that . . ."

"For you? No. No, definitely not. No, God no. It would be weird if I bought you a present. It's not your birthday, is it? See, I don't even know when your birthday is. I've a one-in-three-hundred-and-sixty-five shot of getting it right, right? But no."

I can actually feel the sweat crawling over me as I blather on like the gold-medal-winning idiot I am. Populating the end of each sentence with an odd bark of a laugh.

He asks, although I really wish he hadn't, "You said there was a real reason why you were here?" and I have to rack my brain for an alibi. The emotion of everything means I come up short.

"Did I? I did. Yes. But no, it was just that. Just sorry. I am really sorry, man. I keep calling everyone 'man' today. I don't know why. Anyway. The apologies have been delivered. A load is off my chest."

He nods and points back inside the house. "I should probably go."

"Of course!" I squeal. Then, before he can shut the door on me, I call out his name one last time. The door opens again.

"Happy New Year, Tom."

"Yeah. You too."

Before I walk home and put Tom's grandfather's diary on my shelf to gather dust and be a constant reminder of my cowardice, there's just enough time for me to hear her ask who I was. The way he said "No one."

Ooof. I'll replay that reply until the day I die.

27

Old Friends

Tom

D'Arblay Street, London
January 2, 2017

Things were fine yesterday. Until she showed up unannounced and apologetic. Now I feel anxious again. My old friends have returned: Regret. Fear. Doubt. They're lined up, present and correct.

I've got about five minutes to get my shit together before meeting Cara for lunch. What are these signs? Are they signs? Are they here to tell me Cara's the wrong person for me? That the right one is out there, making podcasts, doing stand-up, and blathering nonsense unannounced on my doorstep on New Year's Day?

Surely it means something that she came to my front door yesterday? Maybe she wanted to tell me something more, and didn't get the chance. Maybe, one side of me answers, or maybe not. The evidence suggests the latter. After all, if there's one thing we know about Jessica Henson, it's that she speaks her mind. If she had something to say, she would have said it. But then again . . .

Let it go, the other voice tells me. You have to let it go.

But I don't want to, I reply.

Then a softer, familiar voice interjects. *And. That's. OK.* Her words of comfort come back to me for the first time in a long while.

"I want to be with Jess," I whisper.

And. That's. OK.

It's OK to want things you can't have. You had a moment. Two of them, in fact, but it didn't work out. It happens. *And. That's. OK.*

But it's time to move on. A week ago, you met someone cool, funny, very into you. Last night she made no mistake in letting you know that. You've done it, Tom. You've got to that place where you don't have to feel nervous anymore. The "you" that you are is good enough.

It's time to put the idea of me and Jess to rest.

Part Four

REVELATIONS

28

Mostly Perpendicular

Tom

South Virgil Avenue, Los Angeles
February 28, 2018

LA is hot as hell and Edinburgh's about to freeze. We've been out here four months now, even though the band's hiatus was only supposed to last two. I get messages from Scott weekly now, asking when I'll be back in the UK so we can start to talk about album number three.

The truth is, I like it here. Even if I'm not sure the feeling is mutual.

If I had a time machine I'd go back to secondary school and tell every boy in my class that there are several downsides to dating a movie star. I'd mostly be doing this to brag that I'm dating a movie star, but I'd also want to educate their teenage minds on how a poisoned chalice actually works.

The downsides I'm struggling with today are intrinsically linked. Cara has been offered a job in Mexico. For three months. Her costar is the unquestionably handsome and terribly behaved Bradley Worth, a British actor who's broken up more Hollywood marriages than Lana Turner and Jerry Lee Lewis combined.

If she was just going away for three months, I'd be unhappy. If she was just on set with this guy for a day, I'd be worried. Add them together and I've found new levels of unhappiness and worry. She appears to be drifting away from me, and the tide is getting stronger.

Our current rented downtown apartment isn't dissimilar to the London one we had at the start of last year. The kind of sub-minimal you could move out of in less than an hour. The majority of my stuff is in Edinburgh, hers in Toronto. We've been living out of suitcases and shopping bags for as long as we've been together.

As she tears around the kitchen, making herself a smoothie before she heads to the gym, I try to corner her for a chat about "The Future." Starting with her plans for the next few months.

"Cara? Have you got a minute?"

Distracted, she ignores my question and asks one of her own instead. "Have you seen the lid for this?" She holds up the clear plastic blender. "It can't be hard to find—we have, like, four things in this entire flat."

"About that . . ." I say, grateful for the segue.

"About what?"

"The flat. Sorry, the apartment. It's a bit bare, isn't it? I mean, when are we going to make it a home?"

She opens the cupboards, still hunting for her errant lid. "Errr. I don't know, Tom. Maybe when I'm back from the shoot."

The inclusion of my name is shorthand for "I'm close to the edge."

"About that, also?"

There's impatience on her face and in her voice. "About what, also?"

"I wondered if you wanted some company when you go?"

She finally stops searching and looks at me with a mix of fear and confusion. Alarm bells start to ring at how much she doesn't want me to join her on set. It's a fight we've had before.

"I thought you were going back to Scotland, to meet up with the band?"

"I was, but I could *not* do that."

"Why, why would you *not* do that?"

"To be with you."

Her tone is that of a mum reprimanding her child with logic rather than anger.

"We talked about this. That's my work. If I was, I don't know, a graphic designer working in an office, you wouldn't come and sit at the end of my desk like an emotional support animal." She slams a cupboard door and raises her voice. "And where is that goddamn lid?!"

Her shout is loud enough to instill fear in me, and she registers my flinch. She centers herself with her eyes shut, her middle finger and thumb pressed together. Years of yoga training in action.

"I'm sorry. I'm just a little strung out at the moment. Can we talk about this later?"

I nod, and I think I've got away with everything lightly. It was needy. She'd made it clear she's going for work. I know some jealousy was creeping in on my part. That she's not angrier is a minor miracle.

But then she adds, "And we'll talk about some other things, maybe, too?"

She looks down at the floor as she leaves and I recognize that our next conversation is going to be longer, and a fair bit more painful.

It's good to see Scott's face again. Even if it does occasionally pause and judder as the Wi-Fi struggles to keep up. We open with the "Can You Hear Me?" Skype ritual, repeated until both parties are convinced they can both hear and be heard in equal measure. It's the video messaging equivalent of saying grace at the start of a meal.

"I can hear you."

"Yep," Scott replies. "I can hear you too. How's the city of angles?"

"Good. Mostly perpendicular."

"What does that mean?"

"I've no idea. I just thought it sounded clever."

He sniggers into the camera and I do the same. There are people you can spend months apart from and within ten seconds of being in their company again, it's as if the time in between just up and vanished like a fart in the wind.

"How's Edinburgh?" I ask.

"Same as always."

"That bad, huh?"

"I see you've been enjoying the sunshine," Scott notes. "You look good."

It's true. For the first time in my life, there's color in my

cheeks. I'm trimmer too, but that's probably not a perma-
nent thing. Over here there's hiking and self-hatred about
your body to keep you thin. But there's also food piled as
high as a mountain and All-U-Can-Eat on every corner.

"I'm feeling . . ." I pause, looking for the right word.
Good probably isn't it. But *OK* will do. "Not bad. How're
Holly and Hayley?"

"They're grand. Hayley's walking now. Which makes the
months where she was immobile seem like a doddle. Now it's
just a constant worry she'll crack her head on anything
harder than a pillow. Our house is like a sponge cake covered
in bubble wrap."

I try to picture myself as a father. All the worry and tension. I attempt to see me and Cara with a baby and a future,
but I can't make the image come to life.

Scott continues, "We have these little soft corners glued to
everything that sticks out at an angle. It'll be handy for if
you ever come over and pass out again. You'll just bounce
straight back up."

His little joke reminds me that it's been years now since I
had anything close to an anxiety episode. Jess's words *"And.
That's. OK"* still need to be brought out on occasion, if I
start to feel the signs. Every time I use them, they do the job.

"And how's Cara?"

My face does the talking for me.

"What happened?"

I tell him about how I've been a little clingy lately and it
seems to be pushing her away. I tell him about the job she's
been offered and who's on set with her. I tell him about the
run-in we've just had.

"She wasn't angry," I tell him. "Just . . . disappointed."

He winces and the screen freezes, trapping Scott in an expression that, if I'm reading it correctly, might spell certain doom for me and Cara. I look at the tiny square of myself in the corner of my screen and the usual self-loathing takes over. Who am I kidding? Why can't I make this work? And the one that's sounded louder as the months have worn on: Is this really what I want?

Scott defrosts and I'm suddenly reminded of what this call was about in the first place.

"So, when are you coming home?" he asks. "When do we get to see you again?"

"I'll answer the second question first. In one week. But that's because you're coming here."

"I don't ken, Ken?" he says, his curiosity stirred.

And that's when I get to tell my best friend about our US TV debut.

29

A Pavlovian Response

Jess

Elstree Way, Boreham Wood
March 3, 2018

It's become an addiction. Like a junkie craves heroin or
Gollum worships the ring. I need them to hate me. As long
as they still laugh, I don't mind being the pantomime vil-
lain, throwing out acid-tongued one-liners on panel shows.
Every time I open my mouth it's a coin flip to see whether
it'll be the sound of a studio audience's sharp intake of
breath or laughter they just can't contain.

Because even though the tabloids love to hate me (the
Mirror dubbed me the Meanest Woman in Britain and I've
been called every name under itself by the *Sun*), and even if
the replies on my social media feeds could be used by police
to spot potential offenders of any shape and size—the un-
derlying truth is I make people laugh. That's it. If my job
description had objectives and goals and twice-yearly reviews, nobody could say I fail to fulfill my role. I don't make

everybody laugh. I've made some people cry. As is the way, I can recall instances of the latter much more easily.

The panel-show host turns to me and says, "Now it's Jess Henson's turn. Things you'd like to see in a box . . ."

I have fourteen seconds left to name as many as I can to get points for my team. The points don't matter, of course, but once the show is over the panelists on the losing side do have to pay for drinks. None of us are going to miss a few quid, but we are dangerously competitive. Above all, though, we measure our proverbial dicks by the laughs we get.

"Things I'd like to see in a box. My deadbeat dad. My ex-boyfriend. The Prime Minister's dick . . ."

Each gets a laugh and a "ding" sound indicates another point for my team. The host tells me I have five seconds left and without really thinking I mention the name of a little girl who went missing about five years ago and the audience howl with laughter and rage. I double down on it.

"What?! At least her parents would have an answer. I'm trying to do a nice thing!"

The host yells time and makes some joke about whether or not my last bit will make the edit. The truth is, if a man said it, they'd call him a boundary pusher. Me, I'm just an evil witch.

Before we're finished, we have to re-film some bits for continuity. It's a ball-ache because we're having to repeat jokes we made five minutes ago, trying to make them sound fresh and spontaneous. That the audience still laughs in the exact same way for the exact same joke says more about them than us.

Once we're wrapped, I head backstage to get out of my uncomfortable dress. The other (all male) panelists get to head out for drinks in the same stuff they wore on set. Not so for me. As I round the corner to my dressing room, there's someone waiting. She's holding a clipboard, a radio mic clipped to her jeans. I'm guessing she's a runner or possibly an Assistant Floor Manager. The look on her face tells me she's not here for an autograph.

"Enjoy the show?" I ask, giving her the performance she wants.

She has the face of someone who sucks lemons for fun. She snarls as I try to push past her. "My cousin went to school with the girl you just made fun of."

"Really?" I say, pretending to be shocked. "My mum's cousin went to school with Enya."

"Who?"

"Nothing." I shake my head and sigh. "So, what you're saying is, because *you* have an incredibly minor connection to a tragedy, *I* shouldn't make jokes about it? Is that right?"

She huffs. "No. You shouldn't make jokes about it because it's cruel."

Her words and face and attitude combine to piss me off. I could just walk away, not rise to it. But then she wins, and why should she get to win?

"Did you give this little speech to Chris Sharman and Mark Simmonds? What about Richard Eves and Tony Smith? They say stuff far worse than me, week in and week out on this show. Or is your vitriol just reserved for the vagina'd?"

She shakes her head, like she's got my number.

"You making mean jokes about dead people is feminism, is it?"

I only half believe it, but I say it anyway. "Very much so, thank you."

She looks me up and down with scorn before delivering a line that still cuts, no matter how many times I've heard it. "If that's what helps you sleep at night."

Once Little Miss Righteous is gone, I enter the dressing room, get changed in under a minute and grab my things. Her words echo, but instead of getting quieter with each repetition they get louder. *If that's what helps you sleep at night.* Before I go, I remember to open the drawer and take out the pills that actually do.

Now I generate headlines, I've become Dean's favorite client. Before I might not hear from him for months, but now it feels like we speak every day. In fact, as depressing as it sounds, I think I talk more to him than my mum or Julia. He's without doubt the most consistent male presence in my life, and that single thought makes me want to weep uncontrollably.

There have been men in the past twelve months. More than there were in the entire twenty-nine years before it, but none of them have lasted from sunrise to sunset. It doesn't bother me. This is 2018 and I'm getting to enjoy what women in 2018 get to enjoy. There are zero strings on me. Except Dean. I appear to be tethered to Dean.

He comes out to meet me personally, like it's a big deal he's left his desk for seven seconds. Even before he says it, I know he's going to ask how his favorite client is. Ready for this, I thought up a response en route. I deliver my joke about an octogenarian actor I know he represents and say I haven't seen him since he gave me the clap. He laughs. Even though it's not particularly funny. People seem to do this a lot lately.

As I take a seat, he offers me a drink, grinning as he does so. His happiness seems genuine. It scares me.

"How would you like to go on *The Clive Charles Show* in LA this week?"

"I wouldn't," I deadpan.

"Are you kidding me? He's great! People love him!"

"Neither of those statements is true. And if the second one is, it's because people are morons. He's only famous because the year before last was such a horror show it left an opening for nasty, unfunny monsters to crawl into."

I loathe my hypocrisy.

"Can't you see it, though? You and Clive, head-to-head. Like a Battle Royale of shit-stirrers."

I shudder as I think of the clips I've seen of him humiliating his guests. They're all A-listers with millions in the bank so it's supposed to be OK when he tears them to shreds. But all it really does is perpetuate the myth that the best laughs are at someone's—anyone's—expense.

Hi, Black Kettle and Pot, I'm Jess.

"Did you see that episode with Dani Hare?" I ask him.

"Remind me."

"He got her housekeeper on and made her go through all these intimate and embarrassing secrets. Dani was nearly in tears. It was horrific."

Dean shakes his head and then squints at me suspiciously.

"Jessica Henson. You're not afraid, are you?"

"Get bent."

"You are!" he yelps. "Well, this is a first for me. The fearless First Lady of Put-downs, too chickenshit to go on *The Clive Charles Show*."

I know exactly what he's doing, and he can do it all day

for all I care. A couple of farmyard noises aren't going to persuade me to put myself in the stocks for an hour of car-crash TV.

"Ah, come on. I've already said you would. Don't make me a liar. It's you, some new young Hollywood starlet, the rapper Towerz, and some British band"—he checks his notes—"The Friedmann Equation?"

I have a Pavlovian response to the mention of their name. It's not dissimilar to being on the top of a rollercoaster before a drop. Absolute elation coupled with the very real thought I may throw up.

Dean makes another chicken noise.

"Just book it, you dick. And try and get me first-class flights and a nice hotel."

30

Not Bad Company

Tom

Scott's asked to see me alone, before we meet up with the rest of the band. I'm pretty sure I know what's coming and have prepared myself much better than last time. My appalling reaction to his previous announcement is one of the many instances of shame that play on loop in my cerebral cortex at three in the morning.

"Good flight?" I ask.

"You kidding? I just had twelve hours of the best sleep of my life. Hayley's been in our bed all month. If we put her back into hers, she just waddles back into ours thirty seconds later."

I want to ask why they don't just shut her bedroom door but fear that may be the equivalent of questioning why they don't put their child in some sort of clamp.

"I suppose I should get used to it, though. Which leads

me nicely on to why I asked you to meet me before. Holly, Hayley, and I have some news."

While it didn't take Sherlock to figure out what the news might be, I don't have to act surprised as he tells me they're expecting not only their second but also their third child.

"Twins!" I say, with the requisite amount of shock.

"I know," he replies, slightly scared. "I mean, we always wanted three, so it's just speeding things along, really."

I give him a proper hug.

"So," I say, knowing we have to get to the next piece of news eventually.

News that I'm guessing I'm not going to be celebrating nearly as much as this first piece. If my instinct is right, and they're here to tell me what I think they're here to tell me, I haven't a clue how I'm going to react. The idea of being on my own, truly on my own, isn't something I want to think about.

Scott sees my worried expression and says, "Please, try and remember that this is just a discussion. No decision has been made by anyone."

Brandon and Colin wait in the corner of the hotel's bar, half-drunk drinks in front of them, two full pints by the empty chairs for me and Scott. It's midday, and the place is pretty empty. Still, I wish we were back at the old warehouse. Everything momentous that ever happened to the band happened there. I want the symmetry of the band breaking up to be at the place where we formed. But alas.

Scott begins. "Like I said on the way here, nobody has decided anything. But we have been talking over the past couple of weeks and—"

I cut him off. "You're thinking it's time to call it a day?"

Brandon, Colin, and Scott catch each other's eyes, playing tennis with an invisible ball, looking at each other for some explanation of how I guessed. I put them out of their misery.

"It's just a gut feeling. The last rehearsal we had. You know if you're all tired and you're just not hitting it that day, or if it's something else. It felt like something else."

My calm reaction has them all perplexed. I can see it on their faces, Scott's most of all.

"You really want to call it a day?" he asks.

"No," I reply steadily. "I just don't think I have it in me to change anyone's mind. It's what it is."

The three of them look down at the ground. I've disappointed them somehow. Given them a reaction they didn't predict. I get it. I do. This band was everything to me. But you can't keep someone with you who wants to leave.

"Do you want me to persuade you?" I say, with a mild laugh.

It lifts them slightly. Scott says, "Yeah, I think we did."

"But it wouldn't have done any good, would it?" I ask.

Nobody answers. Everyone picks up their pints, takes a drink, and sets them back down at exactly the same time. Without another word being said, we know The Friedmann Equation is no more. After a healthy dose of silent drinking, we start to discuss our legacy like a quartet of absolute idiots would. Scott's the first to speak, as ever injecting a bright, optimistic take into proceedings.

"Two studio albums? That's decent. It's all Stone Roses had. And Neutral Milk Hotel."

"Not bad company," Colin agrees.

"Who else?" asks Brandon.

The three of them bounce names off each other and argue the toss over each other's choices. I stay quiet with a sadness I'm not brave enough to articulate. And a fear I don't know how to explain.

"Some absolute hammer legends only got one," says Scott.

"Thunderclap Newman," says Colin.

Brandon offers up, "Minor Threat. The Monks . . ."

"I knew you'd say The Monks," replies Colin.

I silently add to the list of two or less: Joy Division, Jeff Buckley, Amy Winehouse. The extenuating circumstances in each case isn't something I want to think about right now. Therefore, it's all I can. Even if I bury these fears way down, I'm sure they'll crop up again in the early hours of the morning. To quieten my own mind—and to join the conversation for the first time in about five minutes—I add The La's to our "One Album Wonder" discography.

These three men who I see as the embodiment of masculinity start to belt out "There She Goes" in a surprisingly harmonized way. That we haven't had a singer in the last three years is starting to feel like something of a missed opportunity.

"The La's?" Colin says. "I did not have you down as a soppy bastard, Tom Delaney."

As Brandon gets Colin in a headlock and wrestles him off to the bar for the next round of drinks, it strikes me that despite the years of us all being together, living in each other's pockets for short, sharp intervals of time, none of us really know each other. As men, we hide who we are. We put on a show. You only know you've got a true friend when they ask you what's going on under the surface. When they ask questions like this one from Scott.

"How are you feeling about *The Clive Charles Show*?"

I laugh. "I hadn't thought about it. Not in the last hour at least. Becoming a quasi-uncle for the second time and then realizing I need a new job have taken up most of my brain space."

"And seeing her again?" he asks.

I offer Scott my best squint of puzzlement. There are only really two "hers" in my life and I saw one of them a few days ago. He clarifies who he means and it spins my head.

"Jess. This'll be the first time you've seen her since when?"

"Why would I be seeing Jess again?"

Scott's eyes widen.

"I suppose there are three bits of news, then."

31

Fangirl

Jess

West Alameda Avenue, Burbank
March 6, 2018

He's the reason I signed up to this root canal of an interview, but I'm still surprised to see Tom in the here and now. He looks different. Like there's sunshine in his skin. The glow hasn't transferred to his disposition, though. As he fiddles with his kit, I see the same worry lines around his eyes. I watch him for a moment, enjoying the dopamine hit of what *could* happen when I say hello. Before the inevitable letdown of hearing about his celebrity girlfriend and his new LA life. He looks up from behind his keyboard, sees me, and grins a big goofy grin. Maybe there is some sunshine in his character after all.

"Jessica Henson."

I bow and address him in the same manner. "Tom Delaney."

"How long has it been?"

My mind goes back to that New Year's Day. The sniffly

walk home where I wouldn't make eye contact with anyone in case I lost it completely. The way I fell into Julia's hungover arms. How she told me that however much some things might seem a right fit, sometimes the moment gets away. How, after that, I resolved to make life even more about the work. To become the BIG STAR Julia always believed I would be. I sometimes wonder who's more disappointed with who I am now.

"How long has it been?" I repeat. "Ages and ages, I'd say."

"Look at us now," he says, far more melancholy in his voice than this phrase would suggest.

"I know, right? The Beatles and George Carlin both played this stage." We look over to the presenter's chair. "And now that douchebag is hosting. The world's gone to hell in a handbasket, Tom."

The studio audience start to enter and fill up the benches. We both jump and hide behind the curtain, not wanting to shatter the illusion of the guests being pampered Hollywood-style before the show.

"That was close," Tom says with a smile.

Behind the faux-velvet drop scene hanging from the rigging to the floor, Tom and I are closer than we've been since the night we met. The night he rested his head on my shoulder. The night he almost kissed me.

I take a step back. "How's the wife?"

"She's good," he answers. "Busy. Although, you know, we're not married."

"I know." I shrug. "Just a joke."

"You seeing anyone?" he asks, before immediately falling over his tongue. "I mean, not that it matters. I mean, it's your business. You don't have to answer that."

Bless him. Two albums and a couple of world tours and he's still the same Tom. Or is he? There's something about him that's changed. Before I can figure it out, a *"pssst"* comes from behind us and we turn to see a pretty pissed-off floor manager beckoning us out from our hiding spot.

"You're needed in makeup," he tells me. To Tom, he tuts and says, "You know there is a green room for you to hang in before the show?"

"See you in a bit," Tom says.

I flip him a peace sign for no discernible reason as I'm dragged off to look beautiful for my brutal trip into the Colosseum. I catch a glimpse of the audience.

The lions are hungry.

The studio audience love the man I hate and are indifferent to the man I love. Whenever Clive Charles opens his mouth, they screech with glee. When Tom and his band played their opening number, the audience shuffled in their chairs, restless and bored.

Did I say I love Tom? It's because I do. As I watch him from the guest sofa, sitting at the center of the stage, it strikes me for the first time. It's not just a crush. It may never be reciprocated. But I love him. He's a beautiful man. Talented. Kind. And I love him more with every second I'm in his presence.

Clive Charles on the other hand can go jump in the nearest septic tank wearing a helmet made of lead. So far, I've been largely ignored as he's tried to make Towerz his new best friend.

Clive pulls his head out of Towerz's colon long enough to

ask the audience, "Are we ready for another song by The Friedmann Equation?" The crowd holler and hoot, but only because their hero is speaking. The couple of times I have spoken since recording began, the audience have laughed in the same way they do for him. I don't feel good about this.

I have the best view in the world for the next four and a half minutes. As they play, I try to forget about where I am and who I am and how I got here. I think back to Edinburgh and before I got the wrong end of the stick and exploded. I think back to my angry reaction at the airport. My furious hostility on the podcast. You can see the pattern clear as day. It's a miracle Tom acknowledges my existence, let alone looks genuinely pleased to see me.

As they finish their performance, the punters once again unmoved (bar the small contingent of superfans in Friedmann merchandise in the front row), Clive reads the room.

"The Friedmann Equation, ladies and gentlemen, if that's your sort of thing."

The crowd guffaw in reply.

"You got a microphone over there, guys?" he asks the band.

Scott picks one up and turns it on. The tool looks alien in his hand as it screeches out a little feedback. Once it's under control, Scott offers a meek "Hello. Hi."

Without missing a beat, Clive asks, "Ever thought of writing some actual songs?"

More sniggers.

As self-deprecating as Tom, Scott says, "It wasn't our forte. We do have a little announcement though for fans watching, here and at home." This piques the host's interest.

"Please, proceed."

"After careful consideration . . . we've made the collective decision to call it a day. Officially. A farewell tour and then The Friedmann Equation is no more."

"Hey, that rhymes!" interjects Clive. "Maybe if you'd actually written some lyrics you could keep it going a bit longer."

My face must be a picture because I see Clive studying it. Looking for weakness. I can't keep the emotion out. There are extenuating circumstances, but this band's music means the world to me. Even when Tom's been a ghost, his music has been by my side. I will miss them so much, and I'm showing it. Clive pounces.

"I thought I just saw Jess Henson's bottom lip wobble there!"

I have no option but to own it. "I'm a fan. What can I say? They will be missed."

The band turn to me and take a little bow. It's a touching moment, immediately ruined by the berk to my left.

"All right, fangirl. Don't forget to get your T-shirt signed after the show."

I snap back. "I'll put it next to the autographed pair of your dad's panties I have. I got them on eBay for twenty-five cents."

Clive slaps his desk in merriment. "Zing! I love this chick." He looks down the lens. "Well, that's the end of Part Two. Quite a revelation on *The Clive Charles Show*. Stay tuned because we've got tons more. See you after the break."

32

At Ease

Tom

West Alameda Avenue, Burbank
March 6, 2018

The talk-show host is a loathsome individual. He sneers and looks down on everyone who isn't earning what he is, completely convinced his success is from his own awesomeness and nothing to do with dumb fucking luck, or the fact that he went to a posh boys' school and his family had "connections."

I know for a fact we only got booked on his show because the producer's daughter is a big fan. In hindsight, announcing our decision to split on this particular program might not have been the best move. At least me and Jess got to sort of share a stage, even if it was just for one night only. I sometimes think there's an alternative universe (in which I can keep my foot out of my mouth long enough to make a semi-good impression) in which we shared a stage a lot. The Comic & the Band. Jessica Henson and The Friedmann Equation. Touring the world. It's a nice dream.

I see Clive crack open a beer and pour it into a pint glass (it's sort of a gimmick of his) and I long to be backstage drowning my sorrows. But we've got the closing number to do, and here, well, here I get to see Jess take center stage. She's finishing up a three-minute routine that's filthy and offensive and I hypothesize how much will make the final cut. The audience laugh, but I can't say I'm in love with her material. It's smart and mean. Clever and nasty. Each to their own, goes the saying, but it's nothing like the stuff I know she can do. She finishes up to a roar of applause and takes her seat again, ready for the grilling from the host that can make or break someone this side of the Atlantic.

"Jessica Henson? Jess? Can I call you Jess?"

Through shiny teeth she tells him, "I couldn't care less, Clive."

"You're famous for not really giving a crap?"

Jess does a canny, dead-eyed Barbie doll impression, complete with stiff arms and bimbo eyelashes, before delivering the line "I didn't realize I was famous. Is that what all this is?"

Clive circles again.

"You seemed quite sincere when that band said they were calling it quits?"

Scott mouths to me, *"That Band"*? I reply with a rude gesture that I hope isn't picked up by any cameras. Jess looks in our direction and catches my eye.

"Like I say," she says. "I'm a fan."

Clive continues. You can see by his body language he's up to something. Planning something sinister. And then he reveals it. "You do a lot of jokes about your dad in your routine. He left when you were young, right?"

Jess shifts. She's trying not to show a weakness, but that was an uppercut that's left her stunned. She emits a meek "He did."

"Does he ever try and get in touch?"

She sits up, stronger now.

"Occasionally. But I've made it pretty clear he can get—"

"Careful now," Clive interjects.

"Stuffed. Why do you ask? He's not here tonight, is he?"

As the audience laugh and Jess gains a bit of confidence for the battle ahead, the host looks annoyed. His irritation triggers something in Jess, as she gets an inkling of what's to come. Clive Charles snickers and looks over to the cronies around him who he pays to laugh.

"Did someone tell her?"

Jess looks like she's been hit by a ten-ton truck.

"Are you serious?"

"I think we may have found her weak spot!"

I take my eyes off the backstage monitor to see Jess in the flesh. She's crumbling under the light. The atmosphere in the whole room changes. The audience start whispering to one another. This is what passes for entertainment, is it? Despite her bolshie and confrontational mask, every single person watching can see a scared little girl, blindsided by an abhorrent, bullying man.

Her voice trembles. "So, is he here?"

Clive replies, "We'll find out after these messages."

As the feed goes dead, Jess blinks twice, stands up, and marches toward Clive with violence in her eyes. Security preempt any danger and flank the host, who reaches for his pint. Before he can get to it, Jess unclips her microphone, wraps the wires around her battery, and in one swift move she dunks the recording equipment into Clive's glass. I see the glass smash on impact. I also see Jess quickly hide her bleeding hand.

Before I run off to find her, I ask Scott if he minds being a man down for the final song. He tells me he couldn't give two shits right now, and lets me know if I don't go after her, he will.

I follow droplets of blood backstage until I see her burst out of her dressing room, coat in hand. She banks left, running down the corridor, toward the exit. She pushes a fire door and a small alarm sounds. Neither of us pays it much attention as we step out into the bright LA sunshine.

She's walking too fast for me to keep up and so I have to call out her name. She doesn't stop walking.

"Jess, please?"

"Seriously, Tom. Now is not a good time."

I stop, ready and willing to take her at her word and leave. But then she stops too. I catch up to her and ask if I can at least help her sort out her hand. She nods. I usher her into a local burger joint and through to the bathroom in the back. While she runs her hand under a cold tap, I nip out to the bar and ask for their first-aid kit.

The cut isn't deep. The running water seems to have cleared the blood and stopped it flowing. All that's left for me to do is wrap her hand with a bandage. I try for a joke to calm the fire raging inside me at the mere touch of her skin.

"Thank God for unisex bathrooms, eh?"

I follow it up by asking her if she's OK. She nods and replies that she's fine. Says it was nothing, really. Knowing how many times I wish someone had asked me if I was OK more than once—how honest I might have been if they had—I ask again.

Her face cracks, the facade vanishes. She throws her arms around me. Despite willing this moment into existence many, many times, this is not how I wanted it to be. Even with the Californian heat, Jess is shivering. She takes a step back and wipes her eyes.

"Who even does that?" she asks.

"You want me to go back there and smash his face in?"

"No." She wipes away a few more tears and laughs through them. "I mean, you're a big guy, Tom, but you strike me as soft."

"I'd be offended if it wasn't true."

She carries on through the tears, "I bet you punch with your thumb inside your fist."

I grin, happy to let her tease me. I can be the butt of any joke if it makes someone feel a little better, and right now Jess needs to feel a little better. I take her hands in mine.

"How about I set fire to his house?" I offer.

"You'd probably kill a maid or something by mistake."

"Might help with the music. That level of guilt."

"Yeah, but you wouldn't last a day in Sing Sing."

"So no to punches in the face. No to arson. Anything I *can* do?"

She pauses to genuinely consider my very silly question. "If you ever have kids, if they're boys, raise them not to be arseholes. If everyone did that, we'd have a fighting chance."

A sadness overcomes her, and she finally lets go of my hands.

"Man, I'm hungry," she says, a semblance of a plan to move past this awfulness starting to form in her head.

"This place does a crazy-good dirty burger," I offer as we step back out into the restaurant.

"You've eaten here before?" she asks.

"Are you kidding? How do you think I got the first-aid kit so easily? I'm putting the owner's kids through university."

I wave at the nearest waiter and he shows us to an empty table at the front. I pull out her chair for her and she sits.

It's the first time we've ever shared a meal.

I feel at home in her presence. Comfortable. At ease. The nastiness of earlier seems to have disappeared, a load lifted from her shoulders. For some reason, I ask her about Chris, the guy she was seeing a year and a bit ago. She tells me they broke up around the same time I got together with Cara.

"We were on our way to a New Year's party. A load of his friends were over from Australia." She takes a deep breath. "Just before we knocked on the door he asked me to do him a favor."

"Which was?" I ask.

"'Be less Jess.'"

I nearly choke on my meat, salt, and processed cheese.

"Yeah, well," she continues. "I knew before that it wasn't going to be anything long-term."

"Still," I say.

She shrugs and takes a bite of her burger. I think about Cara for the first time since we left *The Clive Charles Show*. "Long-term" certainly doesn't feel in the cards for us after our last sit-down. Cara said I've been overbearing of late and that she needs some space. I don't tell Jess this for obvious reasons. As if by magic, she asks anyway.

"How are things with you and Little Miss Hollywood?"

I shoot her a look that says *Don't* and she immediately apologizes.

"It was a cheap shot. I'm sorry." She wrinkles her nose, an adorable affectation that I shouldn't be concentrating on now.

"What?" I ask.

"What do you mean, 'what'?"

I take a sip of milkshake and tell her, "You do this thing with your nose when you have something you want to say."

"Oh, I do, do I?"

"You do."

"Well, what I was thinking was, I apologize to you a lot, you know."

"I apologized to you first. The Sarah thing, remember?"

"Ha. Yeah!" She squeals as she says it. "That was so lame!"

My face probably looks like it's chewing a wasp, but inside I'm ecstatic at how happy she is. She continues, dropping from high to low in under three seconds. "But the podcast. That was fully awful on my part. I am so sorry."

"I'm OK," I lie.

I realize it's the first time I've openly lied to Jess. It's a white one, but it comes with a weird feeling. I know she doesn't need to know how awful it made me feel. How the mention of musicians ending their lives sent me into a tailspin for far too long.

She continues, "If I'd known, I never would have made a joke about that. I shouldn't have, regardless. It was a dick move. I really am sorry."

As the waiter returns and asks if we need a top-up, I down

the last quarter of my drink and order another. The conversation has me reaching for backup in the form of something stronger. I order that too, and on this, Jess gives me a look. I try to ignore it, but Jess has never struck me as the kind to ignore anything.

"Bad company, am I?" she asks.

"No," I reply. "Not at all. I just fancied a drink."

Not many people would be confrontational enough to say, with a smile, "But you've already had two." Then again, many people aren't Jess.

"That's right," I say, through slightly gritted teeth. "I have had two already."

"Just saying," she offers, all sweetness and light.

I feel like I'm being teased and tested at the same time. Trying to work her out is an exercise in futility. And the best part about Jess—I never have to wait long before she just straight-out tells me.

"You don't need it. Right now, I mean. You don't need it for courage, or for defense, or to help you relax. It's me. I am me. And you are you. And *you* is good."

Almost immediately I make eye contact with the waiter and cancel my drinks. She looks at me as I do this, studying me. I feel like she sees me. Really sees me. The real me.

"You've changed," she says, submitting it like it's a fact, probably because if it was framed as a question, I'd refute it. I try to turn the focus back onto her by telling her "So have you," but it doesn't land.

"Of course I've changed," she says. "Everyone knows I've changed. But you. You seem . . . good. Better. No, 'good' was right."

It takes someone you haven't seen in a while to make you

sit up and notice the change for yourself. I am good. I am better. I want to tell her that she's played more of a role in that change than she could ever know. That thinking about her, wanting to be someone that's good enough for her, is what's made me better. But I know how inappropriate that is. How borderline deceitful to Cara it would sound. And so, I say nothing.

"And this, man. This announcement. You're really calling it a day?"

"We are."

"What's next?"

I see from her manner that talking about me takes her mind off what's gone before, and so—while "me" was never my favorite topic, I relent. I tell her how even before the band came out here I was sure we were heading for splitsville. I say how I've started talking to a filmmaker I like about scoring her next film. As I continue, I notice she's more perplexed about where I am than I am myself.

"I told you you'd changed, but . . . it's hard to marry the person that you were with this guy in front of me. I don't mean to be a Debbie Downer, but that band meant so much to you and now . . ."

"I don't know," I reply. "I'll miss it for sure, but we've achieved things I never thought we would. If you love something, set it free, right?"

She turns pensive at this. Inward. I wish I knew what was going on in her head but now is not the time to push. We share another comfortable silence until I see her nose start to wrinkle and she stops herself.

"Go on," I say with a smile.

"It's about the podcast?"

I fear she's going to bring up my grandad and that'll be me gone until they clear our plates away. I'm relieved when she says it's about the band name.

"The Friedmann Equation?" I say.

"Yeah. Even though it was me that didn't let you answer, I've always wanted to know." She takes out her mobile and pretends it's a Dictaphone, affecting the voice of a prime-time interviewer. "What's the story there, then, Mr. Delaney?"

"Well," I start. "I won't pretend to understand it fully. But the general gist is this guy Friedmann came up with a theory that the universe is expanding. Before that, most scientists thought of everything as static."

"And you like this theory?"

"I do. Very much."

"I sense there's more. Like you have a theory on top of this theory."

I laugh. "You're a pretty perceptive person, Jess."

She leans back in her seat. "So . . ."

"So," I begin again, having waited for this moment since I first came up with the name. "There's a theory that, yes, the universe is constantly expanding, but eventually it'll reach a point in which it'll stop and contract again. Falling back into the Big Bang to start all over again."

"Like a balloon inflating and deflating over and over again."

"Exactly!" The pitch of my voice isn't very impressive, but I'm on a roll. "Now, if this single point of creation that we know as the Big Bang was no larger than a golf ball, if it were to start again, what's to say anything would change at all? If the universe returns to the singularity that started everything—and this is a pretty massive *if*—what's to say we, the humans that live thirteen point eight billion years after time began, won't just continually live out our stories again and again and again? Lives infinitely on repeat."

I watch as she takes a moment to get her head around it.

"And so, in your theory, we'd end up doing the exact same things each time?"

"Yeah. Why wouldn't we? We'd all start from the same place, so why would anything, including our circumstances, thoughts, and feelings, ever change?"

She grabs a chip from my plate and holds it up as if to make a point with it. "I think I like it. But what does Mr. Friedmann have to say about your theory on his theory?"

"He's long dead. Died from typhoid after eating an unwashed pear on his honeymoon."

"Shiiiiitt."

"Yeah."

"And if your theory holds up . . ."

I remind her how implausible it is. "Again, *big if* . . ."

". . . Friedmann will eat that unwashed pear an infinite number of times."

I take another sip of drink and tell Jess, "I never said it was a happy theory."

This time she turns from sad to happy on a dime, leaning forward as if she has breaking news. "But then again, he'll also have his miraculous discovery and his honeymoon—pre-pear—an infinite number of times too."

She smiles broadly at this crazy hypothetical that holds no weight in the real world, happy that this Soviet scientist—

someone she didn't know existed until a few minutes ago—
might get to experience innumerable post-nuptial vacations
with the woman he loved.

"I like your theory, Mr. Delaney. I don't know why, but it
makes me feel less angry at the world. Like there is a plan."

Knowing she's taken comfort in my words, I remind her
of the ones she gave me.

"And. That's. OK."

Her lips press together and her eyes start to water.

"And. That's. OK," she repeats as I watch today and all
the days before wash over her.

"You know you have every right to be angry," I say.

She turns it back to me again. "I can't see *you* angry."

"What, about the podcast?" I remind her, missing the
mark of playful and instead reminding her of one of the bad
times we shared, slap-bang in the middle of what is turning
out to be one of the better. She rolls with it.

"You were pushed. You had every right to be a little vexy.
I'm the one that erupts for no reason." She holds up the ban-
daged hand she's been hiding underneath the table.

"That," I remind her, "was totally justified."

She contemplates it. "Maybe." The weight of her actions
and their consequences is starting to play out again. "But,"
she continues, "I've been carrying this anger for a while
now."

"Anger doesn't have to be a bad thing," I say.

"It depends where you point it, I suppose," she concedes.
"If it pushes people away who you care about . . ." The sentence hangs.

It was early when we entered the diner. It's late now.
There's plenty more to be said, but with full bellies and

drained emotions from earlier events, talk slows to a crawl. She doesn't appear to mind. I certainly don't.

"Where are you staying tonight?" I ask. I mean it innocently but, as ever, it comes out weird.

"I'm not," she replies, lacking the energy to make a joke out of my question. "I have a show tomorrow night. I fly back to the UK in the early hours. Bit whistle-stop, eh?"

The waiter arrives with the bill and I wish he hadn't. It's a marker that this evening is coming to an end. All things do, but I was happy to trick myself into thinking this wouldn't. I pay. She doesn't argue. I don't have anything to grab before we leave. All my stuff is back at the studio, bar my wallet. As we make our way out onto the street, I ask her what time her flight is.

"It's a red-eye. Two a.m."

I look at my watch and see that we still have a few hours left.

I scratch my neck and ask, "Do you want to catch a movie or somethi—"

She says my name. Once. Short and sharp.

I stare at the ground in front of me again, as she scans the road for a taxi she hasn't ordered yet. We both look up. We both take an infinitesimal step toward each other. It's Edinburgh three years ago. Until it isn't. Unable to stay silent any longer, I finally answer.

"I'm seeing someone."

She nods. And smiles. She seems strangely happy with the answer.

"Yes. Yes, you are."

She reaches out a hand and I shake it.

"Until next time," Jess says, matter-of-fact. She flags a

yellow cab and climbs in. The whole thing happens in a blink. It's a moment I'd rather not relive, even once. But I know it's preferable to the pain caused by any alternative.

It's almost 2 a.m. Jess will be in the air any minute now. By the time I wake up she'll be five thousand, three hundred, and nine miles away. Even though I've been staring at my phone since she left, it hasn't made a sound. I put it on charge and climb into bed. The second I'm under the covers, I hear it beep. For all of five seconds, I manage to convince myself I can wait until the morning before I check the message. I throw the covers back, cross the room, and the screen lights up my face. Her name is there followed by a question.

What's the secret to good comedy, good music and good relationships?

I reply with, *That's a good question*. Then I say I hope she has a safe flight and gets home OK, and that I hope to see her soon at one of our Farewell to Friedmann gigs. There's a lot of hope in the message I send to Jess. There's very little in the one I send to Cara minutes later, asking for her to give me a call whenever she can.

33

Better and Better

Jess

Heathrow, Arrivals
March 7, 2018

Julia's waiting for me at the airport holding a sign that says QUEEN JESSICA—SLAYER OF A***HOLES. It perks me up more than a million morning coffees. She throws her arms around me and takes my bag.

"What do you need?" she asks.

"Food. Sleep. To absolutely bollock my agent to see if he knew about this."

She hands me a muffin and rather than wonder the answer, I ask her outright. "What did I do to deserve a friend like you, Julia?"

She stops and puts my bag down, looking me directly in the eye. "You made me laugh when I was sad." She says it with such sincerity, she might as well have been saying *You saved my life*. "Now, we've a taxi outside and your bed is made up. You want some company to tear Dean a new one?" I do. But I decline it. This is my fight and I'm ready for it.

In the cab, I start to mull over my twenty-four hours in America. My mind keeps coming back to Tom. There was a lot we didn't say when I left. The thing that's troubling me the most, however, is how he's going to cope with the band splitting up. I know how much it all means to him. I hope he's got someone he can talk to about it all. For people like Tom, bottling it up is like setting a timer for when you'll explode. It might not be for a while, but it will happen. Maybe it's the same for all of us. I know that right now, I'm a powder keg in the middle of a forest fire.

Lexington Street, London
March 8, 2018

He doesn't come out of his office to greet me today. When I enter, he offers the best impression of sympathy he can muster. It's not good. There's still a little grin hidden behind it, a grin that says *Your misery is gonna make me money.*

"Jess. How was the flight? You like that first-class?"

I don't say a word. Patience is my virtue. I can wait all day to find out if he had anything to do with it, if he masterminded the whole sorry mess. I am a Zen master, I can bide my time . . . no . . . wait . . . I can't.

"DID YOU KNOW?" I scream at Dean across his desk.

He holds his hands up like I'm brandishing a weapon and threatening to take his wallet.

"No. Of course not!" he says unconvincingly. "They told me they had this big surprise lined up, but I swear to God, I didn't know what it was. Cross my heart." He mimes it for added effect, unaware that I'm convinced there's nothing but a very expensive piece of black coal where his fingers just traced. He waits for what I assume he thinks is long enough.

"It's not such a bad thing, is it?"

I shake my head and mutter, "Unbelievable."

"Look at it this way. You walked out. You stood up to him. People are writing it up as a win for the underdog."

I know full well that he's blowing smoke up my hole. I've read the comments, the think-pieces. "Bitch can't take a joke" seems to be the consensus. Closely followed by "She got what she deserves" in second place.

Dean strolls around his desk and sits on the edge of it closest to me. "Look," he says. "I have your dad's number. If you want it. The producer of *The Clive Charles Show* forwarded it to me after you bailed."

My look to Dean could sink ships and burn them under the waves. He holds out a piece of paper with the number on it and continues, "It doesn't have to be on TV or anything. You get to choose the place and time. I think it'd be good for you."

I snatch the number out of his hand, with the purpose of screwing it up and throwing it back in his face. But something stays my hand. It's Tom. Tom and his stupid idea that we've lived our lives before. I picture myself in a surreal case of déjà vu, looking at this number, calling it, and finding myself face-to-face with Frank Cartwright. The man who walked out on our family before my fifth birthday.

"I'll do it," I tell him. "My way."

I put the piece of paper in my pocket and stand, looking into Dean's soul as I do.

"You promise you didn't know what they were planning?"

"Promise," he says.

Curzon Street, London
March 13, 2018

Last night's set was a disaster. I've tanked on stage before, but this was fresh-out-of-the-gate-student-with-delusions-of-grandeur-first-ever-show tanking. The audience started out on my side, but they turned as each minute ticked by. It wasn't just that my mind wasn't on it—distracted by what today would bring—it was more that I didn't believe in what I was saying. Looking back on myself with anger, it's hard to know if I ever did.

I told Dean I'd do this my way. I know he thinks there's mileage in this. Either a story I can sell to the papers or a re-creation we can stage for the cameras, but neither of those things will ever, *ever* happen. I picked both the venue and the time. There's a quiet café in Mayfair that's even quieter at eleven in the morning, the time I told Frank to meet me there. I arrive fifteen minutes before and find a table in the corner.

As I wait to see if he'll show, it dawns on me I don't know what he looks like. We don't have photos of him around the house, and what little memory I have of him from my childhood has thankfully disappeared over the years. I know he's a white guy in his late fifties and nobody who's turned up so far fits that description.

And then he does. He's shorter than I imagined he'd be. Shorter than me for sure. He's recently shaved, and I can tell from his irritated skin that it's a rare occurrence. He holds his hat in his hand. A little on the nose, I suppose.

"Jess," he says, as meekly as he can manage. It's almost a whimper.

"Frank?"

He nods. I ask him what he wants to drink and he looks absolutely shocked at my civility. He asks for a Coke. I show him to his seat and head to the counter. As I wait for our order to be poured, I watch him from afar. His small frame is hunched over the table. I might be projecting, but he looks bent and broken. I return with our drinks and take a seat.

"How are you?" he asks.

"I'm good, thank you. You?"

Again, he looks baffled that I'd make an inquiry into his well-being.

"Erm. Yeah. I'm not too bad. Not too bad."

The talk couldn't be smaller. He asks if I got back OK from LA last week. Instead of making a lame joke that "No. I actually got caught in the Bermuda Triangle on the way," I simply nod and say, "Yes. The trip was fine." I ask him the same and he says he was never there, that *The Clive Charles Show* was supposed to be a video setup. He reveals that he's not allowed to travel to America and I don't ask the reason. I'm pretty sure I know it. After a gap, his revelations continue.

"I wanted to be a comic."

"Yeah?" I reply. "Who'd you like?"

"Richard Pryor and George Carlin. You like them?"

"Yeah," I agree softly. "Big fan of both."

Another flashback to his youth comes in the form of a Rolling Stones track playing over the pub sound system. "This song," he says, pointing to the sky. "One of my favorites. I saw them in '71."

"I saw them last year," I divulge. "Probably not the same as in their prime, but they were good." We both take a sip from our drinks at the same time. I can see the corners of my mouth in his.

With a smile, he says, "Turns out we have a lot in common."

I let a short burst of air out of my nose.

"I've hated you for a very long time, Frank."

He smiles again. "Then we have that in common too."

I have to give him that. That's a good line.

"I might have liked having you around when I grew up."

He shrugs, gaining a little confidence from our rapport. "Well, it's not too late."

For the first time since he walked in, my blood is up. The rage I feel right now is akin to those mothers who can flip over cars when their child's in danger. I'm seconds away from beating him to death with our drinks tray. But as quickly as the anger comes, it fades.

"Yes, Frank. It is too late."

A memory of me and Mum and my brother flashes to mind. We're watching a football match. Dom's choice. And a man in the crowd gets hit in the crotch by an errant ball. The randomness of it. The way it took Dom by surprise. The number of replays the camera crew decided to show of it . . . It had each of us. Totally. Completely. That memory of the three of us holding on to one another, tears streaming, struggling for a lungful of air against the laughter, it gives me a much-needed inner peace.

"I'm sorry," I say.

"Why are you apologizing?" he asks.

"Because I know how it feels to be let down. I'll never forgive you for walking out on us. Ever. After today, I never want to see you again. I hold no ill-will towards you . . ."

"But . . ."

I place my open palm up as if I'm halting traffic.

"This is my turn to speak. You want to make amends, try sending Mum a check for eighteen years of child support. Actually, double that, thirty-six years. I forgot about Dom. But then he's not on TV, so I'm guessing you did too. You will never be my dad, Frank. OK?"

Saying it makes me feel better and better. Then worse. And then better than ever. I expected myself to be so much angrier. But it's clear that anger won't do me any good here. I like the power I have from being calm. This man has no hold over me. I should no more waste my time and energy on him than I would on the guy who mixed up my coffee order three days ago. This man sitting across from me is a stranger and it was his choice to be one. But before I say my last goodbye, there is a bubble of anger. And two things I still need answers for. There may be a connection between them.

"When did you give my agent your number?"

"A week ago, I think. Yeah, just before the show. We talked a bit about whether it would be good for your career if it was on TV or not. If it means anything, I didn't think it was a great idea."

"But you did it anyway?"

I try not to put too much malice in the question, but his reaction says I have. He looks down at the remnants of his drink.

"Frank?"

He looks up. Nods. And with one look, he foresees my next question.

"You want to know why, don't you?"

As much as I tell myself I don't care what his answer is, I still do.

It's my turn to nod.

He begins, "Having children is easy. Raising them is hard. It was just too hard for me."

For the very first time I have pity for this man in front of me. For his lack of strength. The voice that told him he wasn't good enough. The story he told himself.

In that moment, before we say our last goodbye, I resolve to never take the easy way out ever again. No matter the consequences.

"Goodbye, Frank."

Part Five

ENDINGS

34

Phoebe Cates

Tom

Transcript of WTKX-FM The Late Hour—Online and on the waves—Guests: The Friedmann Equation / Host: Chuck Hearne

CHUCK HEARNE: Devoted followers. Beloved listeners. This one is going to get emotional. I'm joined today by the two founding members of The Friedmann Equation as they embark on their farewell tour. Everybody's favorite post-rock guitar band from Scotland—

SCOTT WALDEN: Second favorite. Third, maybe.

TOM DELANEY: I'm not sure we'd make my top five, actually.

CHUCK HEARNE: Listener, if you didn't know, those far-too-modest voices interrupting my well-written opening monologue belong to Scott Walden and Tom Delaney. Tom, Scott, welcome to the show.

TOM DELANEY: Thank you very much for having us.

CHUCK HEARNE: Let's go back if we can. To where it all started.

SCOTT WALDEN: The days of Phoebe Cates?

CHUCK HEARNE: Phoebe Cates?

SCOTT WALDEN: Ha. Yeah. When we first met and formed the band, Tom and I were adamant we'd be called "Phoebe Cates."

TOM DELANEY: There were two reasons why.

SCOTT WALDEN: Yeah, one, it was the name of the actress in *Gremlins* and so we thought it was a *delightful* nod to our favorite band, Mogwai. Two, we both creased every time we imagined a stadium announcement saying—

TOM DELANEY: "Please welcome to the stage, Phoebe Cates!"

SCOTT WALDEN: What can I say? We were young. Our first singer, he took the point of view that "Phoebe Cates" was the stupidest name he'd ever heard of for a rock band featuring four white guys from Edinburgh and said the only people who would turn up at our gigs were folkies expecting to see "some warbling totty with an acoustic guitar."

CHUCK HEARNE: Was he correct in that assumption?

TOM DELANEY: Clairvoyantly so.

SCOTT WALDEN: As I remember, Tom eloquently told him it was "our sodding band and the name stays." I think our fifth gig was the last for our first singer.

CHUCK HEARNE: How many singers have you had?

TOM DELANEY: Three in total. I'm not sure we can mention the second singer for legal reasons, can we, Scott?

SCOTT WALDEN: My God, I haven't thought about him in years. You tell this one.

TOM DELANEY: So, by about, like, 2011, we'd ditched "Phoebe Cates" and were called "Our Sodding Band." Again, let's remember, we were very young. Early twenties. And what's worse than men in their early twenties, right? So, our second singer, let's call him "Taylor," he was very attracted to being in a band with a semi-expletive in the title. He wore black trench coats and carved very angry, very politically incorrect things into his arm. We'd have been fine if his anarchic streak stopped at the odd bit of swearing and un-PC DIY tattoos, but—

SCOTT WALDEN: It did not.

TOM DELANEY: No. Unfortunately for all involved, it did not. His love of illegal activities reached a high point when he "allegedly" set fire to a pub that stiffed us on our playing fee. Last I heard he's "allegedly" serving five years in Saughton Prison.

CHUCK HEARNE: Sheesh. Some of you out there might be surprised to learn that your third singer, the one who left before you became The Friedmann Equation and decided to go fully instrumental, was none other than Christian Lockheart.

TOM DELANEY: Mad, isn't it? Fair play to him and his million-dollar houses.

CHUCK HEARNE: A smidgen of jealousy?

TOM DELANEY: More than a smidgen for a while. But c'est la vie and all that. Nah, if he's listening, and I'm sure he isn't, all the best to you.

CHUCK HEARNE: Now we're at the birth of Friedmann proper, that seems like a good point to take a break and listen to your chosen track. Scott, what's your choice?

SCOTT WALDEN: Just one choice? You're an evil bastard, Chuck. OK. I'll have The Boss, please. "Dancing in the Dark."

CHUCK HEARNE: Why this one?

SCOTT WALDEN: It reminds me of good times on tour.

As we sit listening to Bruce unable to start a fire without a spark, I'm reminded of another legend who said it best. Miss Joni Mitchell. You don't know what you've got, etc. Since our decision to go our separate ways, the band has been having the kind of fun we used to have way back in the days of "Phoebe Cates" and "Our Sodding Band" (Molotov cocktail–wielding frontmen notwithstanding). We're making more new music, looking forward to rehearsals, and enjoying each other's company more than we have at any point in the last year.

When I last spoke to Jess, three months ago, I put on a brave enough face to convince her I was OK with the decision. Or maybe I was struggling with the first emotion of grief: denial. It's fair to say that whoever said there was an order to it, can stick it up their hole. Because not a day goes by where I don't have some feelings of anger, bargaining, and depression all swirling to try to win the fight in my head.

The high of being together with the band in our final throes has made the lows of being alone much worse. My mind has been awful to me since the two big decisions were made. Even though I could make a strong case for neither of them being entirely within my control, my initial acceptance of them seems extrasupervery premature in hindsight.

I have—as my brain keeps telling me every sleepless night since we called it quits—opted for a life in which I will be alone for the foreseeable future. No band to meet up with. No Cara to come home to. The problem with the foreseeable future is I rarely foresee things optimistically past that. The thought of more solitude makes me sick. And short of half a bottle of Johnnie Walker, there isn't a lot that's getting my mind to shut up.

But it's this sickness that's inspired my biggest breakthrough. I can't keep holding back with how I feel about Jess. Seeing her in LA, being with her again. Just spending a tiny amount of time in the same room as her, made me see what she means to me. She has to know, in a way that is clear and unequivocal. The chances are high that she will reject me, that I'll have to deal with that rejection when I'm at my lowest. But I can't keep it in anymore. No more pussyfooting around on this. But first . . .

CHUCK HEARNE: And we're back. When we left we were discussing your formation and now, regretfully, we're discussing your end.

SCOTT WALDEN: I know, right. It feels weird to say it.

CHUCK HEARNE: Why now, then?

SCOTT WALDEN: I can't speak for everyone in the band, but, well, it's been a pretty intense last three years.

TOM DELANEY: I've been out of the country for a while and . . .

SCOTT WALDEN: But even then, we were still sending music to each other and putting it together. I think, again I can only speak for myself, I think it's fair to say, when we did all meet up again, around autumn last year, it just felt a little different. Like that time before we left was now in the past. I've no doubt we'll all make music again, either together or separately. It's just . . . it just feels like the right time.

CHUCK HEARNE: And now, the end is near.

SCOTT WALDEN: But it's not the end, really, is it? Like with any art form—a book or a painting or a record. It's always there. I take a great amount of comfort in that. And I'll always have my best friend. A lot of bands that carry on when they shouldn't, they lose that.

CHUCK HEARNE: I warned you it might get emotional. Tom, you've been quiet for a bit. Anything you want to add to that?

TOM DELANEY: Nope. I think Scott's said it all.

CHUCK HEARNE: Penultimate question. What's next?

TOM DELANEY: The pub? Er. No. I think, after this, we fly back to the UK for the last run of shows. Then we'll probably take some time off. Try to figure out what fills the gap. The pub? Right? That's what fills the gap?

CHUCK HEARNE: All jokes aside, it's been a real pleasure to follow your band. I wish you all the best with whatever you choose to do next, and we'll be listening. The final track for tonight, chosen by Tom Delaney . . . I do need to ask one last time if you're joking with this—

TOM DELANEY: Absolutely not. It's a banger.

CHUCK HEARNE: OK. So. Here we go. For the first— and probably last—time on an indie music station, you're listening to WTKX-FM, and this is "2 Become 1" by the Spice Girls.

35

Jelly and Ice Cream

Jess

Park Grange Court, Sheffield
June 1, 2018

I'm only back home because Mum told me she has a surprise for me. Since the singular awfulness of three months ago, I've become something of a recluse. Holed up in London. Not really visiting anyone. Even Julia. No agent means no gigs. And quite frankly, the idea of standing up in front of an audience at the moment fills me with dread. That thing I used to love, the crowd, the joy, it's gone now. And I don't know how to get it back.

Being home helps. To be able to walk through this little red door—the same red door I've been walking through since I was old enough to walk; the one I leaned backward on after my first kiss from James Swift; the one I opened after my first gig with Julia—it means so much to me.

I don't know how many years I'll have left of this comfort. This safe haven from all that is messed up. Mum will be sixty next year and it's safe to say her body is closer to ninety.

She's still sober and eating well—she even joined some calorie-counting cult—but she did so much damage to herself in the past, I fear for her future. There's the negativity that's been a little too present of late. She's here now, and that's what matters. Her footsteps echo on the wooden stairs, as the sound of their creak vibrates through to the kitchen.

"Hi, pickle," she says, taking my bag from me and placing it on the kitchen table.

Instead of responding, I grab her and I won't let her go. I start sobbing and keep on sobbing and she doesn't move. She is my rock. Finally, when the taps of my eyes run dry, I look down at her and see her mascara has run too. We each let out a tiny laugh at the state of the other.

"Brew?" she offers.

"Always."

We sit in relative silence as I take in the sounds and smells of the only place I've really called home over the last three decades. As she runs the tap, the pipes behind the walls gurgle and hammer. She puts the kettle to whistle on the hob like it's 1943. I can smell she had sausages for tea and I know she'll tell me the points' worth of each mouthful before I go to bed. There's so much comfort in the familiar it makes me want to cry again. Our cat, Agatha, still going strong, slopes in and rubs herself at my feet. I pick her up and cuddle her close as Mum informs me she's cut sugar out of her tea completely. I want to tell her that all she needs to do now is cut out the milk and the bag and she'll be Kate Moss size in a fortnight, but I don't have the energy. Not even for mild ribbing.

It's the first time we've been face-to-face since I met with Frank. I really don't want to talk about it, but I know we have to. For her sake as well as mine. Like ripping off a plaster, I opt to do it right away.

"Was it the right thing to do, Mum? To meet with him?"

She plops a mug of tea down in front of me and pulls up a chair.

"Only you know that, love. But I can't see how it was the wrong thing."

"I just feel dumb for even giving him that one drink."

"You're not dumb, Jess. You've never been that."

I think about some of the mistakes I've made over the past few years. How I've successfully pushed people away. The missteps with Tom. The "New Me" and how she's made me lonelier than I thought possible.

"I think I've made a lot of mistakes," I confess.

She places her hand on mine and smiles. "Making mistakes doesn't make you dumb. I'm sure even Einstein fucked the cat sometimes."

I hold Agatha out at arm's length and stare into her wide eyes.

"I think you mean 'screwed the pooch,' Mum."

She winks and shoots me with her finger gun, like she's done for the last fifteen years whenever I've corrected her. I'd got used to it so much, I'd stopped thinking about why she does it. Only now do I contemplate the thought that it's her way of saying, *I know a lot more than you think*. She really does.

Her eyes widen and she asks, "Do you want some jelly and ice cream?"

"Mum, I'm not six!"

"But do you?"

I nuzzle Agatha and release her back into the wild of the other room.

"Of course I do."

"With sprinkles?"

I nod overenthusiastically and Mum sets about assembling my toddler's treat. I want to ask when she made the jelly and how long has she had the sprinkles, but I think the answer would make me sad. My guess is she's been storing them. Waiting for this exact moment to come. It takes me less time to eat the pudding than it did for her to prepare it. When I look up from my bowl, I see her waiting, a question on the tip of her tongue.

"Was he what you expected?"

"Not really. I wanted him to be this angry boozehound wearing a string vest with questionable tattoos visible. He just seemed a bit . . . I don't know."

"Weak?" she asks, hitting the nail on the head.

"Yeah. I'm worried I've got that in me."

Her face is pure concern as she shakes her head and corrects me.

"Oh, my love. You are one of the strongest people in the entire world."

I let her know something that's been on my mind a lot over the last few months. The source of much of my pain. "I feel like I'm not allowed to be angry. Like, I'll be judged if I am. And in pushing it down, the anger always finds another way to get out. But with even more ferocity."

She takes my hand again and gives it a reassuring squeeze. "You're allowed to be angry, Jess."

Just as I'm about to thank her for this and everything else, we both freeze as we hear a key in the lock. I jump up and grab a frying pan, ready to whack the intruder, but Mum's grin reminds me that another person owns a key to this house. And suddenly, the surprise makes sense.

She flings the kitchen door open and near sprints into the room to see my brother, Dom, the epitome of a weary traveler, swaying in the doorway. Within seconds he's overbalanced by a one-two of me and Mum hugging him and a ten-stone rucksack on his back. We all end up on the floor in a heap.

"Get off me, you weirdos!" he cries as we pepper him with the missed kisses of four years. Only when he stops struggling do we relent.

"My little boy! Back with us at last!" Mum exclaims. "Look at his tan! He's got skin darker than—"

"DO NOT finish that sentence, Mum."

"What?"

"Whatever un-PC comparison you were about to make."

She flings her hands up in the air. "Fine. I'll get the kettle on."

I help Dom take his bag off and he slumps down into his old favorite chair. He looks more than a little freaked out to be back home. I recognize the worry and he sees it.

"You OK, bro?"

His eyes Manga wide, he replies, "Yeah. It's just I've been traveling so long I'd forgotten what this place looks like." He whispers this next bit so Mum doesn't hear. "I'd forgotten how small it is. How low the ceilings are."

I place a hand on his. "And. That's. OK."

He smiles, takes a breath and repeats the mantra. "And. That's. OK."

We take a moment in silence, before we talk for two hours straight. Mum makes teas at regular intervals, whether we need them or not, as we listen to all the people and places Dom has met and visited over the past forty-six months. Fueled by caffeine and absence, his stories only cease at eight thirty when he asks, "So, how's my big sister superstar?"

"Very fine. Thank you."

"I saw a few of your bits on YouTube. That's some risqué material you've been doing of late. I didn't think anyone had that much hatred for the Muppets."

I shrug and a feeling of shame creeps in. I'm not sure I would have done and said some of the stuff I've said if I'd known he was watching. How did I kid myself into thinking he wouldn't be?

Sensing the sadness in me, he insists, "I wasn't having a go. After all, it's not like you're selling military equipment to developing countries. It's just a few jokes."

His rationale makes sense but does little to quell my self-recrimination.

"I don't want to talk about me. I know all about me. I want to hear about my little brother and his lengthy hiatus from the real world."

"Ah, the *real world*. Now there's a concept!"

Mum reenters with another tea, even though I've still got half a cup from earlier.

"So, what have I missed, Jess? Is he a big hippie now?"

"Sounds like it," I reply.

"And what about the ladies? Has he been waiting until I'm out of the room to tell you about all the shagging he's done?" Dom goes a particular shade of red reserved for when parents talk about sex in any context. "Tell me truthfully,

Dominic, am I a nanna to a hundred little kids in faraway lands?"

"Mum!" Dom cries. "Jess, make her stop."

"Don't ask your sister to help. It's not like I'm getting my first grandchild out of her anytime soon!"

She doesn't mean it to, but her "joke" is a little too on the money. It sends me thinking of everything in my life that's off. It's difficult to say what comes first, the thought of Tom or the text from him that pops up on my phone.

Hey. Really wanted you to know that we've got our last few gigs coming up this week. First Manchester. Followed by London. Then a really small run in Scotland.

    If you can make either let me know and I'll have tickets waiting for you. And a plus one. If you need it.

    Tom x

Dom sees my face light up, smiles, and makes some pop at Mum about "grandkids" that I only half register. I'm too busy scrambling to write back my response. A response that says London would be perfect.

I turn to Dom. "Once you've caught up with your friends and got bored of Sheffield, do you fancy coming to London for the weekend?"

36

Someone Special

Tom

Lower Mosley Street, Manchester
June 4, 2018

Setting up the Farewell to Friedmann tour was easier than it should have been. When the label heard of our on-air decision to quit they were ecstatic, calling it "brilliant marketing." They happily helped us organize the final dates under the illusion that we'd re-form in a few years and cash in again. For them, the quick money to be made this tax year from a well-publicized breakup tour was worth not having an album to put out this year.

We tried telling them that this really was *the end*, but they just kept winking and saying things like "Exactly" and "That's the answer you give if anyone asks." If I didn't know better, if I didn't know this was exactly how their cynical minds worked, I would have said *they* were in denial. Even with less than a handful of dates to go, I'm still certain something is going to sweep in and change the minds of Scott, Brandon, and Colin. That at the eleventh hour they'll have a change of heart and this will be a joke that we reference for years to come. Remember that time we nearly split up?

This denial still fights with the depression and I blame them both for my drinking of late. It just seems that everything is easier to deal with after half a bottle of something expensive with a high ABV. As we come off the stage in Manchester, I can already feel the call to get blackout drunk. With it will go the memories of these so-called unforgettable nights. But with it too goes the feeling of fear and the pain of inadequacy. It's worth the trade-off.

"That was orgasmic!" cries Colin as we enter the backstage area. A small group of record company people and well-wishers are already waiting. They've opened the rider and are drinking at its teat.

Scott rushes in front of me and grabs two beers, then offers me one.

"Here you go, bud."

I decline and wrap my fingers around the neck of a 70cl bottle of Maker's Mark.

His face registers his sadness and I take the beer too.

"Tom's party trick!" yells out Brandon.

I oblige, of course, draining the little can of all of its liquid in under five seconds. Everyone cheers. Except Scott. Scott has the look of a doctor about to deliver bad news or a teacher who's about to tell you you're not achieving your full potential. He's not angry that I'm drinking more. He's just disappointed.

"Cheer up," I tell him. "We're nearly there."

As he watches my glass get fuller and fuller, he says my name short and sharp.

I look him in the eye directly. "Not tonight, mate."

He backs off with his hands in the surrender pose. It's not like I don't know what the most pathetic part of this is. Jess asking for a plus-one to the gig has brought back old feelings of anxiety that I thought I'd put to bed. The pit in my stomach at the thought of her—in her own words—"introducing me to someone special" has me bent double. It could be anyone, I know. A new agent. A celebrity friend. But at three in the morning, when I can't control my thoughts, the person I conjure up is always the new love of her life. The person she's been waiting for all this time.

Since LA she's had zero media presence, social or otherwise. I see her on a few TV repeats, but updates on how she is, who she's with—I guess tomorrow I'll find out.

I open my phone and reread the last message she sent.

I can't wait. x

Knowing that in less than twenty-four hours I'll be saying something, finally making it clear how I feel, has turned me into the frightened boy I used to be. The one I thought I was done with. The solution of alcohol as an anesthetic is as stupid as it is a cliché. Yet my hand still goes for the bottle.

37

Little Miss Poo Fingers

Jess

Between Charing Cross and Embankment
June 5, 2018

Dom's nervous on the Underground. But me, I'm a complete mess. It's a toss-up between the fear of seeing Tom at his gig later and being out in public for the first time in forever. On the latter, I'm sitting waiting for every eye to discover me, to know me, to judge me. For people to, above all things, laugh at me. The one thing I used to want more than anything has become a daily nightmare scenario.

The last three months of hiding have done little to help. My career is in hibernation and I've no idea whether I want to wake it up or not. What little impact my appearance on *The Clive Charles Show* made in the news cycle has moved on, but there's still a subsection of Twitter's darkest warriors who hate me for jokes I've made in the past. Those that are unwilling to forgive and forget. I know of at least one who's started a "Where's the B Jess

Henson?" page chronicling the "movements of an *expletive deleted.*"

"And. That's. OK," I try and tell myself. But right now, it's not working. In an hour I'll see Tom and I just want it to be OK. Instead, my hands are clammy as I clutch the gift I should have given him a year and a half ago. His grandfather's diary, still in its wrapping paper from New Year's Day 2017. The thought of me keeping it secret for so long brings forth new waves of self-hatred.

I look up and see Dom's leg bouncing. His eyes darting around the carriage.

"We're not far from the venue," I tell him. "We can walk the last bit if you like?"

He nods and we jump out.

The Queen's Walk, London
Fifteen minutes later

It's a beautiful June day in London as me and my long-gone brother walk the South Bank. All I want is to enjoy this moment. To forget about the past and focus on the present. I try and lose myself in conversation with Dom, but wind up asking questions about his travels I've already asked before. He's smart enough to know something's up and so he asks me outright.

"What's up?"

"Nothing," I lie. "I'm fine."

"Jess?"

I stop and make my way over to the edge of the Thames.

Behind us the sound of teenagers skating under the Queen Elizabeth Hall bounces off the concrete.

"I'm just feeling like . . . what's that song?" I ask. "King Midas in reverse?"

"Like instead of everything you touch turning to gold . . . you're Little Miss Poo Fingers?" Dom nudges me with his elbow. "Come on, sis. It's not that bad, is it? You've got your friends."

"Friend, singular. Julia is one of the few who still cares for me and she's been away a lot recently working on some co-production. I hardly ever see her."

"You've got me and Mum."

He's trying and, in a way, he's right. I am luckier than most, but I can't deny the fact that I've made some pretty shitty decisions of late. Through my actions and my words, I've alienated myself. Pissed people off. Put on a mask and taken the money. Like a crap highwayman.

"I feel like . . . This will sound *so lame,* but . . . when you have a dream, when you think your life is set out on a path, it's such a crushing disappointment when you get there and the path is lined with . . . I don't know . . . lined with shite. And what's worse is . . . I know it's my fault. I was the one throwing shite on my own path!"

He pulls me in for a hug before releasing me and saying, "You're not even thirty, Jess. That path, shit-littered or not, you can clean that up in no time."

Dom turns, his back to the water, his eyes on the skaters. I look up at him and it's hard to see the little brother I once knew. He's changed a lot over the last few years. Matured. It only makes my backward walk all the more obvious. I need to do something about it. I need to start taking some steps forward. I need to clean that path.

"When did you get so chuffing wise?" I ask.

He grins a big goofy grin, with a faraway look in his eye. Like his trip has given him the answers to life, the universe, and everything.

Finally, he asks, "Are we going in, or what?"

38

The Full Friedmann Experience

Tom

South Bank, London
June 5, 2018

She walks into the room on the arm of a man I've never seen before. As far as I'm aware he is no celebrity friend and he doesn't look much like an agent. My heart is crushed. The ending I had planned for the show is now sitting at the bottom of some great lake. Gallons of water smashing it into irrelevance. I fix my face with a smile so fake I could be arrested for forgery, an impossible imitation of a happy man, and walk over to them.

"Hello!" she says, sashaying across the room, finger pointed at me. "It's Tom, right, Tom Delaney?"

I summon up just enough joy from her mere presence to join in on the joke. "Jessica Henson, as I live and breathe." She turns to the mystery man beside her and explains the joke.

"Tom. I'd like you to meet my brother, Dom. Dom, Tom. Tom, Dom. That sounds like the *Jaws* theme."

"Your brother!" I exclaim in a way that is so painfully uncool and obvious to everyone in the room it makes me want to die. But then I'm so thrilled that her plus-one is a relative I grab him by the shoulder and don't stop shaking his hand. He doesn't seem the least bit freaked out by my behavior, mainly because his eyes are squarely fixed on Jenny Helen, the very attractive lead singer of our support band, A Wolf in Unix. Jess doesn't miss a beat to tease her younger brother.

"All right, Dom. Take a picture of her. It'll last longer and be slightly less creepy."

He flusters easily. "Sorry, sorry. Was that kind of obvious? Do you think she saw?"

"Be cool, brother!" Jess warns him, running her hand a few inches in front of his face like a hypnotist. Dom's uncontrollable horn seems to have hidden my earlier outburst. To make sure it has, I swiftly move the conversation along.

"Are you gonna watch the show from the side of the stage?"

"No way. Got to give Dom the full Friedmann experience—standing among the mopey men, wallowing in their divorced-dad misery."

My cheeks hurt with how much I'm smiling. Her younger brother looks at me like I'm high and I try to introduce him into what's becoming a very two-sided three-way conversation.

"Was she always like this?" I ask him. "Growing up?"

In between glances at Jenny, Dom studies his sister for the right thing to say. She interrupts with a self-effacing put-down. "Growing up suggests growth and . . ." She shrugs as if to suggest there's nothing to see here.

I want to ask if she's OK, she seems different. A little down. But just as I open my mouth to ask, Brandon hollers my name from the other side of the room. I look at the time.

"Oh, shit. I really best be getting ready."

"Yeah," Jess offers drily. "You can't stand here all day talking to your many fans."

"You're coming back, though, after the show, yeah?" I ask.

Dom scans the room and sees the beautiful people within it—present company excepted. He nods so enthusiastically I think his head might fall off. And then he checks with his sister.

"I mean, if that's OK. I'd love to. Jess?"

She shrugs. "Sure."

Dom disappears from my vision as I center my eyes on Jess.

"See you after the show."

"See you after the encores," Dom says.

"No," Jess jumps in. "They don't do encores."

I don't want to correct her but I know I have to. I can't have her leave before the end.

"Actually, tonight, we are."

Her face lights up. "This really is a night of firsts. You're in for a treat, little brother."

I fix my eyes on Jess again. Trying not to beg, but making my words as crystal clear as I can. "So, please. Don't go early."

39

—

Encores

Jess

"I won't go early," I vowed to Tom. But I've no idea if I can stick to that promise. Even as the support act comes to a close, I'm itching to run. Lest I contaminate Tom with my crap.

"We've been A Wolf in Unix!" Jenny yells from the stage. "Thank you!" As they leave the platform, the crowd filters out for refills. I nudge Dom, the pixie figure of Jenny Helen still burning into his retinas, and find us a quiet spot near the dormant speakers.

"You a fan, then?" I say, enjoying the opportunity to tease my brother at length for the first time in a long while.

He scoffs and returns fire. "You're one to talk."

"I don't follow."

"You don't follow?" he says, incredulous. "You and Tom? You were doing your trademark *I like you so I'll insult you* thing."

"I don't do that."

"You do do that. What's going on between you two?"

I look down into my warm can of eight-quid beer. "Nothing."

"Are you kidding me? That guy's crazy about you! When I walked in, he gave me the biggest evil eye I've ever had in my life. Then when you said I was your brother, I thought he was going to rip my arm off with glee."

"Shut up!" I say it as a joke, but I genuinely mean it.

Shut up, Dom. I can't. Not today. Not now. I can't.

He studies my face. "All teasing aside, was there, is there something going on?"

I don't know where to start and so I start at the beginning. At Edinburgh. We move swiftly through to the airport and Australia, the podcast and the TV taping. All the while, I replay the almost-moments. The could-have-beens. I tell him that yes, I love him. Or at least, I'm as in love with him as anyone I've never actually been with. And then I tell Dom the clincher. That nothing can happen. That right now is not for us.

"I don't get it," Dom says.

"I feel like I'm getting further away from the person I should be. You saw him in there. He's assured. Together. But that's not who he's always been. At times he's paper-thin. If I latch on to him now, with all my aimlessness, all my problems, I could end up really hurting him and that's the last thing I want to do."

Dom wears a puzzled frown and I can see that maybe he's not as grown-up as I thought he might be.

"But if you like him . . ."

"Then I want what's best for him. And right now, that's not me."

"Maybe he can help?"

"I don't want him to help. I don't want anyone to fix me, but me."

He shakes his head one last time and drains his drink.

"I don't know, sis, helping doesn't always mean fixing."

I know he means well, but again my brain is telling him to shut up. It's unjustified and, what's worse, he may have a point. But still it cries, Shut up, Dom! Coming here was hard enough. I need resolve for this. Not romanticism.

An hour and a half later and the place is electric. Hair-on-the-back-of-your-arms electric. I'm saying this as a fan, but it genuinely feels like every single person in this room will have an "I was there" story to tell about tonight. The set closer is their first single. A reworking of the song I heard in Edinburgh. The finished product I heard in a café in Sheffield with Julia years ago. The one that momentarily brought Tom and me back together.

They leave the stage to thunderous applause but they're not gone long. The four members return to take another bow, and Tom makes his way to a piano, a microphone by its side. I see Scott grin to him from across the stage.

"Hello," Tom begins. "This is very un-us, making speeches, encores and such, but it's the second-to-last show, so jettisoning any mystique we've built up is fine right now. You all know Scott . . ." The audience holler as Scott raises his hand. "Don't you just. And Colin and Brandon. It's only been a couple of years that we've been doing this in front of people. But we did it for years before, trying to get here. Seems a wee bit mad that we're stopping now. But sometimes it's for the best."

He swallows as he tries to get the next bit out.

"Someone incredibly dear to me once asked me what the secret to good comedy, good music, and good relationships is. I figured it out the other day. It's—"

"Timing!" yells out Brandon, to laughter from the audience.

"Yes, Brandon. Timing. Now's the time for new things to start. The time for people to start saying what they believe. With that in mind, here's a song *with actual words,* that hopefully says something."

To three simple chords and a pensive melody, Tom hunches over the piano and sings. It's not a voice for karaoke, it's not smashing ranges, but my God there's absolute emotion in every word. I truly believe every syllable he utters. His lips press up to the wiry frame of the microphone. And the words flow forth.

All again
I'd do it all again
Wrong steps and revelations
Time after time
I'd do it all again

Hours lost
Seconds found
Treading water, above the ground
I'd do it all again

A leper, a volcano
The first of spring, the last of snow
For you
With you
I'd live it all again.

Tom steps away from the mic, the applause exploding around us all, and takes a bow. "We've been The Friedmann Equation. Thank you and good night."

40

Hold On

Tom

South Bank, London
After the show

The adrenaline running through my body could power a lightning storm. I feel invincible. Like I could take on any empire. Send all the king's horses and I'll turn them into glue. The backstage area is like a party. Alan, our manager, is there handing out little party poppers. He gets flustered when we arrive and yells to everyone to make them go bang. A pathetic stream of paper spurts from fifty or so little pieces of plastic. The smell of mini-pyrotechnics manages to over-power the *other* smell of smoke in the room.

Alan comes bounding up. "That was amazing! Like, one of the best shows I've ever seen!" His enthusiasm is very Alan, but even allowing for that, he's right. It was a once-in-a-lifetime show.

"Thanks, Alan."

"It's all right," he says meekly. "It's just a few party poppers."

"I don't mean that. I mean, for everything. You took a chance on us years ago and you fought for us and—"

He throws his arms around my waist. Which considering the size of him and the size of me must look pretty peculiar from anywhere else in the room. Once he releases me, instead of heading straight for the spirits and drinking until morning, I make a conscious decision that I'm going to hold on to the memory. I'm going to make it count.

And to do it, to really make it count, I need to find Jess.

41

And Yet

Jess

South Bank, London
After the aftershow

Dom and I arrive in the actual backstage hangout and I immediately send him on a mission to get me some Dutch courage. I need to give Tom his present and get out. I need to go home and start "de-shitting my path."

The room is tiny and run-down with chipped paintwork, big iron radiators, and one big ratty sofa. The whole thing is filled with smoke—legal and otherwise—and it's quickly apparent why they don't bother keeping on top of the furnishing. I see him. I see Tom on the other side of the room, talking with a woman who has to be a model. If she's not, her careers adviser gave her terrible advice.

He looks up, sees me, and gives the beautiful creature in front of him the international "Sorry, one minute" mime. It might be my imagination, but it feels like he's actually running over to say hi.

"Tom, wow. That was ... amazing. You've just been

holding that in your arsenal until the last week of shows, yeah?"

He blushes and beams at the same time.

"I was so convinced you wouldn't make it. Or something would come up. Or I don't know. I'm really glad you're here." The model gives me a death stare from across the room and I feel incredibly powerful right now. Tom notices and asks if I want to get out of here. Go somewhere a little quieter.

"There's a backstage to the backstage to the backstage?" I ask.

"Sort of. Follow me."

I check to see where Dom is and find him flirting outrageously with Jenny Helen, both of them stroking each other's arms in turn. Go, little brother, I think as Tom leads me out of a door I hadn't noticed before.

After a few more stairs we're back on the main stage staring at an empty concert hall. We pass a technician wrapping cables as a couple of cleaners sweep up the sea of empty plastic pint cups. After less than a minute, they leave us completely alone in the huge room, our voices echoing when we talk.

"I like coming back down here after shows," he says. "It's a completely different place. Like when you take down the decorations after Christmas."

"I feel like jumping down and dancing to Cat Stevens, like Penny Lane in *Almost Famous*."

"I love that movie."

Of course you do, I think. Not allowing myself to fantasize about him and me curled up on a sofa, watching Cameron Crowe movies and feeding each other popcorn and his hands on the small of my back . . . and *goddammit* this is going to be tough.

He tells me, "They've taken the mics away, otherwise I'd ask you to do a set for me."

"The early, funny stuff, you mean." Which, if I'm honest, is a little mean considering how he's made it clear (clear for Tom, anyway) that he isn't a big fan of my recent material. That makes two of us.

Even though my last sentence had an edge to it, nothing seems to be harshing his buzz. Nothing fading his grin. He looks like a kid at Christmas. Maybe it's a post-gig glow, but whatever he has going on, it's luminous.

"So?" he asks.

"So?" I reply. Then before he can answer I turn my back and stroll around the stage. "I'm sorry to hear about you and Cara." Elaborating no further in case an even bigger lie escapes my lips. "Was it your choice or hers?"

His face lights up a fraction. "You know, you're the first person to ask that. Even Scott just massively assumed I was the dumped. What's with that?"

"I mean . . . society? She is breathtakingly beautiful." I'm very nervous about asking this next question but I find the courage. "So . . . you broke up with her?"

He looks shocked at the information in the question. Like he's only just realized he did.

"I did."

"And how are you feeling about that?"

He looks confused and replies, "I'm good with it. Especially now."

He steps toward me. The hope in his eyes. I have to put a stop to it.

"Tom."

"Jess."

He kisses me and I melt into him. I knew this would be a night of firsts. His touch. His taste. I don't believe wild horses could drag me backward right now.

And yet.

And yet.

"I'm sorry."

I break away from him and watch as the only word he wants to say forms on his lips.

"Why?"

"I don't know!" I cry. "I just . . . it's not right. I'm not right. I don't know who I am or where I am or what I'm doing."

None of my non-answers are helping him. I can see his hurt turning to anger.

"What do you want, Jess?"

"I . . . I want some time. Just a little more to sort myself out."

"So, it's like before Australia all over again? Someone's whispered in your ear, have they?"

"That's not fair! That was different. That was you and Julia deciding for me. This is me, knowing what's best for me." I try again to take his hands in mine, but he won't let me. "And what's best for you, Tom. I'm not it. Not now."

"You get to decide for both of us, then."

He's turned petty. Sarcastic. The look I give him must be withering because he's started to chew his cheeks. He's ready for a battle and I'm ready to give him one.

"Maybe you're not as grounded as I thought you were."

"Grounded!" he yells, his voice echoing off the concert hall walls. "Me? Don't be cruel, Jess!"

"I'm not being cruel!"

"And I'm not grounded! I've lost my band. I'm alone. I'm afraid to be me. But I feel like I can be me around you. You're the one thing—"

"Don't say it."

There's enough harshness in my voice to make him stop. I don't want to be cruel. This is supposed to be kind. But I can't stop myself from saying what I think is true.

"If you think I'm the only good thing in your life, then maybe you're not ready for *us* yet either."

The cruelty is contagious. I can see it in his eyes. There's no pause before he says the next bit, it's not thought about. It's said on instinct.

"And maybe you'll never be ready, Jess. Because then you'd have to accept some happiness in your life." As soon as the last word is said, he turns and leaves.

Dom walks onto the stage, calling Tom's name as he exits it. He gets no reply. In one of his hands he's carrying two pint glasses, pinched together. In his other hand I see he's holding a phone number. But the smile those digits might have brought him is lost when he sees my tears.

"What happened?" he asks.

"Oh, you know," I say, wiping away tears. "Just classic Jess, hurting people with her words again."

He takes a step toward me and I hold out my hand to stop him.

"Please, Dom. I think if you're nice to me again I'm going to completely fucking lose it. No more hugs."

"You want to get home?"

It's the first question I've been sure of all night.

"I do."

But before I can, there's one more thing I need to do. Just

one small thing I have to deal with. Something I should have done on the first of January 2017. I find the band's dressing room, locate Tom's old familiar coat, the one I first saw in Edinburgh, and place inside it the diary that belonged to his grandfather, the diary that belongs to him now. I scribble a dozen words on a piece of paper and tuck it into the first page. I hope, whatever the future brings, Tom finds some comfort in it.

42

What If

Tom

Rutland Street, Edinburgh
June 10, 2018

I am ill-equipped to cope with loss. My grandad's death was my first real encounter with it, although my parents often tell a story of when I was two and I had whooping cough so bad I turned a horrific shade of violet. With nobody in the hospital room to help, my dad was forced to stick his fingers down my throat to remove the gunk that was choking the life from me.

I'm thinking of loss (and of the past and of my grandfather) because the last week has felt like the last three years have been erased. I'm back in Edinburgh in the none-more-temporary accommodation of a three-star hotel. I've lost my band. A girlfriend. My identity. Jess. The confidence I gained from finding my success is gone. I could barely look at the face of the checkout girl as she bagged my bottles. My little oblivion-giving bottles.

The film I was supposed to be working on has been

"pushed back." I tell myself I can't write music to footage if I don't have any footage to set it to. I tell myself there's nothing to do. There's too much void in my life to fill it with reason and so I am unreasonable to myself. Years ago, when we first started living the "band life," Scott and I made some promises together.

First was, we would not drink alone. Second, we'd take at least one day off drink in a five-day period. All rules I've broken when I choose to. And alone—alone there's no one here to see these promises kept. I make more anyway. I begin by telling myself I won't drink until the evening. Then the goalposts are moved to the afternoon. Every rule I make is made to be broken. And now it's noon, and in front of me sits a small can of beer. That's all it is. A small can.

I once saw a video of a centimeter-high domino knocking over another over two meters tall. In between the smallest and the largest were ever-increasing sizes. It was shared around social media with comments about *the power of the individual* and *what we're all capable of.* To me, it was a frightening thing. A question of "What if the first domino is wrong?"

The what-ifs of my life have always been negatives. "What if I fail?" "What if she laughs at me?" "What if I can't hold on to my thoughts?" But this next one, this next might save my life. I see two versions of my future play out, like I'm watching them on a cinema screen.

Version One—I pull back the opening on the can and drink greedily. I begin to read the diary Jess left and ignore her note. My grandfather's words from the great beyond are the only ones I listen to. I don't know what I expected, what I hoped for, but the words in it are gray, scared, lonely.

The first drink is done in no time at all, but there are another five in the fridge. The small numbers on their sides encourage me to keep going; they tell me there's no danger inside them, that they're just a treat. But even these small numbers make me feel lonelier, while at the same time tricking me into thinking a greater amount of them will reverse the loneliness. Their purpose is to drown me.

I switch off the stereo that keeps me company. The hum of the empty fridge, the only sound in the flat. The small drinks are gone but they were just the support act. I've seen this gig before, and the headliner is waiting. I fill another glass with something stronger, bigger numbers, and empty it almost as quickly. I lie down hoping this will be the start of the rest I need. I wait.

My head feels heavy. Like it's filled with rocks. With the sleep not coming, I stagger into the bathroom and search for something else. Anything else to make the rest come and the pain stop. Anything to help me sleep.

A darker image fills my head. Where the small can of beer once stood, now there's a bottle of pills. The only thing left standing as the fallen bottles and cans litter the table and floor. I scan the label. My vision is blurry but I can make out it says to take two. I watch myself ignore this advice. I try to find Jess's words. They're lost to me now.

My head feels worse. Like the rocks inside my skull are sliding down a ravine and back up the other side. A Sisyphean perpetual motion machine. I'm woozy and panic fills my blood. Real panic. My eyelids suddenly feel like anvils are attached to them, pulling them to the ground.

I keep watching as we shift location. I'm walking up the path toward my parents' house, each step like the summit of

Everest. The pills swirl with the alcohol. The main ingredients of both swim in my bloodstream. Soaked through in the twelve steps from the taxi to my parents' front door, I press on the doorbell and wait.

My father answers, takes one look at me, and pulls me in out of the rain. It doesn't take long for his face to show the panic mine can't. I want to tell him I'll be OK. I just need a rest. But the words won't come out. He screams for his wife to call someone as I sink to the floor. He asks me repeatedly to tell him what I've taken. I see the outline of my mother on the phone, pacing up and down at the bottom of the stairs. She says words but I only catch the numbers and my dad's reaction to them.

And for the second time in thirty years, my father has his fingers down my throat, trying desperately to figure out a way to animate my lifeless body. He cries like I've never seen him cry before.

But this is only one version of events. Because I'm still staring at that first small can. Unopened. A ring of water creeping from its base.

Version Two—the one I will ultimately choose—begins with the can returning to the fridge and instead of my grandfather's diary in my hand, it's the note Jess left me. I read it over and over again. I pin it to my wall. Then I shower, get dressed, and go for a walk. I fill my days with trips to record stores, visits to the cinema. I work on music that is mine and when work is finally asked of me, I do it to the best of my ability. I shop and I buy food that makes me feel good. I call my parents and offer them apologies. I finally see that his father's death had more of an impact on my dad than on me. That I'm here if he wants to talk about how *he* feels. We arrange to meet more. I visit Scott and his family and I become a real "uncle." I don't date yet; I'm not ready. But I know that one day I will.

I will never tell anyone, because I don't think they will believe me, but I do. I firmly believe I owe my new life to Jessica Henson and the note inside my grandfather's diary that reads . . .

Choose not to be afraid. You are you. And. That's. OK.

Part Six

BEGINNINGS (II)

43

I'm Trying

Jess

I'm nervous. I never used to be nervous. When I was younger, I didn't care what anyone thought of me. Genuinely. Then when I was pretending to be the Queen of WhoGivesAToss-ville, there was no need for nerves. It wasn't really me up there. At least that's what I told myself. Now, though, now I feel like me. And it's making me very scared of what people will think.

I arrive at the Manchester studio just in time for a quick meet-and-greet with the two presenters, Subha and Jeremy, in the green room. She's incredibly pretty. Not beautiful. But pretty. She has dark skin and funny ears and a little crop of jet-black hair. Her presenting partner looks like an English Patrick Bateman. A British Psycho capable of live-reporting on his own murders without the authorities touching him. In years to come we'll all say, "Do you remember that Breakfast

TV host? How did we not see it?!" There's literally nothing behind his eyes.

"New Old Jess" would have five minutes of material on this. She'd go out swinging with witty putdowns, jokes about his appearance, wanting a fight—and she'd get one. It would help sell tickets to the new show and nobody would challenge her on it. Nobody except herself. In the quiet of the night, "New Old Jess" would hate herself. "Just Jess" sleeps better.

They're finishing up a segment on farming—specifically, how the tradition of handing down the farm to the next generation is becoming a thing of the past—and I'll be on straight after that. I try to think of a joke about my mum bequeathing me her comic timing on my sixteenth birthday but abandon it just as the camera swings into position for a close-up.

Subha smiles into the camera and reads her autocue flawlessly. "Our next guest is a comedian you may think you know, but her new Edinburgh shows suggest otherwise. Jess Henson Version One was a controversial, opinionated, often crude comic. But with her new one-woman play, *Happy/Sad,* and her interview show, *Jess Henson Asks,* she's redefining our expectations. As she says, 'Out goes the snark and in comes openness, honesty, and sincerity.' Here's a clip of Jess in action."

They show the safest, most family-friendly part of my act. I cringe at it out of context, but then remember a couple of the reviews my new agent sent me last night. I'm allowed to have faith in myself, and a timid twenty-second clip isn't going to hinder that.

"Welcome to the program," Jeremy says, "Jess, Jessica? What do you prefer?"

"Either's fine," I reply, holding back a thought that pops into my mind about him murdering me in my sleep.

"So, Jessica. Our audience will probably know you best from your TV appearances, shows like *News Unfit to Print* and *The Final Word*. It's fair to say you never really pulled any punches on those."

I shift a little in my seat, aware of what the viewing public might be thinking right now. Oh, it's her. The bitch who says what she likes. Relax, I tell myself. You can't change the past. You can't predict the future. You can only do your best in the present.

"I didn't pull my punches, no."

"And—"

"Quite a lot of people got bloody noses."

Subha leans forward. "You say that with quite a bit of sadness. Do you regret the jokes you've made? The things you've said?"

I take a sip of water, my mouth dry under the studio lights. I've tried not to overprepare what I want to say, for fear I might stumble or leave out a vital piece of information. But I know the bullet points.

"As a comic, there's a value in shock," I reply. "It takes people by surprise. Shifts their comfort zone. It's a tried-and-tested way to get people laughing. But was it the right thing to do? It's hard to make a case for it anymore."

We all know I haven't fully answered her question, so she tries again.

"But do you regret what you've said?"

"Regret's a little like quicksand. If you're not careful you can get swallowed by it. But am I sorry for the things I've said? Yes. One hundred percent."

Jeremy scans his notes and says, "The new show is quite different. Should fans of your previous material skip this, then?"

"If anything, I think they're exactly who it's for. It's just a different kind of funny. I hope."

"But it is funny," Jeremy says, picking up a newspaper and reading. "The *Scotsman* is just one of the papers to give you five stars. Yet almost every review comes with an opening clarifier that 'this isn't the Jess Henson you know and love to hate.'" Jeremy puts down the paper and looks at me skeptically. "How are we to know that this Jess Henson is the real Jess Henson?"

I've thought long and hard about this narrative being formed, that I am a different person. I'd like it to be true, but it isn't. That was still me. I have to own that, if I'm to move on. "It's a fair question," I say. "One I'm not sure I have a definitive answer to yet. It's sort of what the show is about. Amongst other things."

"But you have changed?" Subha asks. I'm glad it's her that asked and not him. From her mouth it feels less combative. My mind searches for an answer. Stopping at highlights and lowlights. Edinburgh. Interviewing Tom. The *Clive Charles* debacle.

"Everybody changes over time," I try.

Their faces show my answer is a little too vague and mystical for ten past nine on a Thursday morning. I accept their expressions and expand my answer.

"Not too long ago, I was talking with my brother . . ." I wave to the camera. "Hi, brother. He told me, 'You'll be amazed how much easier it is to be nice.' He's right. Being mean is hard work. Finding someone's weakness to attack. Wondering how far is too far. There's only one question you ever have to ask yourself when you're trying to be a good person."

"Which is?" Subha asks.

"Will this make someone happy?"

Jeremy sits forward, still playing his part as the more aggressive of the two. "And what about you? Are you happy?"

The pause I make them sit through is uncomfortable for all involved.

"Someone I care about once said that I wouldn't accept happiness into my life."

Subha frowns and says, "That sounds like quite a mean thing to tell someone."

There's another pause, as I scan the room for other faces. The camera people and floor staff are all looking on, all wearing the same faces. You could call it pity. You could call it concern. It depends on your point of view.

"It was said during a fight so . . . I think it was supposed to be a little mean. But, in hindsight, I believe the reason it was said, was out of love. There's certainly an argument to be made that they were hoping it would help me."

"Did it?" Subha asks.

"I think it did." I smile. "So, to answer your question, am I happy?"

I leave a big enough gap before I answer them and myself.

"I'm trying."

The two presenters nod, thank me for my time, and then quick as a flash they're ready for their next segment. I'm whisked off set and into the dressing room. When I'm alone, I look at my reflection in the mirror and say the last two words back to myself again.

44

A Miniature Drum Kit

Tom

Kingsknowe Road North, Edinburgh
August 17, 2018

"A tattoo?" I ask, more than a little shocked at the suggestion.

She clarifies in no uncertain terms, "I am not advising you to get a tattoo. I'm just telling you that I have a client who has one."

I don't hate the idea. I'm just surprised it's coming from my counselor. We got onto the subject after I told her about the brakes I use to get me through periods of anxiety. The calming techniques. The words. Alice told me she counsels an anxiety sufferer who inked herself with a famous quote that brought her stillness. I know exactly the words I would choose.

Alice sits cross-legged in wicker furniture in the conservatory of her Edinburgh house. Her two dogs wander in and out intermittently. It's not quite the Hollywood image of a psychiatrist's couch on the forty-fourth floor of a New

York high-rise, but it's the words that count. And Alice has the best words. We're on my seventh session and I'm already starting to see things differently. Pressure that I put on myself is slowly being eased off. There's still darkness sometimes. There's still fear. But now I have the tools to step back from it.

"This will sound stupid . . ." I begin.

"Nothing is stupid in here. This hour is a stupidity amnesty."

"The two versions I told you about, the version where I kept on drinking until something bad happened. I kind of wish I'd actually gone through that."

She wrinkles her eyes as if to say, *About that stupidity amnesty*. Instead she asks me why I think that.

"Part of me thinks I need to actually experience rock bottom."

"I'd caution against this sort of thinking, Tom." The use of my name makes me sit up and pay attention. "In films and stories, we often see people 'hitting rock bottom,' as you say, just before everything turns out OK. But life isn't like that. The struggles you have will—most likely—always be with you. But it was you that saw that road and made the decision not to drive down it. The idea that you need to hospitalize yourself to prove it is a very dangerous one. You'd be writing yourself a narrative that says you deserve unhappiness."

She leans forward and delivers her next words with composure. "You don't, Tom."

We take a moment of silence, as we often do when something important has been said. I think about her words and find the truth in them. As my mind often does in the silence, it wanders and finds Jess. Or, at least, words by Jess.

"Yesterday morning I heard someone on the TV say that 'regret is like quicksand.'"

She raises her eyebrows, which is something of a trademark for Alice. This elevation of facial muscles always means the same thing. *You think you can get away with that? Be honest. Be truthful.* I relent. "Yes, that someone was Jess Henson."

"I saw it. It was a good interview," Alice replies. "Have you thought any more about reaching out to her? Contacting her?"

I shake my head. "I've thought about it, of course. But . . ."

She fills the void. "But what?"

"This might be a cop-out but I sort of feel like the ball is in her court. Y'know?"

As she nods, it's hard not to feel like Alice has an ulterior motive. It's not her place to suggest I do a thing—like the tattoo, for example—but whenever the subject of Jess crops up, I feel like she's pushing me in a certain direction. When I've challenged her on this in the past, she just replies by asking me why I think that. It's either a sneaky therapist trick or it really is my mind's way of saying it thinks I'm ready to see her.

Over the last few months, Alice and I have talked at great length about how dangerous investing too heavily into something too soon can be. The key, she says, is being someone capable of maintaining a relationship. Anyone can be with another person to stop them feeling lonely, but, she argues, it's more important to make sure the relationship is the right one. Especially when loneliness is a such a personal trigger for anxiety and depression.

I confess to her, "I do have this worry that I'm still not right for a relationship. Of any kind."

"These sessions aren't meant to scare you into analyzing your potential as a partner," Alice reminds me. "You should feel free to voice your doubts here. By voicing them, you'll see how you're stronger than them. You've made huge improvements over the last month. But, yes, you're right. Your history does suggest you should use caution."

The caution she's warning of isn't to stop me doing or saying anything. That's never been my problem. She means caution against thinking that someone else can save me. That having someone will fix me. I'm still a fool on a lot of things, but not this. Only I can save me. Others can help.

Once the clock on the wall ticks over the allotted fifty-five minutes, Alice becomes an entirely different person. It's like she's in character when she's a therapist, and as soon as she's done for the day the wall drops down.

"Where are you off to now?" she asks.

"Aside from the tattoo parlor?"

She laughs and smiles, something she never does "on the clock."

"It works for some. And then?"

"I'm off to do a little shopping. My friend Scott had twins last week."

"Whoa."

"I know, right. Sometimes I think of myself with kids and . . ." I look at her look at her clock. "Sorry. Something for another day, maybe."

Bruntsfield Place, Edinburgh

Despite the toy shop being divided into sections, it's still a minefield of choice. Most of the things are branded monstrosities, all the colors of the rainbow thrown onto plastic noise-emitters. Over the speaker system the most in-your-face type of pop music plays.

I scan the shelves, taking in the names of them all, one by one. There's a few I recognize from my own childhood—*Thomas the Tank Engine* and *Pingu* still seem to be going strong. The rest are a strange combination of words and syllables that don't really belong together.

Paw Patrol
Octonauts
Peppa Pig
Hey Duggee!
The Twirlywoos

A young woman working in the shop reads the look of utter bewilderment on my face and graciously helps me out. She's decked out in the company's outfit of black-and-white T-shirt and dungarees, badges on the straps with more cartoon characters and cheery slogans.

"You look a little lost," she says.

"A bit, yeah."

"What are you looking for?"

"Two presents if possible. One for a two-year-old girl. And something for newborn twins."

I pick up a couple of boxes. One holds what looks like an

alphabet on some sort of wooden abacus, the aforemen-
tioned pig and her friends on each letter. In the other hand I
have a toy drum kit.

"If you like the person," she advises me, "I'd go for the
abacus."

I take her point and put the drum kit back. She leads me
to the newborn section and there I find a couple of cuddly
toys. One shaped like a leek, another shaped like a crab. I
thank her for her help, make my way to the checkout, and
pay.

Coulter Crescent, Edinburgh
One bus ride later

I enter the house expecting to hear the wailing of two infants, one toddler, and the anguished parents of all three.
Instead, the house is in such relative silence I wonder if I have
the right address.

"Come through." Scott beckons me.

I do as I'm told and see the picture postcard of a family
unit. Mother and father looking in over the edges of the
twins' cot, beaming with pride. Hayley makes a mad dash in
front of Scott and toward the sleeping twosome. He picks
her up and plops her on his knee. "And you, my wee pump-
kin?" he asks his daughter. "What do you think of your two
brothers?"

Her reply of "Can I watch something?" isn't quite as endearing as either he or Holly had hoped.

"Watch something?" he asks her. "It's a sunny day. Uncle
Tom is here . . ."

"I feel very uncomfortable with that phrase," I tell him.

"Please?" she begs, bottom lip wobbling.

The two parents exchange a look, both of them hoping the other will back down so they can have some peace while the babies sleep, but neither wanting to be seen as the type of parent who lets their kids sit inside watching TV on a glorious summer's day.

"OK," Holly acquiesces. "Just one episode."

I suddenly remember my gifts and take them out of my bag. Both Scott and Holly seem amazed at my offerings. Hayley tears into the paper and bounces with delight.

"Peppa! Peppa! Peppa!"

"I'd say that's a hit," Holly adds.

"It was either that or a miniature drum kit." I hand the bag over. "There's a couple of things for the twins, too."

Holly gives me a hug and looks genuinely touched. Scott still looks baffled as he ushers me outside through the patio doors, not before grabbing a beer for himself and a sugar-free Irn-Bru for me. As we flop ourselves into two garden chairs, he looks at my drink with overly dramatic disbelief.

"Never thought I'd see the day," he says, fake tutting. "But I'm glad it's here."

I raise my can of fizz in a strange toast and tell my friend, "I've tried gunning one of these in under ten seconds but it just gives me really bad gas."

He laughs and tells me I look good, for probably the first time in our over-a-decade friendship. Off my look he doubles down on it. "I mean it," he says, "you look healthy. Those ever-present frown lines are fading. It's like you're living in color a little more these days."

As odd as it is to take a compliment about my appearance

from him, he's not wrong. It's not just therapy and being off the sauce. I get out of the house more these days. "Exercise" might be an extreme word for it, but I'm walking about more. Getting sunshine and air. I see my parents more these days too. Bridging a divide we all held for too long, for no good reason.

"Thanks again for the presents," Scott adds.

I want to ask him why he's so shocked by a few little gifts. But I don't have to. It just isn't something I would have done, even a few months ago and certainly not at the time Baby Number One came along. Not for any reason other than it wouldn't have crossed my mind. It's nice to have the time to think of others.

He sips his beer and I get a little pang of jealousy at the missed taste of amber. On a hot day like today, I miss it more. We chat for a little while longer. He explains to me the logistics of feeding two babies at once and I tell him how my first-ever film score is premiering at the Sundance Film Festival. I also mention a new young band Alan is managing. I tell Scott I'm thinking of writing a few songs for them.

"They're so young!" I pause before adding, "We were once, weren't we?"

"Aye," he says. "I suppose we were. Who knew you had all those words in you? Nice words too. Soppy words but . . ." He grins and nudges my arm. "You don't fancy singing them yourself, though?"

His question triggers a memory I'd still rather not think about.

"Not really. The last time didn't work out too well."

He takes a bigger drink and addresses the elephant in the garden. "I saw her on the telly, yesterday. Your lass."

"She's not my—"

Scott cuts me off. "I know, I know. So, you've not been in touch?"

"You're the second person to ask that today."

"And?"

I shake my head and look at my friend, needing to change the subject. "Scott."

He play-acts being frightened. "Oh dear, he's using my name, it must be serious."

"I want to say thanks. For being my friend. I just want to say thanks for that."

Having averted my eyes from his face as I spoke, I only now look back at him and see the tears in his eyes.

"Sleep deprivation, man," he sniffles. "It'll mess you up." He takes a bigger sip of his beer and composes himself. "Life's a big bowl of gash, mate. Or at least it can be. People can be dicks far too much of the time. Yourself and myself included. But people are also the ones that'll help you through it. You've helped me through more than you realize too. That's what mates are for."

We share a laugh at the state of ourselves. Both of us pushing back tears into our ducts as if that'll erase them.

"And as your friend, I'd like to point out, that was an absolute world-class bit of steering the topic of conversation away from Jess, there."

I laugh loudly. "I thought I'd got away with it." Nothing much gets past my friend and so I relent. "I don't know. I want to see her. Of course I do. But she couldn't have been more right."

"When?"

"At the gig, in London. She said I wasn't ready for a relationship and I wasn't. If it was up to me, we'd be together and probably unhappy as we'd still be working through our own shite."

"And now?"

My shrug isn't enough of an answer, but it prompts a perfect one from Scott.

"Rewind about five years ago and can you really imagine me and Holly here? After all that on-again-off-again drama? We were like cats and dogs who supported different football teams and liked opposing politicians. But today, we're here. We talked our problems out. Found common ground."

Together we take a glance back at the house, the life he's led to get him where he is. Mortgage. Kids. Wife. I ask him if he thinks he'll miss the road. If he'll miss the life.

"The stuff we got to do—travel the world, meet our heroes, hang out with my friends every day, and get paid enough to buy this freaking place—I wouldn't change a bit of it. I'd live it a million times over. I mean, I've no idea what the future might hold, but now? All I want is to be right here."

He looks at me with a smile.

"D'yae ken, Ken?"

"I ken, Ken."

45

Happiness

Jess

The *me* in charge of organizing two sellout Edinburgh shows tells me I don't have time for the complication of last-minute changes. But as the *me* who wants this, *I* get to decide. At the end of the day, I'm my own boss, what I say goes, and if I want a specific guest for the second of my final shows, I get to ask for it. Considering he's invited me to two of his in the past, it's the least I could do.

If Tom ends up saying no, as he has every right to, Julia has reluctantly agreed to be a stand-in. The audience never know who the guest will be, so there's no disappointment. For them, anyway.

The first invite I send to Tom is one I hope he'll take me up on. After all, he only has to sit and watch the show. Two tickets are attached. There's a plus-one if he wants it. The second invitation, however—the one that asks him to share a stage with me—I'm less convinced he might say yes to that.

After all, the last time we tried this, there was shrieking and shouting and bitterness and resentment. But that was, as I remind myself a lot these days, a long time ago.

I end the note saying, if he can't make it to either, I completely understand. I add in an apology about the way I've acted in the past. Not for three months ago. That, I say, was the right thing to do. Minus the shouting, of course. But I needed that time. For what it's worth, I write, I feel that time has been used wisely.

Once the email is sent, all I can do is wait.

Hill Street, Edinburgh
August 29, 2018

I walk over to the curb and sit my arse down. Tears streaming. Makeup running down my face. Courtesy of Liza. She's done a good job. Everything is as I wanted. The bus stop behind me, the double yellow lines under my feet. You can't see them from the front couple of rows but they help me picture it all. I wanted the stage to have puddles and faux-rain, but it became a health-and-safety issue for the venue. They gave me such a good rate I wasn't going to argue.

I can't see the audience—the spotlight is too bright. I don't know if Tom's here or not. It's probably for the best that I don't know. Part of the act speaks directly to him, whether he's here or not.

This image I'm giving them. A drunk girl sitting on a curb with tears in her eyes and her shoes in her hands. I leave it long enough where I'm just sobbing so that they start to ask themselves uncomfortable questions. The men I've asked for reactions almost immediately envision something horrific befalling this sad figure. The women, as the seconds pass, simply start to see themselves. I make them wait a little longer before my first words. I suppress a tiny burp.

"I just reeeeaaaaallly need a kebab."

You can feel the room decompress in time with the laughter. The tension of my tears, even though they know it's a performance, had everyone on edge. I've been able to convince them that they needn't worry, that they're safe here. Once they start to feel that, I can take it all away again.

Over the past three months I've written and rewritten and edited and fixed and binned every inch of this show, so that every moment is timed just so. The night I told Tom we weren't ready yet, I phoned Julia as soon as I got home. For the first time in the history of our friendship, I asked for help. She met me the next day. The greatest friend the world has ever known.

As is typical for Julia, she wanted to get straight down to work. "What you put out into the world, who you are as a performer," she told me, "is what makes you YOU." She wanted me to start there. She asked me what it was I wanted to say. What the truth of my show was.

We talked about everything. My career over the past half a decade. My childhood. My mum. Chris. My dad. Tom. A lot of it came back to Tom. My first instinct was that the show should be an apology. But Julia was quick to quash that: "It's good to say sorry. Important too. But you don't need a show to do it." She asked again, "What is it you want to say?"

After weeks and weeks shut inside, pen to paper, it was time to present what I had. Julia was first. Just me and her in my mum's front room in Sheffield. Like we were nineteen again. When it was over, she cried. Then I cried. Then we both cried and hugged for about an hour with her trying to get out the same sentence over and over again through the delightfully massive snot and tears.

"I knew it," she told me. "I knew you'd be amazing one day."

She had notes. Of course she had notes. But they were great notes. Without her help it wouldn't be the show it is and these people wouldn't be sitting here waiting for the next words out of my mouth.

"I really don't want it to, but it all started when my dad left."

I stand for the first time, my butt off the curb, and hitch my dress back down. I leave my shoes where I was sitting and start to ramble around the stage. Every night, this opening feels like I'm marking my territory.

"My dad met my mum in a Kentucky Fried Chicken. For those youthful enough to belong to Generation Z, that's what KFC actually means." As I deliver it, I know that the Dad material isn't my favorite part of the show. But it fulfills two crucial ingredients for getting the audience onside. First, and quite unashamedly, it elicits sympathy. Who doesn't want to root for the girl with half a family? Secondly, the "Colonel's secret recipe" punchline, while crude, works very well for getting the first big, full communal chuckle. When every single person laughs in a room it brings them together. It lets them be a part of something. Get one early and it buys you goodwill.

And goodwill is something this show needs. It's not your

traditional stand-up show. It's not a one-woman performance piece either. It straddles a fine line because it has to. I
need it to be personal. A great big picture of me. My heart
on my sleeve and on my chest and tattooed on my inner thigh
for good measure.

Because ultimately, mine is a show about loneliness. And
people fear that word. They worry it's about them. They fear
that even if they're not lonely now, they might be one day.
Fear of loneliness is why people stay with the wrong person.
It's the reason dating is a multibillion-dollar industry. It's
why films and music and books are almost exclusively about
relationships. Little blueprints of how we should interact
with each other. What we should say, how we should say it.
Too many of them peddle the lie that you just need to meet
the right someone. Things might get in the way, they tell you,
but true love will out. Maybe we need more that tell you it's
harder than that.

I tell the audience that for a long time I've considered myself a broken thing. Not worthy of love. By doing so, I hope
the other broken things out there feel less broken. The reviews so far have understood my intent and been more than
kind about it. Critics who have hated my work previously are
now offering me praise. I'd like to say it doesn't matter what
they say, but it does. I need affirmation as much, if not more,
than the next woman. Sticks and stones may break my body.
But words still hurt the most.

Nearing the closing section of the show, I repeat the line
from the TV interview I gave a little over a week ago. Tom's
line. The only part of the show that addresses him directly.
The only part that singles out one of the most devastating

things anyone has ever said to me. Every night, I'm torn between wanting him to hear it and wanting it to remain un-
said.

"Someone once told me, 'You won't accept happiness
into your life.' I've only met this person a few times in my
life. But every time I do, he leaves an impact. You can guess
the impact he had when he said that particular doozy."

It's more of my soul laid bare. More of my truth. And
because of this, the audience respond with a sympathetic reaction. They know. They understand. They get it. They
laugh.

"Here's the thing. He might have been wrong. He might
have been right. That's it, though. Those are the only two
possibilities. Right or wrong. No middle ground. Considering it turned out to be the last thing he said to me, you'd have
to go with wrong, right?"

I shake my head and walk around the stage. The pretense
that I'm considering all this, right here in front of them.
That it isn't something I've struggled with and written down
and decided on as the final portion of this performance.

"It helps us all if we can see things from both sides. That
person who disagrees with your politics? They do it for a
reason that makes sense to them. That colleague who looks
down on you? She probably had that same thing happen to
her all her life. That thankfully now-ex-boyfriend who loved
pointing out when you were wrong? He was never taught
that was wrong. It doesn't stop him being a dick; I just think
with a little more compassion we can see the reasons for
things that upset us."

I pick up my coat from the stool and put it around my
shoulders.

"That guy who said I couldn't accept happiness, I know why he said it. I know him well. Or at least I think I do. And I think he said it because he was finding it hard to accept his own. A lot of us are. I hope, wherever he is, he's closer to being happy now. And I hope you are too. I know I am. Thank you and good night."

46

Trust

Tom

To say I have mixed emotions about seeing Jess on stage is an understatement. Her finale has my stomach and lungs contracting in on themselves. If she'd said any more, I'd have imploded right there in my seat at the back of the venue.

But taking over from these considerations about myself is the overwhelming thought of how Julia was right, all those years ago, that one day Jess was going to be something else. Someone great. Someone who speaks to people. Looking at her now, encircled by fans wanting to know more, wanting to be near her, to give her little pieces of fan art they've made from seeing her new show multiple times, this journey she's been on becomes clear.

She looks up, sees me, and smiles. She raises a single finger to ask me to wait. She doesn't need to. I'm not going anywhere. She signs a few more programs and hugs a few more teary audience members. Then she's walking toward me. She stops an arm's length away.

"You came."

"I did."

"You sure you want to do this?" she asks. "I'd completely understand if you didn't. After last time."

I scrunch my face up. "*Sure* is a strong word. But yeah. I'm sure."

Taking me at my word, Jess explains that the Q&A show is in a different venue, but close.

"It's about five minutes away. But we'll have about fifteen minutes when we get there to get you mic'd up."

"And makeup?" I joke.

"You don't need makeup. I'm not sure I've ever seen you with such color."

Her line isn't flirtatious, but it makes me feel good. Walking alongside her makes me feel good. Knowing she's where she should be makes me feel good.

In the short walk to the venue we chat a little about her two shows, about my music. It's small talk. But far from awkward. I ask about Julia. She tells me Julia's forever grateful I've showed up for this, because Julia hates talking on stage. Especially about herself. Jess asks about the band and what I'm doing now. Before long we're talking about daily life. I like her telling me about what she did today.

The five-minute walk is over too quickly and in a blink we're on the side of the stage, microphones on and ready to chat in front of a roomful of strangers.

"Before we go on . . ." Jess asks. "Are there any topics you don't want to talk about?"

"No," I say, assuredly. "I trust you."

She glances out at the crowd from the side of the stage. Friends and family members sit talking to each other, anticipating an evening's entertainment. There's the buzz that we've both felt many times before. But every now and then, the buzz is extra special. That's the case tonight.

"You ready?" she asks.

I meet her eye.

"For the record," I tell her. "The last thing I said to you, after the gig, the thing about happiness . . . I was wrong."

"And you were right," she says.

"And I was right," I repeat.

"And you were wrong."

She smiles.

"Shall we do this, then?"

47

And. That's. OK.

Jess and Tom

Transcribed highlights of the **Jess Henson Asks** *stage show from the Edinburgh Festival 2018. Closing night show. For wider circulation.*

Applause

JESS: Hello! Hello! Thank you all for coming. Has everyone had a wonderful Festival?

Cheers and applause.

JESS: I legitimately love this place. I'm not sure if there's anywhere I'd rather be. Anyway. Before I get too emotional too soon, I should tell you a little something about this evening's guest. He's not hugely media-friendly so this is something of a coup. Please be nice to him. I know I will be. His band, The Friedmann Equation, were one of Scotland's finest exports. Critically acclaimed the world over and loved by fans who *got it*. And boy, did we get it. Please welcome Tom Delaney.

More cheers and applause.

TOM: Hello.

JESS: Thank you for coming on the show. I think I've mentioned it a few times, but I'm a big fan of the band.

TOM: Well, I'm a big fan of yours. I just saw the new show and it was—

An audience member whoops and yells, "I love you, Jess!"

TOM: OK, I did love it. But maybe I didn't love it as much as that guy.

JESS: That's fine. I pay him. He's a professional whooper.

TOM: What's the going rate for that?

JESS: Minimum wage?

TOM: Plus tips?

JESS: Performance-based tips. So, are you looking for work? After you pulled the plug on one of the greatest bands of all time.

TOM: Now *that's* some hyperbole. *(pause)* I'm lucky. I've had some time off. Not everyone gets that luxury.

JESS: And what have you been doing with that time off? Binging on *The Bachelor*? Lounging about with *Love Island*?

TOM: I wish! No, mostly taking time to . . . God, this sounds wanky.

JESS: Go on.

TOM: Taking a bit of time to get to know myself better. Yeah, that really does sound wanky. That and writing songs.

JESS: And wanking, I would imagine?

TOM: Definitely. Isn't that why we in the entertainment profession picked our jobs?

JESS: Lots of downtime.

TOM: Lots of alone time, yeah.

JESS: Ha. That took a turn, didn't it?

TOM: Are you still doing your Bucketful of Klostermans bit?

JESS: We might have to explain that to the audience. I think about twenty people listened to my ill-fated podcast experiment of 2016. And I'd urge them not to revisit it.

TOM: But "The Bucket" was a good bit.

JESS: It was. To explain, there's an American writer named Chuck Klosterman who likes to make up stupid hypotheticals, and I'd bring these questions out at various points—

TOM: Like the famous "Would you rather fight a hundred duck-sized horses or one horse-sized duck?"— that sort of thing.

JESS: I heard a great one the other day.

TOM: Go on.

JESS: If someone opened a restaurant called Karma where you're only served what you deserve, what would arrive at your table?

TOM: Great question. Just such a great question. OK! Moving on.

JESS: Answer the question, Tom.

TOM: Do I have to?

JESS: I know what *I'm* getting but I think it best to keep things light. So, in your words, moving on.

TOM: I think you'd get a better meal than you think.

JESS: That's a very nice thing for you to say. So, are you missing life on the road?

TOM: Surprisingly not. Which is a weird thing to discover.

JESS: What are the things you miss that you didn't think you would? And vice versa?

TOM: I knew I'd miss hanging out with my mates, so that's not a surprise. Oh! I know! Tucked-in sheets in hotel beds.

JESS: You're a tucker-inner? I never would have guessed that.

TOM: That's the thing, though, I'm not. I hate the tucked-in sheets. But I miss that moment of rebellion where you kick them loose and shout, "Not today, ya quilty bastard!"

JESS: Ha!

TOM: We all do that, right? It's not just me who talks to their linen?

JESS: I had a pretty in-depth discussion with a toaster once, but we can blame a heroic dose of psilocybin mushrooms for that one. Any other hotel room stories you want to share in front of a roomful of strangers?

TOM: Ha. No. I think I'm good there.

JESS: What happens on the road . . .

TOM: . . . is surprisingly boring.

JESS: What about now you're home? Is your liver in shock?

TOM: It might be. I've stopped drinking.

JESS: Completely?

TOM: Yep. *(pause)* I know you *want* to ask, but you're being awfully polite. It's fine. I decided it would ruin me one day and I don't want to be ruined.

JESS: I am so sorry. I had no idea. We really don't have to talk about it, if . . .

TOM: It's OK. Honestly. I'd like to. I think it's good to talk about stuff. Maybe someone else is going through the same thing. With struggles like these, one of the worst things is the loneliness. Thinking that it's just you suffering can make it ten times worse. I was in a bad place. Thought I'd figured myself out, which is a dangerous thing to assume. Someone, ah, someone close to me pointed out I might not be as together as I thought I was. She turned out to be very correct in that assumption.

JESS: And now?

TOM: I pay more attention to what people are telling me. People are smarter than you think.

JESS: Right. That's the half hour mark. But I'm having fun so let's keep going. If that's all right with you?

TOM: Absolutely.

JESS: Shall we take some questions from the audience?

TOM: On your head be it.

JESS: If you have any questions, just put your hand up and we'll get you a mic. Yes. The lady in the yellow jumper.

AUDIENCE MEMBER 1: You've both had quite famous partners . . .

TOM: Oh, Christ. I knew this was a bad idea. The dreaded exes question.

AUDIENCE MEMBER 1: . . . I just, I wondered how it was to date someone—

TOM: Way more famous than you.

JESS: We're the rejects, aren't we?

TOM: I think so. Sorry, please finish your question.

AUDIENCE MEMBER 1: I suppose I just wanted to know, is it tough dating another celebrity?

TOM: Right, no more questions from the audience.

JESS: Tom?

TOM: Oh, I'll go first, shall I? Thanks. Er. Yes, I suppose, is the short answer. But contrary to popular opinion, people in the public eye are actual people. They have the fun jobs that everyone wants. They get paid more than they should in comparison to people who actually do good—you know, doctors and nurses and the like. But underneath they're all the same. They fart and belch and . . .

JESS: Touch themselves.

TOM: That, as we've learned, they do. So, no, I'll completely reverse my previous answer. I don't think it's harder to date someone who is a quote unquote celebrity. Jess? Care to share your thoughts?

JESS: I assume you're referring to a certain Australian comic who's making quite a name for himself of late telling stories about me. I probably wouldn't date *him* again. But, Tom's right. I'm lucky as anything to have this life, but I don't consider myself a wholly different person from before I became a professional comedian. Or a quote unquote celebrity.

TOM: God, I hate that word. Don't you?

JESS: Just a bit. Next question.

AUDIENCE MEMBER 2: I've got one for Jess and one for Tom. Do you see yourself going back on the panel shows? Doing stand-up again? And Tom, have you seen Jess's show?

JESS: I don't see myself doing a lot of TV, of any sort to be honest. I haven't fully decided. I doubt it, though. Not the way I was, anyway. But I do have an idea for a TV show.

TOM: What's it about?

JESS: A boy and a girl.

TOM: I'd watch it. And yes, I have seen Jess's show. It's really good. I was lucky enough to see her years and years ago. We were on the same bill for some crappy *Edinburgh's Got Talent* thing that I really did not want to do. Jess was great then and, well, I think she's great now.

AUDIENCE MEMBER 3: Hi, Tom. Huge fan of your music. And I love your tattoos.

TOM: They love you too.

AUDIENCE MEMBER 3: Do you have any new ones?

TOM: Ha! I do, as a matter of fact. I got a new one done a few days ago.

JESS: Can we see it?

TOM: It's across my arm, so yes, you can. Just need to roll up my sleeve and . . . It's three little words that bring me a lot of comfort when I'm feeling low or anxious or if I'm struggling in the darkness. Like we all do from time to time.

JESS: *(reading)* And . . . That's . . . OK.

TOM: Those words mean a lot to me, so I thought I'd get them inked.

JESS: OK! I think that's a perfect place to end it. Edinburgh Festival, you have been wonderful. Please give a big hand to my guest, Tom Delaney of The Friedmann Equation. See you all next year!

48

Miles Davis

Jess

George Street, Edinburgh
August 29, 2018

The audience was hopefully far enough away to not see the tears in my eyes. But Tom saw them. This I know. I tried to shield them as I shook his hand on the stage. I tried and failed. And now I have to work out a way to tell him. To let him know this mascara-ruining mess is a good thing. That it's the right thing.

Our wranglers don't notice the disloyalty from my tear ducts and a quick wipe gets rid of the evidence. Instead, they herd Tom and me back out into the arena for more smiling and photos and all the bits and pieces of the publicity game that nobody tells you about when you're young and deluded enough to think fame is all that's worth pursuing.

Before he's surrounded by fans wanting selfies, I whisper into Tom's ear, "Can we go somewhere and talk?" He nods eagerly. I whisper into my publicist's ear too. Priming her to tell everyone we have five minutes before we need to go.

The next five minutes might be the longest of my life. They're not the worst. They give me time to watch Tom to see the parts of him that have changed. He's still the shy, anxious person who barreled me to the floor and skinned my knee in the city we're in now. His eyes still dart around the room, but now it doesn't look so much like he's searching for the nearest exit. I see him scratch his beard as another young man, possibly racked with the same self-doubt as him, manages to summon up the courage to ask for a photo of his idol. I can see Tom would rather not, but he balances the joy he'll give with the discomfort that might put on himself. The equation isn't weighted as much to one side as it once might have been.

"Sorry, everyone," the publicist announces gleefully. "Places to go. People to see. Thank you all for coming. A recording of the show will be online sometime next week. Check the Jess Henson website for details."

The three of us exit via the stage door and after some huge thanks and rushed goodbyes, Tom and I are alone. I can feel my hand ever so slightly trembling as we walk the warm streets of Scotland's capital. We amble side by side. No words spoken. Until.

"You know Miles Davis?" Tom asks.

"The trumpet guy?" I reply, curious as to where the hell he's going with this.

"Yeah. He released fifty-one albums. And only four of them were puns around his first name. *Milestones* being the ultimate one. The rest never really live up to that in terms of punna—"

"Tom!" I yell, stopping on the spot. He stops walking too and turns to me. "What are you talking about?"

"Absolutely nothing," he confesses. "I just wanted to talk to you. Are you OK? Your hand's shaking."

"I know."

"Why is it doing that?"

I take my eyes off the floor and look at his. They're hopeful. But no longer desperate.

"It's shaking because I'm scared."

"Why are you scared?"

"Because I like you. I like you *so much*. And I have for a very, very long time."

I hold out my hands and he takes them.

"You've never shook before."

"That's because we've never got to this point before. Not really. Not the point where this could really be something."

Despite us stopping in the middle of the throngs, Festivalgoers pass around us without giving us a second look.

"I haven't always known how to behave when I'm around you," Tom explains. "I've said the wrong thing a lot. And it wasn't because I didn't care or I didn't think it through. It's because I thought about it too much, until there were a million different lines in my head with a million different outcomes if I chose the wrong one. I've never been confident enough to say what I want."

"And now?" I prompt.

Silence.

"Tom, please. Just tell me if you still want me."

"Of course I do. I always have. And I don't care if you say you don't want me . . . I mean, I do care . . . of course I care." Even now, I can see frustration at his own tongue and brain not working in tandem. But he perseveres. "Massively bollocking my words up is probably something I'll always do." He pauses and says, "I've been seeing someone . . ."

My heart sinks and I instantly let go of his hands. He screams the word "No!" loud enough to warrant the attention of a few passersby, which, considering getting attention in Edinburgh is no small thing, seems like an achievement of sorts.

He clarifies. "A counselor. I've been seeing a counselor. Jesus. Why is this so hard?"

"Things that are worth it usually are."

At this, he smiles. "I've been seeing a counselor and we're working on my ability to express myself. I'm teaching myself to try not to panic, to keep the doubt away for long enough so I can say what I mean. It still takes me a little while to get there. I need to be with someone who can let me get there."

I know exactly what he's talking about.

"To be with someone who doesn't attack?" I ask. "Someone who doesn't bite your head off?"

"Yeah," he says. "I suppose so."

"I can be that person," I reply. Before adding in a disclaimer. "Probably."

He furrows his brow. I think it's as angry as he can get, and he looks pretty damn endearing when he does it. He asks me again. "Jess?"

"I can. I can do that. But there are plenty of things about me that won't change."

His eyes go wide and he yells "Good!" to more stares. "Because as I may have mumbled before, I like you. I like you being *you*. I think you're the best when you're *you*."

He looks at me and he sees me. Really sees me, like no one

I've met before. This man has been near me at my best and at my worst, and he's still here. It's been a long and winding road but we're here. Together.

"I want to kiss you," he tells me.

"I am not angry with you for wanting that."

"Good," he says.

"Good," I say.

And then he does. He holds me close and his lips touch mine, and my hands are on his face and it feels right. After years, actual years, of missed opportunities and messed-up moments, it feels better than right. Like the waiting has given it more value.

Finally, the time is right.

49

Perfect Timing

Tom

George Street, Edinburgh
August 29, 2018

A few roads over is the curry house where I first met Jess. There's a version of our story in which the men who jumped me on that same night left us alone. There's a version where I came clean about my made-up girlfriend early on. There's another where she listened to the words in between the words I spoke. Where she was slower to anger. More forgiving. A version where she didn't put her guard up and I didn't fluff my lines. But I don't want any of those. Because none of those versions end with this moment, timed to perfection, right now.

We're back in the same place we started. We're the same people. Just with slightly different outlooks. Who's to say any other version of Tom and Jess would have been able to make a go of it if circumstances had fallen in their lap. Who's to say this Tom and Jess will.

Watching Jess on stage, and then being on stage with her myself, I could see Julia was right all those years ago when she said Jess would do something amazing. Something to blow us all away. I'm proud to know her. And proud I saw I could be a better person for knowing her. Not that there isn't room for improvement. Kissing her—here and now—I have absolute certainty that perfect timing isn't about circumstance. It's about who you are. There's a reason couples who get together at a certain point in their lives make it work. And a reason others don't. Jess and I have ironed out some of our worst creases. We've another gazillion to work on, but with confidence, patience, and kindness on our side, I have hope. She steps back and looks at me with love.

I am no longer afraid.

No longer afraid of who I am and whether I'm good enough. No longer afraid of the what-ifs.

Jess kisses me again. This time with passion and desire and longing. It doesn't take long before we're back in her flat, in her room, and in her bed. After, we stare up at the speckled ceiling, our hearts beating frantically, but in time. I'm short of breath. I was the first time I met Jess Henson.

"That was exceptionally good timing," she notes.

She lies naked across my chest, in the groove of my neck and shoulder, burying herself deep.

"What are you up to now?" I ask.

"I had a thing," she replies. "But I don't really want to do the thing."

"So, you're free?"

"As a bird."

"And what about next week?"

"No plans."

"You want to hang out then?"

"Sounds perfect to me."

Epilogue

Tom and Jess sit across from each other in a café they both feel they know but can't quite place. To their credit, the location has changed a lot over the past four years. New staff, new décor, bold experiments with the menu that have failed and triumphed in equal measure. Everything old is new again.

Tom likes it. He likes this part of Sheffield. He likes that it reminds him of his grandfather, and he likes that it's the place where Jess feels most at home. Where she can be herself. He has a feeling that, if he's able to give enough time over to it, he could one day call it home too.

In their shared flat they work on their own projects, sharing ideas, seeking advice, supporting one another. She still teases him, of course. Only now the teasing centers around his weird sleeping habits and domestic peculiarities. Over food and drink, they often discuss his strange theory that the two of them have lived out these moments an infinite number of times (and will live them out an infinite number more). They are both content that, to their senses, this world, and everything in it, is fresh and new and surprising.

They both know they have big decisions to make, but now is not the time. Plans are for tomorrow. Today is for living. There is no distance between them anymore. From above, you can see they are exactly when, where, and who they both should be.

Acknowledgments

This book has been—as many books are—a battle against self-doubt, fear, and more than a few interruptions. I didn't fight this alone, and it was only won with the help of the following people.

First, always, Nina. Your support and love make everything possible. Eleven (11!) years and counting. Thanks for all the encouragement, the time, and, especially, the "pick-me-ups."

Oscar and Isaac: "How you doing boat!"

This book is dedicated to my parents. They didn't give me everything I wanted, they gave me everything I needed. And that's a much better thing to have. Love you both. We are insanely lucky to have you.

To the magnificent Hayley Steed. Whether in London, visiting Norwich, or becoming a bona fide Welsh woman, it always feels like you're in the next room ready to fight for me. How was I ever so fortunate to get an agency like Madeleine Milburn in my corner?

To Jess at Headline. This one has been a wild ride. But

worth it. For every note and prod and "Are you sure?," this book has your name in it and on it. Thanks, also, to everyone at Headline, including, but not limited, to Alara Delfosse, Ellie Morley, and Viviane Basset.

Hilary at Random House and Iris at HarperCollins, your input, as ever, has helped turn that first messy thing into something much, much better. One day, I'll get on a plane and thank you in person.

Big thanks to my first readers, Jake Marcet and Suzanne Sharman. I ask a lot of you both and you always deliver. Time and time again. I'll try and make it easy to get through the early bits next time.

My other writing buddies. Lewis Swift for the Lockdown Tuesdays. Kate Davies for talking me off the ledge countless times. Mike Walden for making me feel like I'm a peer. Hannah Harper for helping start all this. And Rob Perry, I can't wait to see my name in the back of *Dog*.

I was fortunate enough to get an invaluable insight into an industry I've never been a part of from Jack Burton. The Wolf Number forever. Thanks to Alexandra Haddow for the nudge to see a word-for-word stand-up set in a novel was an act of folly.

Finally. To those who have made me laugh or made music I love, this book is my love letter to you and your world. The list of artists who inspire me would fill another book entirely, but I'd be remiss not to give a full-blooded (and fast-blooded) mention to the words and music of Frightened Rabbit.

If you're not a fan, give them a listen and you will be. Once you are, visit tinychanges.com and see the most excellent work their founding member, Scott, has inspired.

Perfect Timing

OWEN NICHOLLS

Random
House
Book Club

Because
Stories Are
Better Shared

A Book Club Guide

Questions and Topics
for Discussion

1. When Tom and Jess first meet at the Edinburgh Festival, their spark is immediately apparent as they spend the evening getting to know each other. Have you ever experienced an instant connection like that, where you thought about someone constantly even after just a brief meeting?

2. Unfortunately, things between Tom and Jess go awry quite quickly after Scott reveals to Jess that Tom has a "girlfriend." Have you ever been in a position similar to Tom's, where lying seemed like the easier thing to do, only for the lie to derail something else? If so, what happened?

3. After hearing Tom's song on the radio, Jess is determined to find Tom's "girlfriend" and tell her the truth. In Jess's position, would you have reacted similarly, or would you have brushed it off instead? Why or why not?

4. A miscommunication at the airport causes Tom and Jess to hit another bump in their relationship; have you ever ex-

perienced similar fallout from a miscommunication with a friend or partner? If so, were you able to resolve it?

5. After Jess's stint in Australia, her style of comedy takes a very different turn. Even though she doesn't really like what she's doing, she feels compelled to keep going because it is what everyone expects of her. Have you ever felt compelled to fulfill someone else's expectations the way Jess does? Do you understand why she kept it going for as long as she did, or do you think you would have stopped sooner had you been in her position?

6. Tom also struggles with expectations, though his struggle is more about the expectations he sets for himself. We see him fighting with his anxiety and with his concern for what others think of him. We also see him struggle with his need to be successful like his grandfather, but also fearful he'll walk the same tragic path as him. Do you think Tom copes with his struggles in a healthy way? Why or why not? If not, what would you do to cope in a similar position?

7. Throughout the novel, the reason Tom and Jess can't be together is because they are never in the same place in their lives, be it in regard to their careers, their other relationships, or their own personal struggles as they make their way through their twenties. Do you think it is important that both parties in a relationship are on the same page in these regards? Why or why not?

8. At the end of the book, Tom and Jess finally seem to have found the perfect timing. Do you think their individual expe-

riences and personal growth, which we see throughout the novel, will mean they will have a better relationship than if they had gotten together that first night they met? Why or why not? What importance do you think timing plays in relationships?

ABOUT THE AUTHOR

OWEN NICHOLLS is the author of *Love, Unscripted* and a screenwriter with a master's degree in scriptwriting. He lives in Norwich, England, with his partner and their two sons.

ABOUT THE TYPE

This book was set in Sabon, a typeface designed by the well-known German typographer Jan Tschichold (1902–74). Sabon's design is based upon the original letterforms of sixteenth-century French type designer Claude Garamond and was created specifically to be used for three sources: foundry type for hand composition, Linotype, and Monotype. Tschichold named his typeface for the famous Frankfurt typefounder Jacques Sabon (c. 1520–80).

RANDOM HOUSE BOOK CLUB

Because Stories Are Better Shared

Discover
Exciting new books that spark conversation every week.

Connect
With authors on tour—or in your living room. (Request an Author Chat for your book club!)

Discuss
Stories that move you with fellow book lovers on Facebook, on Goodreads, or at in-person meet-ups.

Enhance
Your reading experience with discussion prompts, digital book club kits, and more, available on our website.

Join our online book club community!

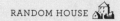 randomhousebookclub.com

Random House Book Club ™

Because Stories Are Better Shared

RANDOM HOUSE